For Love
&
Grace

KENDRA NORMAN-BELLAMY

BET Publications, LLC

http://www.bet.com

NEW SPIRIT BOOKS are published by

BET Publications, LLC
c/o BET BOOKS
One BET Plaza
1900 W Place NE
Washington, DC 20018-1211

All Kensington Titles, Imprints, and Distributed Lines are available at special quantity discounts for bulk purchases for sales promotions, premiums, fundraising, and educational or institutional use. Special book excerpts or customized printings can also be created to fit specific needs. For details, write or phone the office of the Kensington special sales manager: Kensington Publishing Corp., 850 Third Avenue, New York, NY 10022, attn: Special Sales Department, Phone: 1-800-221-2647.

BET Books is a trademark of Black Entertainment Television, Inc. NEW SPIRIT and the NEW SPIRIT logo are trademarks of BET Books and the BET BOOKS logo is a registered trademark.

ISBN: 1-58314-549-4

First Printing: November 2004
10 9 8 7 6 5 4 3 2 1

Printed in the United States of America

*This book is dedicated
to the undying memories
of Jimmy Lee Holmes,
the best tenor in heaven's choir,
and Elder Clinton
and Mrs. Willie Mae Bellamy,
my dear parents-in-law.
Remembrance of you all
will forever remain in my heart.*

ACKNOWLEDGMENTS

Lord, first I thank you for extending your gift upon me and giving me an opportunity to share it with the world. To my husband, Jonathan, and my daughters, Brittney and Crystal, I love you all. You are my greatest inspiration.

To my parents, Bishop and Mrs. H.H. Norman, thank you for your prayers and for bringing me up to know the ways of the Lord. Without you and your guidance, I hate to think where I might be today. To Crystal (Albert), Harold (Gloria), Cynthia (Terry), and Kimberly . . . thanks for your undying support. Chance made us siblings—hearts made us friends! To my godchildren, Courtney, Mildred, and Jon-Jon . . . Mommy loves you.

Love to my dearest friends Heather, Gloria, and Deborah. I don't see you every day, but I know that you're always rooting for me. To the Holmeses and the Bellamys, you've truly given new meaning to the term "extended family." How did I get so blessed? Shunda and Jamill, time and space won't permit me to say it all. Just know that I love you dearly.

Terrance, you're still my favorite cousin. Thanks for always having my back and for not once doubting my gifts and abilities. To my longtime friends Torrance, Andrew, Darlene, Angie, Carla, Amy, Yvette, Tan, Joycelyn, Terrilyn, and Anquinette, I love you all.

Much love to my spiritual family at Revival Church, Inc. (Bishop H.H. Norman), and Church of God By Faith Ministries (Pastor Wayne Mack), and my supporters at Genesis Underwriting Management Company (Atlanta), The Care House, and Circle of Friends II Book Club.

To BET Books (New Spirit), this is the beginning of a beautiful relationship. Thank you for loving my work, believing in me, and helping my dream to become realized. Thank you, Glenda, for being a wonderful hands-on editor.

Last, but not least, to my all-time favorite songsters, Brian McKnight, Melvin Williams (The Williams Brothers), and BeBe and CeCe Winans . . . your positive and uplifting songs defeated writer's block and kept me going sometimes deep into the night as I worked on this project. Thank you.

CHAPTER 1

Derrick and Greg stood quietly by Derrick's mother's grave. She had been lowered into the ground and the crowd was beginning to thin. Several people patted the two young men on the shoulders as they walked away and headed for their cars.

Derrick Madison and Gregory Dixon had been best friends since grammar school. Mrs. Madison had been like a mother to Greg through the years. In his preteen and teen years, he'd stay at their house about as much as he stayed at his own. It killed him to see the pain that his friend was going through at the sudden death of his mom.

"It's gonna be okay, Rick," Greg tried to assure him through his own heartache.

"I hope she dies," Derrick mumbled.

"What?" Greg stepped away. "What did you say?"

"I know it's wrong," Derrick said.

"And I know you didn't just say what I think you said," Greg said with visible disappointment.

"Look, man—" Derrick started.

"No, *you* look," Greg interrupted. He lowered his voice and looked around to be sure that no one was within listening range.

"I know this is hard for you, Rick," he began again. "Believe me, I know. I've spent a lot of time with you over the past few days. Ms. Julia was like my own mama. I'm gonna miss her too, but . . ."

"Yeah," Derrick began. "*Like* your own mama. But she *was* my mama. When it comes right down to it, Greg, you still got a mama. I don't. My mama was all I had left in the world and *she* killed her."

Gregory embraced his friend as the tears Derrick had been holding back burst free. Greg fought his own tears in an attempt to be strong for Derrick. He led Derrick away from the grave site as the workers came to complete the burial.

"C'mon, Rick," he whispered. "You don't want to see this."

The two men got into the waiting funeral limousine and headed home. It was a quiet, somber ride. Derrick stared out of the window and watched nothing in particular as the driver periodically glanced at him through the rearview mirror.

"She wasn't all you had, you know. You have a beautiful family and don't you forget that," Greg finally said. "And you don't really want that lady to die."

"Yes, I do have a family. You're right about that part, and I love them dearly. But you're wrong about one thing, too. Because honestly, Greg, I really do want her to die. Why should she live and Mama pay with her life?" Derrick asked angrily.

"God's not pleased, Rick."

"I know." Derrick nodded. "But if I said I didn't want her to die, I'd be lying and God wouldn't be pleased with that either."

Greg made another attempt to get through. "It's not like she meant to do it. It was an accident."

"She killed my mama. That makes her a murderer."

"Stop it, Rick." Greg's voice became stern. "The accident investigation hasn't even been completed yet. We don't know what happened for sure."

"Mama was a good driver."

"All right. I'll give you that. But we still don't know yet. This Jessica person is in a coma, so she can't talk yet and—"

"And what's she gonna say?" Derrick said, showing his own

anger. "If she fell asleep at the wheel or was drinking or just not paying attention, you think she's gonna say that?"

"If she was drinking, that can be proven," Greg pointed out.

The limo stopped in front of Derrick's condominium and the driver reached for his door handle so that he could let the passengers out.

"It's okay, Nelson," Greg called to the driver. "We got it. Thanks a lot for the ride. You guys did a good job today."

"Thanks, G," Nelson said as he watched Derrick walk slowly toward his porch. "He gonna be okay?" he asked.

Greg nodded. "Uh-huh. He'll be fine. He just needs a little time and a lot of prayer. He's not himself right now."

"I know," Nelson said. "I heard."

"Don't repeat it, Nelson," Greg said. "Please. You know he doesn't really mean that stuff. He's just hurting."

"I know, man," Nelson assured him. "That was just an overheard private conversation between two friends. I wouldn't try to make it worse by spreading it. Derrick's an honest-to-God good man. I know he don't mean that stuff."

"Thanks." Greg slid out of his seat and waved at Nelson before closing the door. He ran ahead to catch up with his friend, who was unlocking his door.

"Hey, you two," Sherry said as she gave Derrick a long, warm hug. She kissed his neck and held his face between her hands, as she looked him directly in the eyes.

"Are you okay, baby?" she asked.

"I am now." Derrick tried to smile as he kissed her lips briefly. "You been okay today?"

"Yeah," Sherry answered. Embracing Greg, she put her lips to his ears.

"Is he really okay?" she asked.

"No," he whispered back.

Sherry was a beautiful woman. Back in school, fellow classmates were always amazed at how athletic she was. She was a full-figured girl. Their friends in college used to call her Queen, because of her striking resemblance to Queen Latifah. She had been Derrick's prom date in high school. Prior to the prom, they had never dated. They had all just been very good friends.

In school, the three of them had belonged to the Fellowship of Christian Athletes. Both Derrick and Greg played basketball in high school and in college. Sherry had played on the girls' softball team in high school and was on the volleyball team in college. Derrick, twenty-six, and Sherry, twenty-five, dated throughout their college years and had finally married two years ago after five years of courtship.

Gregory was also twenty-six years old. He and his best friend had so much in common. Not only were they both very much into watching and playing sports, but they were born only a day apart and in the same hospital. That's how their friendship began. Their mothers shared the same hospital room. Derrick, born October 5, was only sixteen hours older than Greg.

That shared hospital room sealed a lifetime bond between their mothers. Greg's mother was Derrick's godmother, and Derrick's mom had been Greg's godmother. Both boys lost their fathers early in life. Neither of them had any siblings, so their friendship was like a brotherhood. Greg's father died when he was only three years old, and Mr. Madison had abandoned his family by the time Derrick started kindergarten.

When they were still in high school and finally able to appreciate the sacrifices that their mothers had made in raising them as single parents, both boys made a pact to become successful so that they could take care of their mothers.

Just a few months prior to Julia Madison's death, she had contemplated moving down South to be closer to her sisters. Julia had injured her hip in a fall and her sisters suggested that she move closer to them. Derrick had begged her to stay. He said that he'd make sure that she got the best care for her injury and he'd run her errands whenever she didn't feel up to it. To his delight, she agreed to stay.

Greg's and Derrick's long-standing friendship had encountered very few threats through the years. They got along well and their common interests kept them close. It seemed as though they had been joined at the hip since they were infants. Both the boys had the same babysitter growing up and attended the same school from kindergarten until they graduated from Georgetown University. Standing at a height of six feet one, Greg was one inch taller than his friend.

"How's Daddy's girl?" Derrick picked his newborn daughter up from her crib and held her close to his chest.

Little Denise had been born just three weeks ago, on Christmas Eve. Because of that, Sherry was unable to attend her mother-in-law's funeral. Derrick sat in the rocking chair by his daughter's bed and hummed as he rocked her.

"Did you eat anything?" Sherry asked him.

"Naa-aah," he whispered. "I'm not hungry right now, sweetie. I'll get something later, maybe."

Sherry touched Greg's arm and motioned for him to follow her as she headed out of the room and toward the kitchen. Greg stood in the doorway for a little longer watching Derrick cradle his daughter as he continued to sing softly to her.

"It's still hard for me to believe Rick's got a kid," Greg said as he joined Sherry in the kitchen.

"He's such an attentive father," Sherry said while sitting at the dining room table and placing a cup of hot tea on a coaster for Greg.

Greg saw a worried look on her face as he joined her at the table and took a sip of the steaming drink.

"Mmmm," he said as the hot liquid went down his throat. "Girl, you still make the best lemon tea this side of—well, this side of anywhere."

"Thanks," Sherry said.

"He'll be fine." Greg was trying to convince himself as well as her.

"I'm worried, Greg. He's been so torn up and distant since Mama died. Sometimes I wake up in the middle of the night and he's not in bed. Usually, I find him sitting in the living room in the dark holding Mama's picture and crying. I never let him know I see him though. You think it was just the impending funeral?" she asked in hopefulness. "You think since that part's over, he'll start to heal?"

"I don't know that it'll be that cut-and-dry." Greg tried to be honest. He remembered his conversation with Derrick at Julia's graveside and on the ride home. "He's bitter. He's so angry with this girl that he's not being reasonable right now."

"I know." Sherry sat up straight. "I sent flowers to the hospital for her yesterday." She lowered her voice and glanced toward her daughter's room. "I want to tell him, but—"

"No. Please don't do that, Sherry," Greg whispered in a pleading voice.

"You think I was wrong?"

"No, sweetie," he assured her. "It's not you. I think what you did was very considerate. I just don't think he's ready to hear that. It wouldn't go over well."

"You're right. I know you're right. You know, I just don't like keeping stuff from him."

"I know. I'm not trying to make you do that. You do what you want. I'm just saying."

"No. You're right," Sherry said. "He's not ready. I'll wait until the time is right. I just wish he could see that this girl is near death and needs our prayers too. You understand, don't you? I'm not being insensitive to Mama's death, am I?"

Greg reached across the table and grabbed her hand and smiled as he shook his head. "No. You're absolutely right. That's what I was trying to tell him today at the cemetery and on the ride over here. We don't even know all the details yet," he said as Sherry nodded in agreement.

"But somehow he just wants to blame her for everything," Greg continued. "From the little we know, it's pretty clear that she hit Ms. Julia, and it wasn't the other way around. I guess that's all Rick needs to know to draw a verdict. I know he's gonna get through this—I just don't know how or how soon."

"It's definitely going to take God," Sherry said. "I spoke with Daddy last night. He said I'll just need to be supportive, patient, and prayerful."

Sherry's parents lived in Newark, New Jersey. They'd moved there shortly after she graduated from college. She'd been brought up in the church all of her life. At first, her father had been apprehensive about accepting her relationship with Derrick. They broke up several times during their first year together. All of their disagreements seemed to involve religion. During their freshman year in college, Derrick didn't attend church very often, and when he did he always walked away confused or finding fault in something that went on.

As much as Sherry tried to get him to understand God's will and to explain the Bible's teachings, it wasn't until his mother had a heart-to-heart with him one night that Derrick made up his mind to give it a try. He wasn't what one would call a mama's boy, but he was very close to his mother and respected her highly. He admired the way she raised him in their single-parent home.

Greg's salvation came almost a year earlier than Derrick's. Like Sherry, Greg had been brought up in the church. His mother was very involved in church activities and functions. He had always attended services, but didn't make the decision to accept Christ until the summer after graduation from high school.

Greg prepared to leave as he finished his tea and placed his empty cup in the kitchen sink. He walked to Denise's room where Derrick was preparing to put her back into her crib.

"I'm leaving, Rick," he whispered as he walked in to kiss the baby's forehead.

"Isn't she beautiful?" Derrick remarked as he admired his sleeping daughter.

"She is," Greg agreed. "Must've got it from her mama."

Derrick laughed softly. "Yeah, right. Admit it, man, you know I'm pretty."

"Dude, don't be believing them lies Sherry be telling you." The friends shared a brief laugh.

"I hate that she'll never know her grandma," Derrick said sadly.

"Yeah. Me too."

"I guess Ms. Lena will have to be a granny for her." Derrick referred to Greg's mother.

"You know Mama would be all too happy to fill in." Greg shoved his hands in his pockets and took a deep breath. "I need to check on her first thing in the morning. She didn't do too well at the services today."

"Yeah, I saw her," Derrick said.

"If you need anything at all, man, don't fail to call me." Greg embraced Derrick firmly and patted his back.

"Thanks for everything," Derrick said.

After kissing Sherry's cheek, Greg walked to his car and headed home. Sherry looked at Derrick and smiled.

"You're blessed to have a friend like him, you know."

"Oh, don't I know it?" Derrick placed his arm around her waist. "I owe you an apology," he continued after a pause.

"What for?"

"Because today, for a split second, I forgot how blessed I was to have you and Dee," he explained as he thought of his conversation with Greg at the cemetery. "I was so consumed with thoughts of never seeing Mama again that I forgot that I still had someone to love and lean on. You've been so wonderful to me and you didn't deserve that." He sighed heavily. "Forgive me?"

"Oh, sweetheart." Sherry saw the tears in his eyes and knew that they were only partly due to his forgetting about their daughter and her. It was also the heaviness of his heart over his mother's death. She hugged him tightly and said a quick silent prayer.

"You don't have to apologize," she whispered. "I've never lost a parent, so I don't know what it's like. I can only imagine the pain that you're going through. There's no need to ask for forgiveness. Dee and I love you very much and we understand."

"When I was a teenager," he said as he wiped a tear from his eye, "I used to wonder what it would be like if anything happened to Mama. I don't know why, but sometimes it would just come to my mind."

"I think we all think about that," Sherry said as she held his hand. "Especially as our parents get older."

"I guess so," he continued. "I always knew that it would be hard. Me and Mama were real close. Still, I had no idea it would be like this. I expected her to live a full life and die in her sleep or something. You know, die of old age. But I wasn't prepared to have her life snatched away by some stupid careless driver."

"I know, sweetheart," Sherry said. "We just have to believe that God doesn't make mistakes and this happened for a reason. We just have to wait and see what the reason is."

"There are some things that I don't believe God has anything to do with, Sherry, and this is one of them."

"I wonder what Mama was doing driving around at that time of day anyway," Sherry said thoughtfully. "She usually doesn't drive much in the evening hours without you or Ms. Lena or somebody in the car with her."

"What does that matter?" Derrick snapped. "A woman has a right to drive any time she pleases. That ain't got nothing to do with the reason for the accident. The accident wasn't caused because she was driving. People drive every day of the week and at all hours of the day. This woman in the hospital was the cause. Period."

"Okay," Sherry said quietly as she stepped back and prepared to walk away.

"Baby," Derrick said as he gently grabbed her arm. "I'm sorry. I didn't mean to raise my voice. I'm sorry."

"It's okay." Sherry smiled. "Let me fix you something to eat."

"No," he said. "I don't want anything to eat right now. I want you. I *need* you."

"Sweetie," Sherry said as she kissed his hand. "We can't. It's way too soon."

"I know. I'm sorry," he said as he sat on the sofa and rubbed his face with his hands while fighting the tears that pressed against the back of his eyes.

Sitting next to him, Sherry ran her fingers through his hair lovingly. "I can hold you if you'd like," she offered.

Derrick nodded silently and welcomed her warm embrace. The tears he had been fighting had finally won the battle. Sherry held him tightly while he wept in her arms. Her own tears flowed as she tried to comfort him.

"I love you, sweetie," she whispered in his ear.

"I love you too, baby." Derrick's voice trembled. "Please be patient with me," he pleaded. "Please."

"We're going to get through this," she assured him. "Whatever it takes, we're going to get through this. And we're going to get through it together."

CHAPTER 2

"Really, son, I'm fine," Lena Dixon told her only child for the third time. "I know I broke down quite a bit at the services, but God's beginning to give me the strength I need to go on without Julia in my life."

It had been three weeks since the funeral and Greg had been making it a point to go by on a regular basis and check on his mother. Mrs. Dixon had always been a strong woman, but in recent years she hadn't lost anyone as dear to her as Julia Madison. Greg worried because Ms. Julia was the only close friend that his mother had.

"You know," she continued, "I picked up the phone one day last week to call her and then I remembered she was gone."

"It's only been a few weeks, Mama. It's going to take some getting used to," Greg said.

"I know. You been checking on Derrick?"

"Yes, I have," Greg said. "He's doing better. If he could get over his animosity for the other driver he would be able to move on with his life a little easier."

"I can imagine how he feels. I guess it's normal to want to see some type of justice carried out for the person responsible for your mama's death."

"Yeah, Mama, but he's taking it too far. It's not only about justice with Rick. It's malice. He's handed this woman a sentence and hasn't even heard the trial yet."

"Is she still unconscious?"

"Yeah. She's been in and out of consciousness for too long now. They're beginning to worry about long-term effects if she pulls through this."

"Is she brain-dead?"

"No. According to her staff of doctors, she's not. She'll wake up slightly and briefly, but they can't get her to be coherent at all. She took a bad blow to the head."

"How do you know so much about her case?" Lena asked.

"We had a meeting about her case two days ago. It seems that there's a good chance she'll be moved to Robinson Memorial."

"Your hospital?"

"Yeah. I spoke personally with Dr. Grant and that's what he thinks is going to happen. At Saint Mary's they don't have the experienced staff that they need for her case," he said. "So they may give her to us."

"Are you gonna be her doctor?"

"I understand she may need surgery done to relieve pressure from her brain." Greg sank slowly onto the sofa and rubbed his eyes. He had had a full day at the hospital.

"If she indeed needs that surgery," he continued, "I'm sure I'll be the man, or at least one of the men. I'm certain that Dr. Grant will be on hand as well, being that he's the head surgeon."

Greg was the newest surgeon on the staff at Robinson Memorial. He was still working as a resident, but he had made the headlines one year earlier during his first week on staff when the chief of police took a bullet to the head in a shoot-out near the White House. Even the experienced staff surgeons said it was a lost cause. Against their best advice, Greg, the youngest and only black surgeon on staff, removed the bullet and was credited with saving the veteran's life. The president had honored him along with other local heroes during a special ceremony a few months later.

"Have you talked to Derrick about this?"

"Not yet. I don't see the need to unless I know for sure. Even then, I don't know."

"You gonna have to tell him, Greg."

"No, Mama. Actually, I don't. It's not his business who I treat at the hospital. I don't need that added pressure. It's not gonna make a difference. If this woman is placed in my care, I'm going to do my best to save her. Rick's not gonna want to hear that."

"Poor baby." Lena sighed. "He's trying to cope, but he's having a hard time. If he really prayed about his feelings, God could help him."

"I know," Greg agreed. "But he's not hearing God or man these days. He just wants her to pay."

Lena Dixon began humming an old hymn as she started cooking dinner. Greg loved to hear his mother sing. It reminded him of his childhood days. She would always hum as she cooked or cleaned house. She'd even sing in the shower. She didn't have the greatest voice, but she loved singing and he loved hearing it. The sweet sound of his mama's voice could still be heard faintly as he drifted off to sleep.

Lena looked at her son's long body, as he lay stretched across the couch. She shook her head and laughed softly.

"Boy, if you don't look just like your daddy," she said as she draped a blanket across him. "Sho didn't get that height from me," she said as she looked at her five-foot-five, thin reflection in the mirror on her living room wall.

She rushed to answer the phone to prevent the ringing from waking her child. It was a member of the church calling. There was always somebody calling to make sure she was all right. She didn't want to be rude, but she was coming very close to just telling them to leave her alone. Yes, she missed Julia, but God had given her peace. She knew where her friend was. She had no doubts about that.

"I just want to know that you're doing okay, Sister Dixon," Mary Gillis was saying from the other end of the phone line.

"Well, thank you, Sister Gillis," Lena said while rolling her eyes toward the ceiling and hoping dearly that this phone call would end soon.

"Yes, Lord," Mary said in what seemed to be the most pitiful voice she could conjure up. "I sho do miss Sister Madison and I said to myself, if I miss her I know you do even more so. Y'all were so close and now she's gone forever. You'll never get to see that smiling face again."

"Yes, I do miss her, Sister Gillis," Lena responded. "I'll always miss Julia, but I know she's with the Lord, and as I see it, she's doing a whole lot better than the rest of us who still have to deal with all the mess going on in this here world."

"Well, yeah, that's true," Mary agreed. "But just look at how she died. So tragic, and so soon after the holidays. She probably never even knew what hit her. Now that son of hers is living in a world of his own and that poor grandchild of hers will never even know what she looked like. Oh, Lord, it's just so sad!" Mary broke down in tears.

"Sister Gillis, it's okay," Lena said. "Don't worry 'bout me and my grief. Just see 'bout yourself and everything will be okay."

"Ooooooh, yes, Lord," Mary wailed. "You just be strong, sister. And remember I'm always here for you."

"Thank you, Sister Gillis. I'll keep that in mind," Lena said as she ended the conversation and hung up the phone. "Well, Lord," she said as she looked toward the ceiling, "I'm glad I got you to depend on, 'cause if that phone call was my means of encouragement, I'd be in a bad fix."

Dinner was almost ready now, but Lena hated to awaken her son. He needed every bit of rest he could sneak in throughout the day. Yet, she knew he was hungry and needed to eat.

"Greg," she called as she set the table.

She watched him stir briefly as he turned over to his other side and pulled the blanket close around his neck.

"I'm sorry, baby, but you've got to wake up now," she said as she shook his shoulder gently. "Dinner's ready."

"Okay, Mama." Greg stood up and stretched his body. His mother laughed as he dragged his tired body into the bathroom to wash his hands and face.

"Maybe you need to take a vacation and get some rest," Lena called to her son from the kitchen.

"I'll be okay, Mommy," Greg teased in a childlike voice as he sat at the dining room table. "I knew the hours were like this when I chose the profession. I just catch a little shut-eye whenever I can."

"As long as you think it's worth it," Lena said. "Saving lives and making folks feel better must be pretty rewarding."

Greg smiled. "It is. Of course there will always be those patients that when you meet them you wonder why God bothered to plan their existence. For instance," he continued, "a few weeks ago, this trifling guy came in who had been in a fight with some friend of his. His arm was broken in two places and he had a bunch of pretty bad bruises on his face. He said that his friend had caught him in bed with his wife and they got into a fight. He said his friend pushed him down a flight of stairs. He claims to have won, but that just made us wonder what the friend looked like. He didn't want to press any charges, so we patched him up and sent him on his way."

"You know what they say," Lena said. "There's one in every bunch."

"Yeah." He laughed. "But all in all, it's a noble profession and I believe it is my true calling."

"I remember us talking 'bout it when you decided to go to medical school," his mother reminisced. "I want you to know I'm proud of you, son, and your daddy woulda been too. Eight years is a long time to spend in college right after twelve years of regular schooling."

"Thanks, Mama," Greg said, beaming. "I have you to thank for all those years of schooling."

"Me? Boy, you had a full scholarship. It's not like I had to pay for it or nothing," she said, laughing.

"But you were my encouragement and inspiration. You'll

never want for anything, Mama. I'll work my whole life to keep you comfortable."

Ms. Dixon walked away from the kitchen to the dining table and gave Greg a long, warm hug. She blinked back tears at her son's words.

"I'da had ten more babies if your daddy had lived and if I could have been certain that each and every one of them would have been just like you."

"Whoa, Mama. I would have liked a sibling or two, but ten?"

"Well, if they were all like you, there wouldn't be a problem."

"Thank you, Mama." Greg smiled.

Lena placed Greg's plate in front of him and her own on the place mat next to his. The two of them held hands and said grace. They ate in silence for a few minutes.

"You're finished with work for today, right?"

"In this profession, Mama, there's no such thing," Greg said. "For today, my normal rounds are finished. I go back in at 11:00 tonight, but I could be called in at any time."

His mother looked at him with a worried expression. "Greg, this job won't prevent me from having grandchildren one day, will it?"

"Ma'am?" Greg was confused.

"I mean, with all this working, when you ever gonna have time to meet and court a nice young lady?"

"You're kidding, right?" Greg laughed.

"No. I'm serious."

"Mama, I see female doctors, nurses, and hospital employees all day long. If I wanted to date right now, I could. I just haven't met anyone that I'm interested in yet."

"You want to marry a doctor?"

"Not necessarily." Greg thought deeply as he spoke. "As a matter of fact, that's not my preference. I'd rather marry someone in a different profession than myself. Maybe a less stressful profession."

"You know quite a few of the sisters at church have their eyes on you," his mother pointed out.

"And how would you know this?"

"Oh, baby, I see the eyes cutting your way all the time. They ain't even discreet about it. That Evelyn is so transparent it's ridiculous. She practically throws herself at you. And she's always speaking to me and pretending to want to help me out. All that 'Mother Lena, you want me to carry that Bible for you?' and 'Mother Lena, would you like a fan?' I just be wanting to say, 'Gal, get out of my face. You ain't getting my son. And wear a longer skirt with them knobby knees!' "

Greg doubled over with laughter as his mother mimicked Evelyn Cobb. Evelyn was indeed very obvious in her attempts to catch the eye of the congregation's only eligible bachelor who practiced medicine. Greg tried to be modest, but he realized all too well that he had quite a number of female fans at his church. Many of them were nice and a couple of them even fit his criteria for a nice mate, but none of them impressed him enough for him to ask them out. They all fell short in one respect. They were chasing him. He'd decided a long time ago that whenever he decided to pursue a relationship, he would be the aggressor.

"Well, Mama," Greg said, "Miss Cobb isn't one for you to worry about. I don't know who I'll marry one day, but I know who I *won't* marry."

"Thank God she's not a prospect." His mother sighed in relief.

"You never thought she was, did you?"

"No. Well, at least I was praying that she wouldn't be the one."

"Your prayers have definitely been answered," Greg assured her as he ate the last of his vegetables and handed the plate to his mother, who was now clearing the table.

"You know I ain't never been all in your business. Well, not since you got out of high school anyway," Lena Dixon said. "I don't try to run your love life or nothing. You're a grown man and you got to make those major decisions on your own," she continued as Greg joined her at the sink to rinse the dishes as she washed.

"I know, Mom, and I appreciate that."

"I have to admit though," she added, "I do want you to meet a nice girl and settle down one day. I don't wanna be one of those mothers-in-law who can't get along with her son's wife, either. I want to like this girl and I want her to like me."

"How could she not like you, Mama?" Greg smiled at his mother's dreamy-eyed comments. "As a matter of fact, if a girl can't get along with you, as sweet and wonderful as you are, then she's not the girl for Dr. Gregory Paul Dixon."

"Hush, boy." His mother laughed with a blush. "You sound like a mama's boy. No woman wants to marry a man who compares her to his mama."

"Well, then I guess I won't be hooking up with a wife any time soon."

"Don't say that, sweetheart," his mother said in a disappointed, almost whiney voice.

The high-pitched sounds of Greg's pager delayed his response. His mother shook her head as he reached down and grabbed it from his pocket. He looked at the number and smiled at his mother.

"Duty calls," he said.

"I knew it was the hospital," she said. "Don't work too hard, Greg."

"I'll do my best, Mother dear," he said as he kissed her jaw. "Thanks for dinner, and don't worry," he continued as he put on his coat and grabbed the keys to his car. "In God's own time, you'll get your daughter-in-law."

"And grandbabies?"

"And grandbabies, Mama. Lots and lots of grandbabies." Greg laughed as he kissed her again and dashed down the stairs toward his car.

"If they turn out anything at all like their daddy, they'll be some of the smartest, sweetest, prettiest kids in the world," Lena said with pride as she watched the gold Jaguar pull away.

Greg picked up his cell phone and dialed the number from his pager. Dr. Simon Grant picked up at the other end.

"Grant," Greg said, "I'm on my way. What's up?"

"Don't run any red lights, Dixon." Dr. Grant chuckled. "We're having a mandatory meeting and you need to be here."

"Okay. What time does it start?"

"As soon as you get here. Everybody else is already here."

"I'll be there in ten minutes."

"That soon? Okay, then I'll gather everybody else together. Just meet us in the seventh-floor conference room."

"Gotcha."

With a swipe of his card, the security gate to the parking garage lifted and Lena Dixon's little boy turned instantly into Dr. Gregory Dixon. The elevators at Robinson Memorial were always busy. It seemed to take forever to get from floor to floor.

"Good evening, Dr. Dixon," the receptionist said in a flirty, almost singing tone as Greg passed her desk on his way to take the steps.

"Evening, uh . . ." Greg hesitated.

"Creshondria," she said with a smile.

"Oh, yeah." Greg waved as he entered the stairwell. "I knew it was something crazy," he mumbled as he dashed up seven flights of stairs. He stopped briefly at the door of the seventh floor to catch his breath.

"Dixon—you made it." Dr. Grant smiled and shook Greg's hand as he met him walking down the hall.

Greg really admired Dr. Grant. The popular hospital shows on television Greg had watched as he went through medical school usually portrayed heads of surgery as extremely impatient and short-tempered with their residents. Greg knew that the portrayals were somewhat accurate, but was thankful that he didn't have to deal with that so far in his own experience.

"Did I hold you guys up too long?" he asked Dr. Grant.

"Not at all. Believe it or not, Dr. Merrill still hasn't gotten here yet, and he was on the fifth floor finishing up when I called you."

"Well, he *is* nearing retirement age, Grant," Greg said, chuckling.

"You've got a point there," Dr. Grant agreed.

The two doctors joined the three waiting colleagues in the conference room. Dr. Merrill came in as they all settled around what they called the "chat table." An orderly placed a glass of water in front of each doctor as Dr. Grant put X-rays on the medical board and turned on the light so that the X-rays could be seen by all of them.

"Water," Dr. Neal observed. "Looks like we're in for the long haul."

"This is not as bad as it looks," Dr. Grant responded. "Most of this we've already prepared for. In short, we got our critical patient from Saint Mary's today."

Greg closed his eyes as though to block out the thoughts of what was inevitably to come. He could only imagine Rick's anger when he found out that he was caring for the woman who had possibly caused his mother's untimely death.

"I need for each of you to be on hand for the surgery," Dr. Grant continued.

"Has surgery been scheduled?" Dr. Lowe asked as he drank his water.

"Not yet," Dr. Grant answered. "Let me make this clear," he continued. "I want you, Dr. Dixon, to take the wheel on this one. This is your baby and I know you'll do as good a job as possible."

"Thank you, sir." Greg forced a smile and took a sip of water to ease the dryness in his throat.

"Can you handle it?" Dr. Grant asked.

"If he can't, then we're in trouble," Dr. Pridgen interjected, "because I'm not too proud to admit that he's the best we've got."

"Speak for yourself, Pridgen," Dr. Merrill said. "I've been in this game for over forty years and I'm not about to say that a green Dr. Dixon is better than me."

"That's 'cause you're half crazy, Dr. Merrill." Dr. Pridgen laughed. "You're too old to know any better."

"Old?" Dr. Merrill pounded his fist on the table. "I beg your pardon. I helped to train your smart-mouthed little—"

"Gentlemen." Greg held up his hand. "This is not a contest. I may be in charge, but it's possible I'll have to go to Dr. Merrill for his experienced expertise at some point. I may need *all* of you at some point."

"That's right," Dr. Grant agreed. "And also a great come-back, I might add," he whispered as he leaned in to Greg's ear.

"You'd better believe you're going to need me at some point," Dr. Merrill boasted. He turned to Dr. Pridgen. "And so will *you*, you young whippersnapper."

"You know, Merrill," Dr. Pridgen said, "the fact that you still use the phrase 'young whippersnapper' just proves my point."

"Will you two knock it off?" Dr. Neal whined.

"This meeting of what I thought were expert minds is adjourned," Dr. Grant said. "Now get out."

"What?" Dr. Lowe said.

"You heard me," Dr. Grant said. Though he didn't appear angry, his voice was strong and demanding. "I'd get more done talking to my seven- and eight-year-olds."

"I'm sorry, Dr. Grant," Dr. Pridgen apologized.

"So am I," Dr. Grant said. "I'll put all the information that you need to know in a memo and have it sent to your offices. Now leave."

The doctors quietly packed their notebooks together and headed for the door.

"Except you, Dr. Dixon," Dr. Grant said. "We still need to discuss this case."

"Of course," Greg said as he placed his notebook back on the table and followed Dr. Grant to the lighted board.

"The patient's name is Jessica Charles. She's a black female, height five feet nine inches, weight 130 pounds," Dr. Grant rambled as he flipped through his handheld chart. "Her age is unknown, or at least it was left out of her information," he continued. "You do remember our chat about the specifics of the accident, right?"

"Yes," Greg said. "Traumatic head injury with pressure around the brain area," he recanted. "The patient has been in and out of a comatose state."

"Good memory," Dr. Grant said.

"Any test been run since she's been here?" Greg asked.

"The X-rays on the left are from Saint Mary's and the ones here are what we took this afternoon."

"Looks pretty bad," Greg said as he observed carefully. "Looks like there's a bit of swelling starting now," he continued.

"Good observation," Dr. Grant said. "I wasn't sure you'd notice with it being such a small amount."

"Is that why they sent her to us? The swelling solidified their decision, didn't it?"

"Right again, Dixon. Saint Mary's kept saying they could handle this injury. This subject has already been through one surgery. They thought they had rectified the injury, but apparently they were wrong."

"Can her body stand another surgery, Dr. Grant?"

Dr. Grant turned off the light on the board and took all the X-rays down. He placed them gingerly in separate sleeves and in a folder and handed the folder to Greg.

"I'll let you decide that, Dr. Dixon. She's your baby now. I know you don't need this added pressure, but in laymen's terms, her life is in your hands."

Without further conversation, Dr. Grant patted Greg's back and left the room.

"Thanks for your confidence, Simon Grant," Greg said aloud, "but you're wrong. It's out of my hands. Her life is in God's hands."

He left the conference room and stepped onto an open-door

elevator and pressed the fourth-floor button. It was the ICU floor. To his surprise, the elevator made no stops on the way to its destination. Stepping off on the fourth floor, he responded to several doctors and nurses who spoke as he passed them on his way to room 42.

"Hello," he said to a woman sitting by the bedside. "I'm Dr. Gregory Dixon."

"I'm Mattie Charles," the attractive lady said softly. "Are you my baby's doctor?"

Gregory looked at the woman lying in the bed and suddenly became speechless. There was a band of surgical tape wrapped around her head, a bruise by her left eye, and a tube going into her mouth and down her throat. Bags of fluid stood around the back and sides of her bed, and needles and tubes feeding the liquid were stuck in her arms and in the back of her hands. Her hair was extremely short from its previous shaving, but in spite of it all, Greg only had one thought: *She's beautiful!*

"Are you Jessie's doctor?" Mattie repeated.

"Yes, ma'am," Greg said. "I'm sorry." He was embarrassed and tried to regain his professionalism. "This is my first visit with Miss Charles, and I guess I wasn't prepared for what I now see."

"You look too young to be her doctor," Mattie noted.

"And you look too young to be her mother," Greg responded.

"Thank you." Mattie smiled, obviously flattered as she nervously ran her hands through her hair in an almost flirty fashion. "I was pretty young when I had her. I was just a few years older than she is right now."

"Speaking of which," Greg said, "her records don't give her age. How old is Jessica?"

"She'll be twenty-two on the nineteenth of May."

"I see." Greg made the notation in her chart. He looked back at Mattie. She looked so helpless as she silently stroked her daughter's arm.

"Ms. Charles," he began, "I plan to schedule this surgery as soon as possible. I'm going to take a look at her final tests today, and if I feel she's strong enough I'm going to schedule her for Monday."

"As in the day after tomorrow?" Mattie asked.

"Yes, ma'am. Do you have any questions or concerns that you'd like to discuss with me now?"

"Yes, Dr. Dixon, I do. I got one question and I need to know the truth. Look me in my eyes and tell me the truth. Won't nobody give me a straight answer," she said. "Nobody at Saint Mary's would tell me, and so far, no one here either."

"I don't know if I can answer your question, Ms. Charles," Greg said, "but if I can, I promise to give you the truth. What is it?"

"Is my baby gonna die?"

Greg looked again at the woman lying seemingly lifeless on the bed beside him. The heart monitor on the wall showed her steady heartbeat and her chest rose and flattened as she breathed.

"Look me in my eyes, Doctor," Mattie said tearfully. "She done been like this a long time. What are her chances?"

Gregory pulled an empty chair beside the worried mother and took her hands in his. He could feel the crumpled tissue in her hand.

"Ms. Charles," he began as her tears flowed, "if it were up to me, I could say without hesitation that your daughter will pull through this and everything will go back to normal before you know it. You want the truth? Here is the truth." Greg released the mother's hands and held his open hands in front of her.

"You see these hands, Ms. Charles?" he asked. "I don't know if you can relate to this or not, but I pray over these hands every day. I've only been practicing medicine full-time for a short while, but I've never lost a patient. That's not to brag. I give God all the glory for it. That's not saying that I never will, but if God be my helper and my strength, your daughter will not be my first."

"A Christian doctor." Mattie hugged Greg tightly. "When Jessie was at Saint Mary's I asked God for a doctor who knew something 'bout Him," she went on to explain. "When I met that Dr. Grasley, I thought God had done let me down. I see now that He didn't. I just had to move her here and meet you."

Greg smiled. "Well, knowing that you know the God I serve just gives me more faith."

"And knowing that *you* know the God *I* serve," Mattie said, "gives me more hope. I thought it was time for me to give up. Now I feel like I can hold on a little longer."

"Yes, ma'am." Greg held her hands again. "You just hold on."

CHAPTER 3

"I don't understand why I can't get any answers here." Derrick slammed the closet door as he and his family prepared for church.

"Baby, don't get all worked up," Sherry said. "You have to realize that the investigation is still going on. They can't release information to you like that."

"She was my mama, Sherry. It's not like I'm some stranger trying to find out what happened. This is about my mama."

"I know, but it's still a police matter."

"You know what I think?" he continued. "I think they're sitting on their hands and doing nothing. I think they're just hoping I'll go away and drop the subject."

"Oh, sweetheart."

"No, really. Stuff like that happens all the time, especially in the black community. That's why we have so many unsolved crimes around. We give up and they drop the matter and file it under *A* for 'Another Senseless Negro Crime.' "

"Derrick, you don't believe that."

"Sweetie, I'm a lawyer. I know how the system works. A lot of things like this get swept under the carpet."

"I know," Sherry said, "but I believe they're trying with this one. They just haven't been able to question the other driver yet. She's still in the ICU at Saint Mary's and still unconscious."

"That's another thing. Why don't they just pull the plug?"

"*Derrick Jerome Madison!*"

"Well, she ain't doing no good for nobody and she's using up our tax dollars."

"Derrick, if you don't take that back—"

"It's true."

"It is *not!*" Sherry slammed her purse on the bed. "That woman is somebody's daughter, maybe somebody's wife and somebody's mother."

"And?"

"What if it were me?"

"What?"

"You heard me," Sherry said angrily. "What if I make a mistake one day and take my eyes off the road for one short moment and in that short moment I hit somebody? What if, God forbid, that person dies in the wreck, what then? Would you stand back and say I should die too?"

"Honey, that's a stupid question. You're my wife. I love you. Why would I want you to die?"

"My point exactly. Somebody loves this lady too. Somebody wants her to live so that they can continue to love her."

"Okay, okay." Derrick held his hands up in surrender. "I see your point, but I still don't like the fact that nothing is being done."

"Who says nothing is being done?" Sherry said as she walked to the room next door and got Denise and laid her on the bed to change her diaper.

"Well," Derrick insisted, "if anything is being done, it's not being done fast enough. It's been several weeks now."

"It's better to do a thorough job than a quick one," Sherry pointed out.

Almost two months had now passed since the accident. Derrick had visited the police station so often that the investigation team was tired of seeing him. Most days they didn't have any new information. Derrick just wanted them to be assured that he wasn't going to leave them alone until a report was finalized.

"So far, all they've been able to tell me is that this other driver didn't even brake. They think that she may have fallen asleep behind the wheel. There were no skid marks from her tires to show she'd braked. Just some that show where she may have tried to swerve at the last minute to avoid hitting Mama."

"So, how could she have been asleep if she tried to avoid the collision?"

"They can only guess that she awakened right before impact. The idiot didn't have sense enough not to drive while sleepy."

"I've driven while sleepy. Am I an idiot?"

"Sherry, will you stop trying to compare yourself to this woman who killed Mama?" Derrick said in an annoyed tone.

"Okay," Sherry said. "*You've* driven while sleepy. Does that make *you* an idiot?"

"Are you making jokes about my mother's death?"

Sherry sighed. "Baby, you know I wouldn't be so cold-hearted. It just seems like the only way I can get you to look at this fairly is to either make the victim someone that you *don't* know and love, or make this girl someone you *do* know and love."

"Changing it hypothetically isn't changing what happened," Derrick said as he took Denise from Sherry's arms. "I got her if you'll get her bag," he said.

"I know, Ricky," Sherry said as she hugged him from behind. "I love you and I just want you to get beyond this."

"I know you're frustrated with hearing about Mama and the accident—" Derrick began.

"No, no, that's not it at all. I'm here to listen to whatever you want to talk about. I'm just worried that you're going to let your anger eat away at your soul."

"I admit that this whole thing makes me angry, baby," Derrick said. "It makes me very angry, but I can handle it. I just need to vent sometimes."

"Like I said," Sherry assured him, "I'm always here for you."

"I know," Derrick said, "and I love you for it. You've been wonderful through all of this."

"I love you too," Sherry said as she kissed Derrick's cheek. "Now, if we're going to get our good seats, we'd better get going."

"Wait a minute," Derrick said as he placed the sleeping Denise in her carrier. He grabbed Sherry's arm and pulled her close to him and began kissing her neck.

"What are you doing?" Sherry asked.

"We've been married two and a half years and you don't know when I'm on the prowl?"

"Derrick, we don't have time for this."

"Then we'll be late," he replied as he loosened his tie and slipped it from around his neck.

"The baby's in the room," Sherry whispered.

"She's asleep," he said as he unzipped the back of her dress and watched it fall around her feet. Pressing his lips passionately against hers, he lifted her onto the satin sheets that graced their bed.

The ride to church was a short one. The Madisons only lived four blocks from Fellowship Worship Center. During the spring and summer months, when the weather was agreeable, they would sometimes walk to church.

"Greg must be off today," Derrick observed as he noticed the parked Jaguar when they finally pulled into the parking lot after their morning rendezvous.

"Yeah, and here comes Evelyn," Sherry added as Evelyn's car sped forward to beat another oncoming vehicle to the spot next to Greg's car.

"Did you see that?" Derrick asked.

"Now, that's a shame." Sherry laughed.

Although they were only a few minutes late, service had al-

ready begun and their normal seats were taken. They were ush-
ered to an empty area beside Lena Dixon.

"This is your fault, you know," Sherry whispered to Derrick
as they sat down.

"Yeah, well, I didn't hear no complaints from you an hour
ago," he responded with a sheepish grin.

"How y'all doing this morning?" Lena asked the two of
them.

"Fine, Ms. Lena." Sherry smiled as she hugged Greg's mother.

"Yes, ma'am," Derrick agreed. "I'm a little tired from my
workout this morning, but other than that I'm fine too." Derrick
winced from Sherry's kick as he hugged Lena.

"You got to start scheduling your workouts for after church,
son," Lena suggested.

"Oh, yes, ma'am." Derrick nodded. "I plan to do it then too."

"Cut that out!" Sherry whispered with an embarrassed smile.

"Where's Greg?" Derrick asked Lena.

"He's in the office speaking with Pastor Baldwin," she said
as she pointed toward the side exit of the church.

Sherry and Derrick exchanged confused glances, but joined
in the worship service without any further inquiries.

"I know it's not normal for me to request special prayer like
this," Greg said to Pastor Baldwin, "but I feel a need here."

"I certainly understand," Pastor Baldwin replied. "It must be
quite a task to go into surgery realizing a person may or may
not pull through it."

"Yes, it is, but that's not the big issue here," Greg continued.
"I've done several surgeries before. I need to be able to be extremely honest with you, Pastor. This is doctor/patient confi-
dential stuff. I need this to stay between the two of us."

Luther Baldwin was the pride of Fellowship Worship Center.
With over five hundred members, the church had come a long way
since he took over leadership fifteen years earlier. Pastor Baldwin
was a sixty-four-year-old husband and father of eight with twelve

grandchildren. Gray-haired, tall, and broad-shouldered, he was full of wisdom and was always willing to share his knowledge with whoever was willing to listen.

"You have my word," Pastor Baldwin said.

"I have a strong prayer life, Pastor, you know that," Greg began as his pastor nodded in agreement. "I always pray before going into surgery. Every person who I operate on gets the same care and attention. Tomorrow's surgery is different for two reasons."

"Go on, Greg," Pastor Baldwin said as Greg paused and took a deep breath.

"I'm performing surgery on the woman who was in the other car that was involved in the accident that killed Rick's mother."

"Mother Madison? Oh . . . I see."

"He—Rick, I mean—has no idea that I'm doing this surgery."

"He's still bitter?"

"Very," Greg said. "I believe that he'd be very angry with me if I told him or if he found out that I'm in charge of saving this girl's life."

"Who else knows about your role in this surgery?"

"Just you and my mother," Greg said. "I plan to tell Sherry."

"Are you sure you want to do that?"

"I haven't totally decided yet, but I think so. I know she won't tell him if I ask her not to, and I want her to help me pray. She doesn't agree with the way Rick is dealing with this. We've talked about this before."

"So." Pastor Baldwin cupped his hands together and leaned forward in his seat. "You want me to pray with you that this surgery goes well and that you're not pressured in any way by the situation surrounding her injuries. And, you need this surgery to go well because you don't want there to be any question that you did your absolute best when the world, so to speak, finds out that you knew and were close to the deceased party in this accident."

"Somehow, I knew you'd understand." Greg smiled.

"I do, indeed," he said, "but you said that there were *two* reasons that you needed this surgery to be successful. You've given me one reason. What's the other?"

"My mama wants grandbabies."

"Say again?"

Greg laughed briefly, sat back in his chair, and leaned his head all the way back and looked at the ceiling.

"My mama wants grandbabies," he repeated, "and I think this is the woman that's going to help me give them to her."

"I'm sorry," Pastor Baldwin said after a moment of hesitation. "You've lost me on this one. I was under the impression that this woman wasn't conscious."

"She's not."

"So, you've not spoken with her?"

"No. Just with her mother."

"Yet you feel . . . something for her?"

"Yes."

"Love?"

"I would say yes, but I don't want you to think I'm completely crazy. All I can tell you is that I walked into a hospital room and saw a seemingly lifeless body lying in a bed with needles in her arms and tubes down her throat and I was swept off my feet. That's never happened to me before."

"I'll say," Pastor Baldwin agreed. "You see live women who smile in your face every Sunday and it doesn't move you body or soul. Then you meet a near-dead woman who's hanging on to life by the tips of God's fingers and you're thinking up baby names for your children."

"Sick, huh?" Greg laughed.

"No. Back in the country where I grew up, we called it the leash syndrome."

"The leash syndrome?"

"Yeah." Pastor Baldwin laughed as he reminisced. "When I met Clara she was fourteen years old, had a faceful of mud and a missing tooth in the front from a game of football that she was playing with her big brothers. We had just moved into the neighborhood a couple of weeks earlier. The other kids laughed at her and thought she looked funny. I thought she was beautiful. From that day on, I followed her around like a puppy with a leash around his neck."

Greg laughed. "Thus, the leash syndrome."

"Exactly."

The two shared a warm laugh. Pastor Baldwin's face turned serious again.

"Sounds like they're about finished with worship service," he said. "Why don't we go inside? I'll say a special prayer for you during altar call, and I'll do that without specifics. Brother Derrick won't know who the surgery is for."

"I really appreciate your listening to me, Pastor."

"I'm always glad to help," he said as the two of them shook hands.

Back in the sanctuary, Greg squeezed between Sherry and his mother.

"Hey, partner," Derrick said. "You okay?"

"Oh, yeah. Just had a little business to take care of."

"Would you like a fan, Mother Lena?" Evelyn Cobb whispered over Greg's shoulder from behind them.

"No, thank you," Lena said through her teeth as she forced a smile.

"Deep breaths, Mama. Deep breaths," Greg whispered.

After the choir sang, Pastor Baldwin took the stand and brought forth a powerful sermon. He had been doing a series on forgiveness for the past two Sundays. Secretly, Sherry had been hoping that the sermons would get through to Derrick's heart, but it seemed that his mind wandered throughout the service. He would periodically glance toward the seating area where his mother used to sit and wish that he could turn back the hands of time.

"Let us all stand," Pastor Baldwin instructed. "I want each of you to think on the powerful God we serve. I'm going to pray for each of you and also say a special prayer over all of the requests that were placed in our request box this morning. In addition," he continued, "I want all of you to help me pray for our brother, Dr. Gregory Dixon. He has to perform a very fragile and tedious surgery tomorrow, and we want the Lord to guide his hands and cradle the life of that patient in His arms of safety."

"Yes, sweet Jesus!" Evelyn said in a loud, high-pitched, almost screaming tone as she raised her hands toward the ceiling.

"Give me strength, Lord," Lena whispered.

"Our Father, our Father, our most righteous Father." Pastor Baldwin began all of his prayers with that same introduction. "We come to you as humbly and as lowly as we know how," he continued. "Lord, we just want to thank you."

"Thank you, Lord," the crowd responded.

Pastor Baldwin's prayers could get lengthy sometimes and this was one of those times. He thanked God for everything from life, health, and strength to deliverance from slavery and the "po house." He prayed for forgiveness of the sins of everyone from the president of the United States to his own grandson, who had apparently been sassy with a teacher at school the previous week.

"Lord," he continued, "touch each prayer request in this box on today. Grant them according to your will." His voice lowered to a solemn tone. "Oh, God, I ask that you touch the hands of Dr. Dixon. He's your servant, Lord, and he's asking for your help and your guidance. Make the hands steady and let every cut be perfect," he continued.

"Please, God," Greg prayed. In a simultaneous gesture of support, his mother grabbed his right hand and Sherry grabbed his left.

"It's gonna be hours of surgery, God," Pastor Baldwin continued. "Keep him alert and keep his mind on you. Let the very sweat of his brow be anointed." The crowd began to get excited. "Let every drop of sweat," he repeated, "be anointed." Pastor Baldwin paused for a moment, then let out a deep groan and continued. "Remove his doubt and remove his fear. God, you said we could do all things through you, for you are our strength! Give him that strength that he'll need. Not only him, but give it to every single doctor and nurse that accompanies him in that operating room. Bless the family of the patient. Give them faith, strength, and hope. Let them know it's gonna be all right because you're in control. We claim it and believe it right now in the name of Jesus Christ. Let everybody say amen."

"Amen," the congregation said in unison.

"Amen," Greg said through a teary faint smile.

Sherry handed him a tissue. "You wanna talk about it?" she offered quietly.

He nodded as they sat. "Just you. Not Rick. Okay?" he whispered in her ear.

Sherry nodded.

"Woooooooooooooooo!" Evelyn suddenly wailed from behind them as she fell forward against Greg's back. He reached over to help steady her.

"Uh-uh. Let her fall," Lena told him. "If she's that caught up, the Holy Spirit will cushion her."

"Mama!" Greg whispered, relieved that the ushers quickly came to his rescue.

As the service finally came to a close, one of the brothers stood and announced that he needed to meet for about fifteen minutes with the men of the mentoring program. That included Derrick, and this would give Greg the time he needed to talk with Sherry. After speaking quickly to a few members, he led his best friend's wife into one of the Sunday school rooms. Lena agreed to watch Denise while they met.

"Greg, what's wrong?" Sherry immediately asked after the door closed behind them.

"Nothing. Not really, anyway," he answered.

"Something's up, I can feel it. What is it that you don't want Ricky to know?"

"She's my patient now, Sherry."

"Who?"

"One guess."

"Just tell me, Greg. Who's . . . Oh, my," she said as she covered her mouth after a moment of thought.

"You guessed right."

"You cover patients at Saint Mary's now?" Sherry's voice dropped to a whisper as though she thought she could be heard by others.

"No," Greg tried to explain quickly. "Her condition worsened at Saint Mary's and they decided it was too much for them. Her mother had her moved to Robinson Memorial."

"Is she the one we were just praying for?"

"Yes."

"Oh, Greg," Sherry said as she paced the floor. "Ricky certainly can't find out about this. At least not now."

"I know. I talked to Pastor Baldwin about the entire situation at hand. He knows not to tell Rick. The only people who know are Pastor Baldwin, Mama, and you. I don't want it going any further."

"I agree."

"Sherry, did I do the right thing by telling you? Are you gonna be okay with keeping this for now?"

"Yes, Greg. Don't worry. I'm glad you told me. I want to help you pray on this one. In spite of Mama's death, I want this woman to live. Have you seen her?"

"Yeah."

"How bad is it?"

"Real bad. She's pretty banged up. They operated once at Saint Mary's but they didn't get the job done."

"Is she white or black?"

"She's black." Greg smiled faintly as he thought of her. "And quite beautiful, I must add," he continued. "She actually reminds me of someone, but I can't think of who it is. Whoever she is though," he said, "she must be beautiful too. Anyway, her name is Jessica Charles. She's a college student about to graduate with honors with a major in music. She's five feet nine, 130 pounds, and twenty-one years old with a birthday coming up on May nineteenth—"

"You like her," Sherry said, interrupting his rambling.

"What?"

"You like her," she repeated. "I can see it in your eyes."

Greg looked at Sherry and held her hands in his. "I have to save this girl," he said. "I need you to help me pray that God helps me save her. I want to ask God to let His will be done, but I'm afraid of that prayer. I want her to live."

Seeing the glistening of emerging tears in her friend's eyes, Sherry hugged him tightly. It was a side of him she'd never known before.

"We've already prayed, Greg. I don't believe the outcome will be any different if we pray for God's will to be done. I think His will is for her to live. Now we—that includes you—have to have faith to believe that it's done."

"You're right," Greg said as his cell phone rang.

"That's probably the hospital," Sherry observed.

"Hello," Greg said as he wiped away the threat of tears. He laughed softly. "Thanks," he said into the phone. "We're on our way out."

"The hospital?" Sherry asked.

"No. It's Mama. She said the men are out of the meeting. She didn't want Rick to find us in here."

"Okay," Sherry said as she headed for the door. "I'm going to walk around to the restroom and go back into the sanctuary from the other door. I'll continue praying with you, Greg."

"Thanks, sweetie."

Greg stayed in the room a moment longer to get himself together before he walked out to meet the others. He was stopped by an all-too-familiar voice calling his name. He turned to face Evelyn Cobb, who today wore a short blue skirt that barely covered her thighs. She was a fairly attractive twenty-four-year-old saleswoman. At five feet ten and wearing high heels, she stood almost face-to-face with Greg.

"Hi, Evelyn," Greg responded as she rushed to catch up with him.

"Hi." She stood so close to him that Greg thought she was going to try and kiss him.

"How are you?" he asked as he stepped back.

"I'm fine. I just wanted you to know that I'll be saying a special prayer for you and your surgical duties tonight before I go to bed."

"Thanks, Evelyn. I really appreciate that."

"And tomorrow," she continued, "I'm going to be on a special fast for your success."

"Thanks, Evelyn, but that's really not—"

"And *then*," she interrupted, "when it's all over, I'd be happy to have you come over for dinner. I'm sure you'll be hungry after such a hard day's work."

"Thanks, Evelyn, but—"

"I hear you love meat loaf. My mama says I make the best meat loaf in Washington."

"I'm sure it's delicious," Greg said. He only liked his mother's meat loaf because she made it special for him—using ground turkey instead of beef. He didn't dare tell Evelyn that, though. She'd be sure to try and match the recipe. The beeping of his pager had never sounded so heavenly. He looked at the number. It was his mother's cell number. She was coming to his rescue once more.

"Excuse me, Evelyn," he said knowingly, "I need to make a phone call." He took out his cell phone and dialed his mother's number.

"Boy," she began as she answered his call, "ignore that fast-tail girl and let's go."

"Yes, ma'am," Greg said in a business tone. "Is it serious? Do you need me to meet you right now?"

"Boy, don't make me come over there."

"No, ma'am," he continued, "that won't be necessary. I'm on my way."

He closed his phone, quickly excused himself from Evelyn, and met his mother at the car.

"Thanks, Mama." He kissed her cheek.

"Just get in the car and take me home," Lena instructed as she pushed him away. "I don't know why you don't just keep walking when she calls you."

"Mama, I don't want to be rude."

"With some people, you have to be," she said. He held her door open until she got into the car, and then walked to the driver's side.

"Mama, she knows I'm not interested in her."

"How does she know? Have you ever told her?"

"Not in so many words, but she'd have to be quite ignorant to believe that I am. I never show her any affection and I've never asked her out. As a matter of fact, I've never even spoken to her unless she spoke to me first."

"I'm telling you, son," Lena said, "even if she don't think you like her, she at least believes she's got a chance."

"Well, she's wrong."

"I know that and you know that, but Evelyn don't. You gonna have to just be flat-out frank with her. You should've nipped it in the bud a long time ago. If you don't stop her voluntarily, you'll be forced to one day. That's when it'll be ugly and you don't want that."

"Don't worry, Mama. I'll handle it."

CHAPTER 4

"I've got to get some sleep," Greg said. He turned over in his bed and looked at the clock on his nightstand table.

He had missed the evening services at church because he had to get up at 5:00 A.M. to get to the hospital and prepare for the 6:30 A.M. surgery. Thinking he needed the extra sleep, he had watched the 6:00 P.M. news, taken a long hot shower, read a few Scriptures, said his prayers, and crawled under the covers at 8:30 P.M. Since then, he'd done nothing but tossed and turned. His body was tired from the long hours he had pulled the previous week. His eyelids felt heavy enough for him to fall asleep, but he couldn't seem to do it. He looked at the clock again. It was two minutes before midnight.

Greg pulled on a pair of blue jeans and a white pullover sweater and slipped on his socks and tennis shoes. It only took him about twenty minutes to drive into work each day. With its being after midnight and with almost no traffic on the roads, he made it there in twelve.

"Hi, Dr. Dixon," a female doctor said as he passed her in the hall of the fourth floor.

"Hi," he responded. He didn't even know her name.

When he reached room 42, he slowly pushed the door open and walked in. One light was on in the corner of the otherwise darkened room. Greg expected to find Ms. Charles sitting by her daughter's bedside, but she was nowhere in sight. The heart monitor still showed a steady heartbeat and her breathing pattern still appeared normal. It was a good sign. Greg hesitantly reached forward and touched Jessica's head. She had been freshly shaved for surgery.

"You've been like this for a long time, beautiful," he whispered as he touched her hand. "You're holding on for a reason. The reason is that it's not your time to go. You're going to pull through this and God's going to help me to help you do just that." He continued, "The saints prayed for me and for you today, and I have to believe that God heard and is going to honor that prayer."

Wrapping both his hands around her hand, he noticed her hospital identification band. Her full name was printed as Jessica Grace Charles.

"Grace," he whispered. "A beautiful name for a beautiful woman. May I call you Grace?" he asked as though expecting her to open her eyes and answer.

Kneeling by her bedside, he began to pray silently. Tears that he couldn't control streamed slowly down his cheek as he spoke to God within his heart. Finally feeling a sense of peace, he ended the prayer, released her hand, dried his face, and walked slowly from the room. He slipped out of the hospital as quickly and quietly as he had slipped in.

When he finally climbed back into his bed at home, it was 2:00 A.M. He fell asleep almost immediately.

A few hours later, he awakened in fear. Had he overslept? Sitting up quickly, he looked at the clock. His alarm would be going off in two minutes. Greg breathed a sigh of relief. He had gotten less than three hours of sleep and felt surprisingly rested.

"Good morning, Dr. Dixon."

"Hi, Laquanda," he said on his way to the stairwell.

"Cre-*shon*-dri-a," she enunciated slowly with her usual smile.

"Oh, yes," Greg said. "Whatever," he mumbled as he pounced up each flight of stairs.

"Good luck, Dr. Dixon," Dr. Pridgen said as they passed each other on the fourth floor.

"Thanks," Greg responded as he headed toward room 42.

"She's not there," he heard a voice behind him say. He turned to see Mattie Charles walking up the hall behind him.

"Good morning," he said as he extended his hand to greet her. "How are you, Ms. Charles?"

"Oh, please." She shrugged. "Call me Mattie."

"I think I'd feel a bit awkward calling you Mattie," he admitted.

"Okay," she compromised, "what about Ms. Mattie?"

"I can do that," he agreed. "How are you this morning?"

"I'm as well as could be expected, I guess," she said. "They done already took Jessie out of the room."

"I see," Greg said.

"I'm glad you're doing this surgery, Dr. Dixon."

"Thank you." Greg could see the concern on her face in spite of her confidence in his abilities. "I've prayed, Ms. Mattie," he continued. "I believe it's going to be okay."

"I know." She smiled.

"So, you still have faith with me?"

"Oh, of course," she said, "but that ain't what I meant. I meant that I know that you prayed. I saw you kneeling by her bed last night."

"Oh." Greg was confused. He hadn't seen her in the room. He remembered her chair being empty.

"I had gone down to get some coffee," she continued to explain. "When I came back, I saw you kneeling by the bed in silent prayer."

"I'm sorry," Greg said. "I didn't know you were here. I didn't mean to interrupt your time with Grace."

"Grace?" Mattie asked.

"I read it on her wristband last night. Is it okay to call her that?"

"If you want." Mattie shrugged. "Don't nobody else call her that, though."

"Then Grace it is." He smiled. "As I was saying," he continued, "I wouldn't have taken so much time if I had known you were still here sitting with her."

"Oh, please don't apologize. I needed to see that. I needed to know that someone was praying for my baby besides me," she continued. "I know you told me that you prayed over your hands, but I didn't expect to see you praying over your patient."

"I don't usually do that," Greg said as he leaned against the wall and folded his arms. "Last night was a special case. I'll be sure to explain it to you later, but let's just say that I felt led to do it that way."

"Thank you, Dr. Dixon."

"Well," Greg said as he looked at his watch, "I have to get going now. You'll be in the waiting area, right?"

"Yes. Will I know something soon?"

"This surgery may take several hours, Ms. Mattie. Just try and be patient. I'll send a nurse out to give updates as often as necessary. When it's over, I'll come out and speak with you myself."

"Okay," she said with new tears in her eyes.

Greg stepped forward and took the worried mother into his arms. "It's okay to cry, Ms. Mattie," he told her, "as long as you keep a prayer in your heart and believe that God is going to be there. He's going to guide these hands. It's going to be all right."

"I don't know what I'll do if I lose her," she said with her head still buried in Greg's chest. "We were finally becoming really close after all these years."

"If God be with me," Greg said as he released her and began to walk away, "the two of you will have plenty of time to secure your close relationship."

Mattie Charles watched as her daughter's doctor walked away. His face was set with determination and confidence and his strides were quick and long. She knew that God was able to bring her daughter through the surgery, but it helped to hear it from the doctor who would be holding the knife.

Walking slowly into the waiting room, she stood by the window watching cars and school buses drive by on the streets below as the rest of the world went about its busy schedule. For about forty-five minutes, Mattie could do nothing but watch the happenings of the community from the fourth-floor window of Robinson Memorial.

"Mattie Charles?"

Mattie turned, expecting to see a nurse coming to give an update of Jessica's surgery. Instead, she looked into the face of a woman dressed in regular clothes.

"Yes?" she answered.

"Hi, I'm Lena Dixon," she said as she extended her hand. "I'm Dr. Dixon's mother."

Mattie smiled. "Well, I see he didn't get his long legs from you."

Lena laughed. "No, those came from his father."

The two women sat in a quiet corner of the waiting area. There were several other people in the room with them, but no one was doing much talking. Everyone seemed so concerned about whomever they were waiting to hear news on.

"Did you come by just to see me?" Mattie asked.

"Well, my son told me how serious this operation was, and I was just sitting at home praying and I just thought that maybe you didn't want to be alone during this time," Lena said. "Now if you want me to leave," she continued, "then you just tell me and I'll leave and won't have no hard feelings."

"No, Ms. Dixon." Mattie shook her head and smiled. "I'm glad you're here, and I'd be glad for you to sit with me."

"Well, if you want me to stay, then the first thing you have to do is call me Lena."

"I will, if you call me Mattie."

"That's your name, ain't it?" Lena said. "I didn't plan to call you nothing else."

"Mrs. Mattie Charles?" The two women looked up to see a young nurse standing in the doorway of the waiting room searching for a reaction from the proper person.

"I'm Mattie Charles." Mattie raised her hand to get the nurse's attention.

"Hi, Mrs. Charles," the nurse said as she walked over to the corner where they now stood.

"Hello," she responded with visible caution. "How's my daughter?"

"Jessica is still in surgery," the nurse began, "but Dr. Dixon asked me to come and let you know that everything is going well. Her blood pressure is stable and she's continuing to breathe on her own."

Mattie breathed a sigh of relief. "How much longer is it gonna be?" she asked.

"I'm not sure, ma'am. It's only been an hour and these types of surgeries can take a while. It may be several more hours, but Dr. Dixon has told me to give you an update at least once each hour."

"Will you let him know that I'm here with her?" Lena asked. "I'm his mother. Tell him that I came to spend some time with Mattie while the girl was under the knife."

"Yes, ma'am," the nurse replied as she walked away.

"You all right?" Lena asked as Mattie sank into her chair silently.

"Yeah," she began. "You know, I have so much to thank God for. My Jessie ain't never gave me no problems. She was always a good girl in school and at home. For a long time I wasn't even a decent mama to her, so she was always closer to her grandmother up until she died a couple of years ago."

"What do you mean you weren't a decent mother?" Lena sat down next to her.

"I mean, I was on the streets when I got pregnant with her," Mattie explained. "I left home when I was sixteen. Left with a boy I thought loved me. I remember Mama telling me that I was gonna end up with my heart broke. She was sho 'nuff right, too.

He was twenty years old, had his own car and his own run-down apartment. He stuck with me for a year and then one day just threw me out on the streets. He had done found himself somebody else."

"Was he her daddy?"

"Oh, no. He was just the beginning of my troubles. Jessie came along much later in my life. But, at seventeen I was on the streets with nowhere to go and I didn't know nobody."

"You mean at the age of seventeen, your mama wouldn't let you back home?" Lena asked. "Even if you said you was sorry?"

"I'm sure she'd have let me back," Mattie said. "I was just too proud and selfish to let her know that she was right. For years I just lived wherever I could and with whoever would let me. It's a wonder I didn't have twenty or thirty kids."

"Did you eventually go back home?"

"Eventually, but not till after I had done got myself knocked up." Mattie shook her head as if the thought of it all disgusted her all over again. "Mind you," she continued, "I was a grown woman by then. I think I was 'bout twenty-seven or so when I gave birth. To this day, I can't tell you who her daddy is. I was able to narrow it down to two possibilities though."

"Jesus," Lena responded in shock.

Mattie laughed at her expression. "Yeah," she said. "Once she was born, it was pretty clear to me that her father was white. I was only with three of them and only two in the time frame of the pregnancy. I admit, it got pretty bad for me there for a while. Of course, I don't have to tell you that back in our day, being unwed and pregnant wasn't something that folks smiled at. Add to that that the daddy wasn't black made matters worse. Being that I was an adult didn't matter at all. I was single, pregnant, uneducated, and unwed."

"So, when did you finally marry?"

"Never did."

"Never?"

"Never," Mattie repeated.

"Didn't she just call you *Mrs.* Charles?"

"Yeah, but I guess that's 'cause I didn't have time to tell her this story."

"So," Lena said, ignoring Mattie's sarcasm for the moment, "you never got married and never had any other children?"

"No. My mama raised her for the first three or four years of her life. I didn't know nothing about being nobody's mama."

"What made you grow up?" Lena asked.

"Jesus," Mattie answered with a laugh. "By then I was 'bout thirty years old. Finding God completely changed my whole life around. I settled down, got my GED, and concentrated on trying to become a mother that my baby deserved. She was such a good daughter."

"What you mean by 'was'?" Lena asked. "Why you talking like she dead or something? Your girl got the best doctor that this hospital has and she got the prayers of the saints."

"You need to calm down," Mattie said emphatically. "I know 'bout how good her doctor, who just happens to be your son, is. And I know 'bout the prayers that have been sent up for Jessie. I didn't mean it like that. I just meant that she was good as a child. You're mixing my words up."

"Oh," Lena said. "I guess I misunderstood."

"I guess you did."

"Well, now, you did say 'was.' "

"That's because she *was* a child, but now she *is* a grown woman."

"Fine," Lena said. "That's just not the way it sounded. Maybe you should express yourself a bit clearer."

"Or maybe you should be a better listener," Mattie mumbled.

"Well, now, hold up, sister," Lena responded. "Don't catch all that attitude with me. I'm here to help you out."

"Don't do me no favors."

"Well, this is a nice time to tell me that. I done spent the past hour here trying to be a help."

"I didn't ask you to come."

"You didn't ask me to leave either."

The ladies' raised voices had begun to draw attention from others who were waiting. Noticing the stares, Lena picked up her purse and coat and walked to the opposite side of the room and sat in an empty chair. An equally embarrassed Mattie sat in her own chair and stared out the window. A light rainfall had begun.

"Hi, Mrs. Charles."

"Huh?" Mattie jumped as the voice startled her.

"I'm sorry," the nurse apologized. "Are you all right?"

"Yes," Mattie said as she adjusted her skirt and stood. "You here to tell me more about Jessie's surgery? How is she?"

From across the room, Lena tried unsuccessfully to hear the conversation between the nurse and Mattie.

"I'm sorry it took me longer than it should have to come out and update you. I didn't notice that more than an hour had passed since my last visit."

"That's okay, sugar," Mattie assured her. "How is she?" she asked again.

"Everything is still going well. She's been a strong trooper," the nurse said with a smile. "She's not out of the woods yet, but the worst of it is over. There was one point where she lost a lot of blood, but that's fairly normal and we've replenished her supply."

"So what you're saying is that she's going to get through this surgery okay."

"Well, of course, I can't say that for certain," the nurse clarified, "but she has the best doctors in there with Drs. Grant and Dixon."

"I agree." Mattie smiled.

"Well, I'm going to get back now. I'll be back in an hour or so to let you know any further details."

"Thank you."

Lena quickly sat back in her seat in an attempt to appear uninterested in the conversation that had just taken place a few feet across the room. She assumed that everything was okay since Mattie calmly returned to her seat and picked up a magazine and began reading.

In spite of her desire to know the details of Jessica's surgery, Lena kept her distance and continued to sit quietly in the corner. She wasn't sure she even liked the sassy-mouthed woman whom she barely knew, but she didn't want to leave until she was certain that the operation was successful. The minutes passed as she sat watching the others come in and out of the waiting area. Looking at the clock on the wall, she noticed that nearly three hours had passed since the start of the surgery. She picked up a magazine from the table and began reading.

"Hi, Mama," Greg whispered as he stood by her chair.

"Hey, baby." She smiled as she stood and hugged her son. "I didn't even see you walk in."

"Kelly told me that you were here."

"Who?"

"The nurse."

"Oh," Lena said. "How is the girl? Is the surgery over?"

"Where's Ms. Mattie?" Greg asked without answering his mother's questions. "I thought you were with her."

"I was, but we had a little argument and I moved over here. She's over there." Lena pointed across the room at Mattie, who was still reading her magazine.

"Well, I don't know what kind of argument the two of you had, but if you want to hear about the surgery, you'll have to come back over here with her," Greg explained. "It's her daughter and she's the one I need to give the details to."

"I don't think she wants me over there," Lena said.

"Well, I'll fill you in later then," Greg said as he walked toward the opposite side of the room.

Lena sat back down and watched as Greg approached Mattie. He spoke her name softly to get her attention. "Ms. Mattie."

"Dr. Dixon," Mattie said as she stood quickly. "How is she? Is it over?"

"Yes, ma'am," Greg responded, "it's over. Grace came through the surgery fine."

"Thank you, Jesus," Mattie said as she hugged Greg tightly. "Oh, Dr. Dixon, thank you so much," she continued.

"The next few days are very critical," Greg explained as he sat down and motioned for Mattie to sit beside him. "She's going to remain in the ICU until I'm comfortable with moving her to a regular room. She has several stitches in the back of her head from the incision. I'm confident that she will be okay, but the road to recovery may be a lengthy one. Our main concern is to get her to wake up. She's been semiconscious or unconscious for a long time and getting her awake and coherent is at the top of our agenda."

"I understand." Mattie nodded as she sighed in relief. "Thank you again. When can I see—"

"Emergency! Dr. Dixon, please return to operating room number nine immediately!" a man's voice said over the hospital speakers. "Dr. Dixon, your immediate assistance is needed in the OR."

"Oh, my God," Mattie gasped. "It's my baby, ain't it?"

"Just stay here," Greg instructed as he got up and ran from the room.

"Oh, my God!" Mattie wailed.

Lena raced to her side and sat in the seat that her son had suddenly made vacant. She placed her arms around Mattie's shoulders and spoke softly to her to try and calm her down. Mattie covered her face with her hands and laid her head over on Lena's shoulder and continued to cry uncontrollably.

Greg's long strides made double time as he raced down the hospital hall while being careful not to collide with any of the passing doctors or patients. The double doors to the operating room swung open as he pushed through and turned to enter the room that he had left only a few minutes earlier.

"Kelly," he panted as she met him at the door, "what's wrong?"

"She's seizing," Kelly said frantically. "Dr. Grant is trying to get it under control, but it's pretty bad."

Greg rushed past her and saw two assistants holding Jessica down as her body jerked violently. Becoming increasingly concerned about the fresh stitches, he cradled her head as the others continued to try and control her body.

"How long has she been seizing?" Greg asked as Dr. Grant rushed to her side with a syringe.

"It's been a little more than five minutes," he said. "I'm going to give her a shot of midazolum," he continued. "Hold her mouth open so I can squirt this inside."

Kelly tried prying Jessica's clenched jaws apart while Greg assisted by holding her head as still as he could. The seizing had been going on for too long, and concern was showing on Greg's face. He closed his eyes and began to pray inside as he continued to hold her head steady.

"Ugh!" Dr. Grant grunted as the syringe fell from his hand and burst onto the floor. Jessica had knocked it from his hand at the moment that he began to administer the medicine. Only a small drop touched her lips.

"Get me another syringe!" he ordered.

Let the very sweat of his brow be anointed. Greg remembered Pastor Baldwin's words during the prayer in Sunday's service.

"Wait a minute." Greg held up one hand.

"We don't have a minute," Dr. Grant said.

"Hand me that cloth," Greg said to Kelly.

"Excuse me?" Kelly said, seeming confused.

"What are you doing, Dixon?" Dr. Grant asked. "We can wipe up the floor later!"

"The cloth, Kelly!" Greg repeated, ignoring Dr. Grant's comments. "Hand me the cloth!"

He took the cloth from Kelly that had been used to wipe the perspiration from his forehead during surgery, and laid it across Jessica's forehead. Her body took one last hard jerk and she relaxed against the operating table.

"What the—" Dr. Grant began.

"Turn her head so I can check the stitches," Greg instructed.

Kelly and two others in the room turned Jessica's head as Greg placed his protective gloves on his hands. The stitches were still intact and her vital signs slowly returned to normal.

"Thank you, Jesus," Greg whispered as he eased her head back onto the table and picked up her chart to make notes.

"What just happened here?" a stunned Dr. Grant asked as the others quietly stood in wait for an answer from Greg.

"I believe we all just witnessed a miracle," Greg said with a smile.

"Or," Dr. Grant began, "maybe the little medicine that made contact kicked in. We'll never really know, right?" he said as he motioned for the others to disperse.

"Oh, *we* know, Dr. Grant," Greg said. "You know as well as I do that there wasn't nearly enough medicine going in to begin to stop what we both know was a grand mal seizure. You can choose to ignore it if you like, but you know me. I give credit where it's deserved and God gets the glory for this one."

"Listen, Dixon," Dr. Grant said, "I know how much you believe in God and all, and frankly, so do I, but I suggest you stick with the medicine theory when you talk to the family. I think they'll be able to accept that better and they won't go home thinking we allowed a nutcase to operate on their relative."

"Thanks for your suggestion, Dr. Grant," Greg said with a laugh. "However," he continued, "this family will understand the miracle theory just as well."

Dr. Grant walked out of the room shaking his head. Only Greg and Jessica remained in the room. He picked the cloth off of the table where Kelly had moved it in order to check Jessica's vitals following the seizure. Burying his face in the cloth, he quietly thanked God for stopping Jessica's seizure.

"Well, Grace," he whispered as he took her hand in his, "we're going to take this one day at a time. With God's help, we made it over the first hurdle. I plan to be right here with you every step of the way, so don't you dare give up on me. You hang in there."

"Is this patient ready to be moved?" one of two assistants asked as they entered several minutes later with a bed.

"Yes," Greg said as he stepped away from the operating table.

The men carefully lifted Jessica from the table and placed her on the prepared bed. Greg handed them the chart to place on the end of the bed and they began pushing her from the room.

"Wait a minute," Greg said. He walked over and placed the cloth under Jessica's head and motioned for the orderlies to take her away.

"Just in case," he whispered as the doors closed behind them.

Realizing that it had been over half an hour since he left a crying, worried mother in the waiting room, he washed his hands and headed back down the hallway. As he entered the now half-filled room, he saw his mother and Ms. Mattie holding hands and praying together quietly in the corner where he had left them sitting. He walked over to them and placed a hand on each of their shoulders. They both slowly turned and looked up at him, expecting the worst but hoping for the best.

"Your prayers have been answered." Greg smiled. "She's going to be okay."

"Oh, thank God," Mattie said as she collapsed on Lena's chest and wept.

"She's okay?" Lena asked.

"Yes, ma'am," Greg said with a tired smile. "She's still unconscious, as she should be at this point, but she's fine."

Mattie stood up and hugged Greg's waist tightly. She remained speechless as her tears continued to flow.

"You're welcome," Greg said, understanding the meaning of her embrace.

He sat her down in her chair and Lena moved over so that he could sit between them.

"Ms. Mattie," he began, "I need to fill you in on all the details, so I need you to listen to me, okay?" He continued as she nodded. "Grace suffered a grand mal seizure. It was pretty bad and, honestly, kind of scary for a while there. With God's help, we got her calmed down and her vitals are fine now. I'm not sure if these seizures will remain a part of her recovery or not. I'm going to order another MRI as well as a CT scan and a comprehensive panel of blood tests. I'm hopeful that this won't be an ongoing concern, but I must tell you that it's not uncommon for a patient who has suffered the head injuries that Grace has and who has gone through this type of surgery to have recurring seizures."

"Grace?" Lena looked at Mattie. "I thought her name was Jessica."

"It is," Greg said before Mattie could. "Her middle name is Grace and that's what I decided to call her."

"That child's name is Jessica Grace?" Lena asked. "What kind of name is that?"

"Ma," Greg warned, "do I need to send you back to your corner over there?"

"Sorry," she mumbled.

"They can be treated, right?" Mattie asked. "The seizures, I mean."

"Absolutely."

"But you're not saying for sure that she's going to keep having them," she added.

"Oh, no," Greg said. "Not at all. As a matter of fact, with the two of you praying for her, I believe we can claim total healing."

"Amen," Lena agreed.

"When can we see her?" Mattie asked the question she'd started to ask before Greg had been called away.

"She's just being set up in her room now. As soon as they have her totally prepared and settled, I'll come back or send someone else back to let you know."

"Thanks again, Dr. Dixon," Mattie said as she placed her hand on top of his.

"You look tired, son," Lena said. "Are you okay?"

"Yes, Mama," Greg responded. "I didn't get a lot of sleep

last night and the surgery took a lot out of me, but I'm fine," he said as he stood to his feet. "I'll let you know when you can come in and see her," he told Mattie as he walked out of the waiting area.

Mattie and Lena sat quietly for a moment, not quite know-ing what to say after Greg left the room. Mattie took a deep breath.

"I'm sorry I raised my voice," she said.

"No," Lena said. "I'm the one who should apologize. I should understand the stress that you've been going through over the past few weeks. I didn't handle it the best way I could have."

"Yeah, but I don't have no right to take out my stress on you," Mattie responded. "You were just trying to help and I didn't show no appreciation for what you were doing."

"Well, now, that is true," Lena agreed.

"Umph," Mattie grunted as she glanced at Lena from the corner of her eye.

"You want some coffee?" Lena offered.

"Thank you. I like it with sugar, but no cream unless they got some kinda flavored cream."

"Honey, this is not McDonald's," Lena said. "I'll just bring you some sugar and cream and you can flavor it however you want."

"Old battle-ax," Mattie mumbled as Lena walked away.

Shortly after Lena returned with the hot drink, Greg walked in and motioned for the two of them to follow him.

"I'd appreciate it if you could cut today's visit short," he briefed them as they walked down the hall together. "She's a bit swollen from the surgery, but keep in mind that that is normal. Also, I'm a wholehearted believer that patients who are uncon-scious but have normal brain activity can hear what you say when you talk around them," he continued as they stood at the door of Jessica's room. "Therefore, it's a good thing to keep the conversation positive."

They walked quietly into the dimly lit room. The nurses had

attached all the necessary bags of fluid on the stands and her medicine dripped slowly into the tubes that led to her veins.

"Well, isn't she a pretty one?" Lena remarked as she walked over and touched Jessica's forehead.

"Yes, she is," Greg agreed.

"Thank you." Mattie smiled. "People always did say that she looked like me."

"Now, that I don't see," Lena said sarcastically.

"Yeah, well, this doctor son of yours must be the spitting image of his father, 'cause he sho didn't get none of his good looks from you," Mattie responded.

"Ladies," Greg warned again.

"Sorry," they both mumbled as Greg held in the smile that tugged at his lips.

"Jessie, baby," Mattie started as she held her daughter's hand. "You done good, girl. The Lord pulled you through this one and your mama sho is thankful for it. Now, you just need to open them pretty eyes so you can thank Dr. Dixon yourself. He'll be expecting to hear your appreciation when you come to. Ain't that right, Dr. Dixon?"

"Yes, ma'am," Greg said softly, "but seeing her open those pretty eyes would be thanks enough."

CHAPTER 5

Detective John Morrison massaged his temples in an attempt to keep calm as Derrick once again walked into his office demanding updated information on the accident that took the life of his mother.

"Mr. Madison," he began, "I understand your concern—"

"No, you don't!" Derrick interrupted. "You don't even come close to understanding my concern. If you did, you'd have more information to give me."

"The information doesn't fall out of the sky, Mr. Madison."

"You are a detective, for God's sake!" Derrick pounded his hand on Detective Morrison's desk. "Are you and your men even trying to solve this mystery? A woman died in this accident and that woman happens to be my mother. I want to know what happened."

"So do I, but we can't take this investigation any further until we speak with the other victim in the crash."

"Victim?" Derrick said as he stepped back from the desk. "You see her as a victim? She was the cause of the crash! Since when did she become a victim?"

"See, that's what I mean, Mr. Madison. You think you have the whole thing figured out. You'd be happy if I just ended this investigation and had this woman charged with vehicular homicide."

"Yes, I would," Derrick admitted. "That's exactly what it is and you know it. The facts are as clear as day to me. Yet, you're the detective and you can't see what's right in front of your face."

"What are the facts, Mr. Madison?"

"The facts are," Derrick began, "my mother was hit in a near head-on collision by this woman who was apparently not paying attention to the road. You said yourself that she didn't even brake and that she probably fell asleep at the wheel."

"Probable cause is not fact, Mr. Madison. We can't charge anyone with something that we're not sure of."

"So if this other driver dies, or denies falling asleep, then what?"

"Well, as we understand it, she's not going to die. She's had a successful surgery and is expected to make a slow recovery. We're hopeful that we'll be able to speak with her within several days."

"Well, how long before you all plan to follow up with Saint Mary's for the status of her progress?"

"We have to wait for clearance from her doctor," Morrison began. "She's not at Saint Mary's anymore. She was moved to Robinson Memorial several days ago and had the surgery there."

"What?"

"Which part would you like me to repeat?"

"This girl is at Robinson Memorial?"

"Yes. She was apparently moved there after an unsuccessful surgery at Saint Mary's. The staff at Robinson is known for their success in the OR."

"I'm aware of that," Derrick said as he snatched his jacket from the chair and walked from the detective's office.

"I will let you know as soon as we find new information," Detective Morrison called as Derrick continued to walk away.

Derrick jumped into his car and headed to Greg's town

house. In his anger, he didn't even notice that Greg's car wasn't parked in its space. Running up the flight of stairs, he banged on Greg's door. When there was no answer after a few minutes, he ran back to his car and drove five miles eastward, toward Lena Dixon's home.

"Derrick, hi," Lena said as she opened the door. "You don't have to knock so hard—I ain't deaf, you know."

"Where's Greg?" Derrick asked without returning her greeting.

"I guess he at his own house," Lena said hesitantly. "What's the matter with you?"

"The matter is that I have a liar as a friend," Derrick said.

"Now you just wait a minute," Lena warned defensively. "You ain't talking about my boy, I know."

"Yes, I am. I *am* talking about your boy. So, if you see him before I do, let him know that I said it," Derrick said as he turned to walk away.

"I don't know what your problem is, Derrick Madison," Lena said as he stepped off her front porch, "but till you get your attitude straight, don't come knocking on my door again."

Derrick got into his car without a response and sped away. In a mixture of anger and fear, Lena rushed to her phone and dialed Greg's cell number.

"Hello," he answered.

"Greg, baby, where you at?"

"What's the matter, Mama?" Greg sat up straight on the couch.

"Where are you?" she repeated.

"I'm at Rick's, talking to Sherry. What's wrong?"

"You need to get up from over there."

"What? Mama, what are you talking about? Are you okay?"

"Derrick's looking for you."

"I was looking for him too. I just thought I'd wait on him. Sherry said that he went to visit the investigators again."

"Well, I don't know what he found out, but he so mad at you he got smoke coming out his ears."

"At me? Why?"

"I don't know, baby, but I just want you to get from over there and go somewhere else. He called you a liar and told me to tell you that he was looking for you."

"What's the matter?" Sherry asked as she listened to Greg's end of the conversation and read the concern in his face.

"Mama, it's okay," Greg assured her. "I'll be okay. I'm going to wait here for him. He'll come home eventually."

"Ain't you heard nothing I said? I don't think the two of you should be in the same place at the same time. Not with him being angry like he is. I don't know what he upset about, because he didn't tell me, but he very mad, Greg. I don't want you there when he gets home."

"Mama, please trust me to make the right decision," Greg said. "I'll be okay. You just stop worrying. I'll call you and come by your house after I speak with him. I'm sure that I know what it's about. I'll be fine. Please let me handle it."

"Okay," Lena said after a short pause. "Be sure to call me though. I'll be waiting to hear from you."

"Okay, Mama. I love you. Thanks for calling."

"I love you too, baby. Be careful."

Greg sighed deeply, closed his phone, and replaced it in his pocket.

"Greg?" Sherry said.

"Rick stopped by Mama's looking for me. She said he was angry and called me a liar and basically said some threatening things concerning me to Mama."

"What? Has he lost his mind? What's his problem?"

"My guess is that he found out about Grace and the surgery," Greg said.

"Oh, no. How? Who would tell him? I promise, Greg, I didn't breathe a word of it. I wouldn't do that," Sherry rambled.

"I know, Sherry. It wasn't you. I'm sure he found out from the folks who are investigating the accident."

"Why don't you go home, Greg? I'll calm him down when he gets home. Then you can talk to him later."

"No, Sherry. I'll speak with him. I'm not running away from this. I didn't do anything wrong and I'm not gonna act like I did."

Greg remained sitting as Sherry began pacing the floor nervously. She walked over to the window and peered out. Derrick was generally home by this time, but he was apparently late due to the fact that he was hunting for Greg. They had been best friends for a long time, and she hated knowing that her husband was angry enough with Greg to resort to name-calling. She closed her eyes as she saw his Town Car park behind Greg's Jaguar.

"He's here, Greg," she announced as she turned from the window.

"It's okay, Sherry," Greg said as he stood and walked over to her. "Don't worry about it. We'll work it out."

"Is there something you need to tell me?" Derrick demanded as he slammed the front door behind him.

"Ricky," Sherry said, "you'll wake up Dee."

"Well?" he demanded as he walked forward to face Greg.

"Not that I'm aware of," Greg said calmly.

"Don't treat me like I'm some kind of idiot, Greg."

"I wasn't aware that I was doing that, Rick. What's the problem?"

"You tell me."

"Ricky," Sherry interrupted. "Calm down, sweetie. What's wrong?"

"I'll tell you what's wrong, baby. We have a friend who believes in deception and lies, that's what's wrong."

"I have not lied to you, Rick," Greg said.

"So, you're just gonna play dumb, huh?" Derrick tossed his keys on the sofa and stood directly in front of Greg.

"Are you threatening me, Rick?"

"Do you *feel* threatened?"

"Okay, Ricky, that's enough," Sherry said as she pulled his arm.

"Still can't think of anything you should be telling me?" Derrick said as he jerked his arm away from Sherry's grasp.

"No, Rick. Actually I can't think of anything that I *should* be telling you."

"Okay, well, let me refresh your memory," Derrick said as he poked Greg's forehead with his index finger. "Is the woman who killed my mama at your hospital or not?"

"The woman who was involved in the accident with your mother is at Robinson Memorial, yes."

"So why did you lie to me?"

"I never lied to you."

"You didn't tell me she was there."

"It wasn't my responsibility to tell you and, quite frankly, it's not your business."

"Not my business? My mother is dead because of her and you don't think it's my business?"

"No, Rick. It's not your business. What difference would it have made if I told you? Were you going to try and have her removed from Robinson?"

"I had a right to know."

"No, you didn't. Where that lady gets her medical care is no business of yours."

"Who's her doctor?"

"I am," Greg answered without uncertainty.

"I guess you *forgot* to tell me that, too."

"No. You never asked. If you had asked before like you're doing now, I would have told you. You never asked."

"You knew I'd want to know."

"I also knew that it was best that you didn't know. You're proving that right now."

"See what I mean, Sherry?" Derrick said as he continued to look Greg in the eyes. "Our so-called friend has been hiding information from us."

"Ricky, I—" Sherry started.

"Stay out of this, Sherry," Greg said as he held up his hand.

He knew she was about to confess to knowing of Jessica's whereabouts, and he didn't want Derrick knowing of his wife's involvement.

"Did you perform the surgery?" Derrick continued.

"Yes," Greg admitted.

"You creep!" Derrick said as he drew back his fist and punched Greg in the jaw. The blow sent him falling back onto the sofa and the weight of Derrick's body hurling on top of him momentarily held him there.

"Ricky, no!" Sherry screamed as she tried to pull him away.

Greg pushed Derrick off of him and watched him land on the living room floor. Sherry jumped between the two of them as Derrick stood up and started toward Greg.

"I'm not going to fight you, Rick," Greg said as he stood and wiped the blood from his lower lip.

"Fine, Greg," Derrick shot back, "but I'm gonna kick your butt whether you fight back or not. Step aside, Sherry."

"No, Ricky," Sherry said. "This is so childish and so unnecessary. I want you to cut it out right now. Look at what you've done already. He's bleeding."

"Step aside, Sherry," he repeated through clenched teeth.

"No."

"It's okay, Sherry," Greg said. "If beating me up will make him feel better, let him do it."

"No," Sherry said. "Now this has got to stop." She turned to face Derrick. "I will not stand here and watch you make the biggest mistake of your life. Now if you're gonna hit Greg, you'll have to knock me down to do it."

"Stop being silly, Sherry," Derrick said as he took another step forward.

"*I'm* being silly?" Sherry said as Dee began crying in the bedroom. "I'm being silly?" she repeated. "You're fighting your best friend because he did the job he's paid to do and you think I'm being silly."

"I don't have a best friend," Derrick said.

"I'm sorry you feel that way," Greg said.

"I'll bet you are."

"Leave, Greg," Sherry said. "I need to take care of Dee and talk to Ricky alone."

"Please stay out of it, Sherry," Greg said softly, trying to disguise the pleading in his voice.

"You'd better take her advice," Derrick warned.

"I just need to speak with him and calm him down," Sherry responded while trying to assure him with her eyes that she wasn't going to let Derrick know of her knowledge of the situation.

Greg wiped another trickle of blood from his lip, picked up his jacket, and walked slowly toward the door. Sherry walked beside him to be sure that Derrick didn't try to swing at him as he passed. Greg opened the door and turned to face his friend.

"I'm sorry about what happened to Ms. Julia, and I'm sorry that you've chosen to handle your grief this way. I've tried to be here for you in any way you needed. In your line of business, you've defended people who you knew were guilty and won their cases. Yet, we don't even know the details of this accident and you're angry because I did my job by performing a lifesaving operation on a woman placed in my care.

"I'm sorry that you no longer want me as your friend, but I'm not sorry for anything I've done or about the manner in which I handled this situation. Regardless of how you feel about me, Rick, I still love you and I got your back whether you want that or not."

"I don't," Derrick assured him. "Now, get out of my house," he said as he turned and walked toward his crying daughter's room. "Get out and don't even *think* about coming back."

Sherry's tears broke loose as she walked out behind Greg and closed the door behind her. Greg wrapped his arms around her and allowed her to cry on his shoulder.

"It's okay, sweetie," he told her.

"No, it's not. It's worse than I thought," Sherry said through her tears as she pulled back. "Look at you," she continued. "You're still bleeding."

"It's not as bad as it looks," he tried to assure her. "I can feel the cut. It's inside my lower jaw. I'll get some ice for it as soon as I get home. I'll be fine. I know these things. I'm a doctor."

Greg's antics didn't work. Sherry continued to cry softly as she covered her face with her hands.

"Sherry," he said as he pulled her hands from her face and lifted her chin to look at him, "I know this whole situation looks bad and I admit he took it differently than I thought. I never would have thought that he'd actually hit me. However, I *still* know that it's going to be okay. It has to be. God has been with me so far and I'm sure He's not gonna bail out on me now. Somehow, this is going to work out.

"I need you to promise me that you won't tell him that you knew about this," he continued as he lowered his voice. "He doesn't need to know that. I don't want him angry with you. You have to live with him. I don't. Promise me you won't tell him."

"What if he asks?" Sherry said.

"He won't. Not unless you show some sign or give some hint that you knew. I'm not asking you to lie. Just keep handling it the way you have so far. Please, Sherry. Please do that for me."

"Okay," she promised.

"Now, go back inside before your being out here upsets him."

"You're not really going to stay away, are you?" she asked.

"For now, yes. I have to respect his wishes for me not to return to his house. But, I'm just a phone call away if you need me. I mean that, Sherry, okay?"

Sherry nodded and gave him one last hug before going inside. Greg walked slowly to his car and drove away. Since he was closer to his mother's house than his, and he knew she was worried about him, he decided to stop by. She opened the door quickly after he identified himself.

"Hey, baby. You all right?"

"I'm okay, Mama. Can you fix me some ice in a paper towel or something?"

"Why?" she asked as she inspected his face closely. "What happened?"

Greg pulled out his bottom lip and showed her the bloody cut.

"Derrick Madison did this?"

"It was just a scuffle, Ma."

"Derrick Madison hit you in the mouth?"

"Can I get some ice please, Mama?"

"You know where the freezer is," she said as she pointed toward the kitchen. "I got a phone call to make."

"No, you don't, Mama," Greg said as he placed his hand on top of the phone. "I don't need you taking up for me. I'm a grown man. I don't need my five-foot mama fighting my battles for me."

"I'm five feet *five*," she corrected, "and don't let my stature fool you."

"Please, Mama. Let it rest. I'll be okay."

"Tell me what happened," she said as Greg got the ice and placed it inside a napkin that he picked up from the table.

"I stayed at his house and waited on him. He started calling me a liar and accused me of not disclosing information that I should have told him about. He asked me if I was the one who did the surgery and when I said yes, he punched me, knocked me onto the sofa, and started trying to fight. I pushed him off of me and he hit the floor. He wanted to fight further, but I told him that I wasn't going to. He insisted. Sherry stood between the two of us and asked me to leave. Rick made it quite clear that I was no longer welcome in his home and that I was also no longer his friend."

"Jesus," Lena said as she rubbed her forehead.

"Yeah, it got pretty bad. Poor Sherry was caught right in the middle. She wanted to tell him that she'd known the whole time."

"But she didn't, right?"

"I made her promise not to. She said she wouldn't. I think what hurts her most is that Rick ended our friendship over this."

"What you gonna do now, Greg?"

"I'm going to keep living, Mama," he said as he removed the ice from his lip. "Keep living and keep praying. Somehow things have got to work out."

The piercing sound of Greg's pager ended their conversation. His mother wrapped more ice in a cloth and gave it to him on his way out. He kissed her jaw and reassured her that he was going to be fine.

"Good evening, Dr. Dixon."

"Good evening, Shacronda."

"Creshondria," she corrected.

"I'm going to get it right one day," he responded to her delight.

"Evening, Dixon," Dr. Pridgen said as he met Greg in the stairwell. "I thought you were off today."

"I thought so too, but I was paged," Greg responded. "Are we having a meeting?"

"Not that I'm aware of," Dr. Pridgen said. "I haven't seen Grant in the past hour or so. He's probably in his office."

Dr. Grant's office was on the third floor. Dr. Pridgen exited the stairs at the second floor and waved at Greg. Entering the third floor, Greg saw Dr. Grant standing in the doorway of his office.

"Hi, Dr. Dixon," a nurse remarked with a smile as he passed the nurses' station.

"Good evening," Greg responded.

"Dixon," Dr. Grant said as he extended his hand. "Sorry to call you on your day off. I know how few and precious days like this are."

"It's okay, Dr. Grant." Greg shrugged. "That is, as long as you don't want me to stay and start a shift," he added with a laugh.

"No, not at all. Walk with me," Dr. Grant said as they headed toward the elevator. "When was the last time you checked on your patient?" he suddenly asked as they got off on the fourth floor.

"Right before my shift ended yesterday." Greg began to feel panicky. "Why? Is something wrong?"

"Hi, Dr. Dixon." A female doctor smiled as she brushed past Greg. He responded with a quick smile and a nod.

"You know," Dr. Grant said with a chuckle, "when I'm walking with you, I feel totally invisible, especially to the women in this joint. They only see you. I comfort myself by saying it's because I'm married, but somehow I don't think that's the issue."

"Is something wrong with Miss Charles?" Greg repeated.

"Not really, Dr. Dixon. Don't get excited. I only paged you because her mother asked me to. She thought you'd like to see this for yourself."

Dr. Grant pushed open the door to room 42 and Mattie stood and extended her arms for Greg to join her. Greg walked slowly to Jessica's bedside. Her eyes were closed, but the tube going down her throat had been removed.

"They've taken away the temporary respirator," Greg whispered with a smile.

"Yes," Mattie said with tears in her eyes. "Jessie woke up this morning."

"What?" Greg said as he looked back at her.

"She's just sleeping," Ms. Mattie said as she leaned over the bedrail and whispered Jessica's name in her ear.

Her eyelids fluttered as she slowly opened her eyes. She looked toward her mother. Greg fought back his own emotions as he watched her struggle to keep her eyes open.

"This here is Dr. Dixon," Mattie said while pulling Greg close to her side and into Jessica's view. "He's the doctor who prayed for you and did your surgery."

Jessica's eyes slowly met Greg's. Her fingers wiggled as she tried to lift her arm. Greg reached out and grabbed her hand as a tear rolled down her cheek.

"What you gonna say, Jessie?"

"Thank . . ." she whispered slowly, ". . . you."

For a moment, Greg was speechless. He fought tears as he bent down and placed the back of Jessica's hand on his cheek.

"You're welcome, Grace," he finally said through a glassy-eyed smile. "You are so very welcome."

CHAPTER 6

Two weeks later

Greg had told just about everybody that he knew about the miracle of Jessica's recovery. Her progress was slow, but steady, and the joy of it all was tarnished by the missed friendship of Derrick. The only time he saw Sherry now was at church. He took advantage of those moments to share quality time with his growing goddaughter. Derrick hadn't worshiped with them in the two weeks following their confrontation.

"He goes to church," Sherry told Greg following Sunday services, "he just doesn't come here. He says he doesn't want to face you, the pastor, or the congregation who prayed for the well-being of the woman who—as he put it—murdered his mama."

"You haven't told him about your knowing, have you?"

"No, Greg, but frankly, the only reason I haven't is that I told you I wouldn't. Sometimes, I think if I told him and then explained my point of view, he'd get a clearer understanding of it all."

"I believe that's called wishful thinking, Sherry," Greg said.

"Maybe," Sherry admitted, "but I hate to see what this has done to such a strong friendship."

"So do I. Don't you think I miss hanging out with him or just coming over and kicking it with you guys on my off days? Spring is here now and the weather will get warm enough to play one-on-one soon. That's always been our spring and summer sport."

"I know," Sherry said. "Anyway," she added, changing the subject, "how's Miss Jessica doing?"

"She's progressing well." Greg smiled. "I've taken her off of all intravenous meds. She's taking all medications orally now. All of her MRI and CT scans have come back looking pretty good. She hasn't seized since that day in the operating room."

"That's wonderful, Greg," Sherry said. "Is she talking any better?"

"Her speech is still slower than normal, but it's improving every day. Working on her speech is next on our agenda. She's actually progressing better and more quickly than we expected. We're going to start physical and speech therapy with her as soon as we remove the stitches. Ms. Mattie has thanked me a thousand times in the past several days."

"I can only imagine her relief. I mean, just think. Just a few weeks ago, she thought she'd lost her only child. I can only imagine how that must have felt. I don't know what I'd do if something like that happened with Denise."

"I know," Greg said as he handed the baby back to her mother.

"So when are you going to ask her out?" Sherry asked.

"Well, for starters, I think it'd be a good idea to wait until she can actually go out with me. She's got a few more miles to go before that."

She laughed. "Maybe the invitation will give her some incentive."

"You ready to go, Greg?" Lena asked as she joined the two of them by Sherry's car.

"Whenever you are, Mama," he said.

"I told that ol' Mattie Charles that I'd come by the hospital to sit with her and Jessica this afternoon. Don't you have to be at work anyway?"

"Yes, ma'am. I just told them I was going to church and would have my pager if they needed me. I have to go back in."

"Don't work too hard," Sherry said as she strapped Dee into her car seat and walked around to the driver's door that Greg held open for her. "And remember what I said," she continued, "incentive. A girl likes a little incentive every now and then."

Greg smiled as he closed her door and waved as she drove away.

"What's she talking about?"

"Grace."

"What about Grace?" she asked as he helped her into the car.

"She thinks I should ask her out," Greg said as he got settled in the car and pulled out of the parking lot and onto the highway.

"Ask her out? What makes her think you wanna ask her out?"

"I don't know." Greg shrugged. "Maybe it was something I said."

"Keep talking." Lena sat up straight as she stared in surprise at her son.

"There's not much more to tell, Mama. I don't want you blowing this out of proportion."

"Who, me?"

"Yes, Mama. You have a tendency to do that sometimes."

"Are you trying to tell me that you like Jessica? She kind of young, ain't she?"

"Five years, Mama. That's all that there is between us. She's not a child. Daddy was almost ten years your senior as I recall."

"So he was," she admitted. "But keep in mind, you'll have to try and get along with Mattie Charles. There's your drawback."

"Mama, I already get along quite well with Ms. Mattie. It's you who insist on knocking heads with her all the time."

"She's such a know-it-all and she's got a sassy mouth. Always got something to say."

"Yet you can't get enough of her?"

"Oh, I get enough. I just try to put up with her."

"Remind you of anybody you know?" Greg asked.

"Not right offhand," Lena said as she thought deeply. "Who does she remind you of?"

"My mother." Greg laughed.

"Boy, don't make me come over there," Lena warned.

"Think about it, Mama," Greg said. "She's just like you. That's why the two of you argue all the time. When both of you are together, it makes me think of you and Ms. Julia. Always fussing, but can't stop hanging around one another."

"Now I see how Mattie can remind you of *Julia*, 'cause she was another smart-mouth, but me and Julia weren't alike—so me and Mattie ain't alike either."

"Mama, you and Ms. Julia were *exactly* alike. Everybody could see that except, of course, you and Ms. Julia." Greg laughed as he pulled into his mother's driveway and walked around the car to let her out.

"Uh-huh." His mother smiled as he kissed her cheek. "You just get on to the hospital and do your job. I'll be there a little later. And by the way," she continued, "I like Jessie. I agree with Sherry. Ask her out."

Greg smiled as he headed toward the hospital. *Mama actually likes Grace. That's pretty cool. This is the first time she's said that about a girl. Of all the women who have shown an interest in me over the past few years, she's not once admitted to liking any of them. Now the first girl who comes along who shows absolutely no romantic interest in me, Mom likes.*

"Dr. Dixon." Greg heard his name called as he took his changing clothes from his backseat and walked toward the entrance of Robinson Memorial.

Greg returned the greeting. "Dr. Neal."

"Where are you coming from all dressed up?" Dr. Neal asked.

"Had to go and get my praise on, you know." Greg laughed.

"Oh, yeah. I went to Mass early this morning too," Dr. Neal said as they entered the hospital together. "I don't know if you can call that getting my praise on though," he continued with a chuckle.

"To each his own, Neal." Greg patted his shoulder and they parted in separate directions.

"Wow, Dr. Dixon," Creshondria said as he walked toward the front desk, "you look good."

"Thanks." He smiled.

"Uh, Dr. Dixon?" she said.

"Yes?" He stopped and approached the desk.

"Okay," she began, "I know this is the workplace and we don't know each other very well . . ."

Oh, boy. Here goes, Greg thought.

"But I was wondering," Creshondria continued, "if we could, like, go out sometime. You know—maybe after hours for a drink or something."

"I'm sorry," Greg said after a moment of thought, "I'm not good with names, especially if they have more than three syllables. What's your name again?"

"Creshondria." She smiled.

"Can I just call you Shon?" he asked.

"Ooh." She smiled again. "I like that."

Oh, brother.

"Shon," he began, "I appreciate the invitation. I really do, but I don't think our dating would be a good idea. Besides, I don't drink."

"You're not married, are you?" she said. "I mean, I've never seen a ring on your finger and I've never heard you speak of a wife. Not that that really means anything," she rambled. "I know some people don't wear much jewelry to work. I guess I should have asked that question first," she said.

"No, I'm not married," he admitted, to her delight, "but you could say that I'm already interested in someone else."

"Oh," she said. "Well, as long as you're not married, I still have a chance. So I'm not just gonna give up."

"However you want to handle it," Greg said as he waved and continued toward the stairs.

"With your fine self," Creshondria whispered as she watched him walk away.

"Dixon, you're back," Dr. Grant said as they passed each other in the hall.

"I am," Greg said as he headed to his office.

"Did you pray for me?" Dr. Grant called over his shoulder.

"I did," Greg answered.

"Thanks."

"Anytime."

Greg closed his door and quickly changed from his suit into his scrubs. He took a brush and groomed his freshly cut fade. His eyes strayed to a photo that sat on the corner of his desk. It was a picture that he and Derrick had taken together just after Christmas. They were so close then. In just a few short months they had gone from inseparable to invisible. A knock on his door broke his thought process.

"Yes?" he called.

"Dr. Dixon?"

He opened his door to find Mattie Charles standing there.

"Ms. Mattie. Is something wrong?"

"No." She smiled. "I had asked about you earlier and I was told that you had left the grounds for a while. I just saw Dr. Grant and he told me that you had gotten in and were in your office. I just wanted to say hello."

"Well, I feel special." Greg smiled as he accepted Mattie's embrace.

"I'm on my way to Jessie's room," she said. "Are you gonna stop by?"

"Yes, ma'am. I have several patients to check in on, but I will certainly stop by there a little later. Mama said she's coming by today as well."

"Thanks for the warning." Mattie laughed as she walked away.

Checking in on his assigned patients always made Greg realize how blessed he and his family were. Working with critically ill patients had its way of keeping him close to God.

"Dr. Dixon." Dr. Grant caught up with him an hour later while he was in the middle of making his rounds.

"Yes?"

"We have a patient in the emergency room who won't be seen by any other doctor except you."

"What? Who is it?"

"All I know is that the patient is black and female. She probably heard of your successful medical reputation. You can't blame people for wanting the best possible care."

"Is it a serious injury?"

"Could be. She's complaining of severe abdominal pains. Can you squeeze in a few minutes to see her or not? I'll handle it if you can't."

Greg sighed. "No, I'll see her."

"I'll check on a few of your patients while you do that," Dr. Grant offered.

"Thanks," Greg said as he started to walk away. "But leave Grace—I mean Jessica Charles—for me. I need to see her myself."

"Sure thing."

"Hi, Dr. Dixon," Kelly greeted him as he entered the emergency room.

"Hi, Kelly," he responded. "I hear I've been requested by a patient."

"Yes, you have and she's adamant about it."

"Greg!" a familiar voice called.

Greg turned to see Evelyn Cobb walking toward him holding her stomach and slumping over in magnified agony.

"Evelyn," he said, giving her the benefit of the doubt, "what happened?"

"I don't know," she said, "I was eating dinner and started getting these horrible pains in my stomach. I think it's my appendix."

"Do you want me to take her back, Doctor?" Kelly asked.

"Yes, Kelly. Thanks. I'll be there in a minute. Follow her, Evelyn."

"Thank you," Evelyn said as she winced and walked with the assistance of Kelly, who looked over her shoulder at Greg and rolled her eyes in disgust at Evelyn's melodramatic performance.

After getting her charted information from one of the desk clerks, Greg joined Evelyn in her outpatient room and sat on a stool at the edge of the bed. She was sitting on the bed, still in a crumpled position, in the hospital gown that had been provided.

"Okay, Evelyn," he began, "tell me what you were eating at the time the pains started."

"I hadn't even started eating yet," she said while bent over in exaggerated pain. "I had just prepared my plate of cubed steak, rice, gravy, lima beans, and freshly baked rolls and sat to eat with Mom. By the way, I heard that those were some of your favorite foods. Then the pains just came out of nowhere."

"Actually, I don't eat red meat," he said to her disappointment. "I need you to lie back so I can see if I can determine exactly what you're experiencing here."

Evelyn was all too happy to have him assist her in leaning back on the reclined bed.

"Let me know if any of this feels uncomfortable," he said as he began pressing gingerly on her abdominal area.

For several minutes, Evelyn lay with her eyes closed and not responding. After he had tested her entire stomach, Greg began doubting the validity of her explained ailment and wondered if her subtle smile indicated that she was enjoying his touch.

"Evelyn, is none of this hurting at all?" he finally asked.

"Oh. Right there," she suddenly said as he pressed the left side of her stomach for the third time.

"I see," Greg said as he looked at his watch and wrote on his clipboard.

"Is it my appendix?"

"No, that would be your right side."

"Well, I think it's something serious," she said as Greg helped her to sit up straight. "Can you give me an X-ray or something?"

"I don't think an X-ray is necessary, Evelyn," Greg said. "I think you're okay. Maybe it's indigestion, but nothing to be alarmed about."

"But how do you know just from pressing my stomach?"

"Because I'm a doctor."

"Well, *I'm* not convinced," she insisted. "I want to be admitted and I want you to be my doctor to monitor the pain. I can have myself admitted, can't I?" she asked.

"You can, Evelyn," Greg reluctantly admitted. He had to think quickly. He couldn't allow Evelyn to persuade the medical staff to believe she was really ill.

"You could have yourself admitted," he began again, "but I don't think these pains are anything that dinner and a movie couldn't heal. What do you think?"

"Really?" Her face lit up at his words.

"Really." He smiled. "Only problem is, you have to be able to *eat* the dinner and enjoy the movie, and you can't do that lying in a hospital bed strapped to machines and having stomach pains."

"Oh, no," she said. "I feel much better. I guess you were right. A night out was exactly what I needed."

"Then that's what the doctor orders." He smiled again. "Now you get dressed and take this paperwork to the front desk. By the time they get to you, I will have instructed them on the specifics of the dinner and movie invitation and they will let you know."

"Great," she said as she hopped down from the table and hugged Greg's neck. "I don't want to jinx this or anything," she said, "but I knew that God was going to work it out like this. It was only a matter of time."

"He's an awesome God," Greg said as he headed toward the door. "I have other rounds to make. You take care and I'll see you later."

"Yes, you will," she said as he left the room. She quickly got dressed and headed for the receptionist's desk.

As Greg walked down the hospital's halls, he stopped by the waiting room to make a phone call.

"Hello," Kelly answered.

"Kelly—you're just the one I was looking for. I need a huge favor."

"What is it?"

"What's your location?"

"Emergency room front desk."

"Great. Do you see the girl who came in with the abdominal complaints standing in line at the counter there?"

"Uh, yeah, I see the little faker. She appears healed. What'd you give her?"

"Nothing, really. But it's amazing what a little play on words can do."

"Really?" Kelly laughed. "Well, what do you want me to do?"

"Do we still have some of those promotional packets that we were giving out earlier this week?"

"The dinner coupons?"

"And theater tickets. Yes."

"I believe so. Why?"

"Will you have someone at the station give her one of each please?"

"Why?"

"I promised her dinner and a movie if she got better and, by George, she got better. So I'm holding up my end of the deal."

"Ooh, you're bad, Dr. Dixon." Kelly laughed. "I didn't know you had it in you."

"Yeah, well, drastic situations call for drastic measures. Just have one of the girls give it to her."

"Oh, no," Kelly said with enthusiasm. "Please, let me."

"Go for it."

"Thanks," Kelly said as she hung up her cell and approached

the desk as Evelyn stepped up to the window and handed the receptionist her paperwork.

"Ms. Cobb," Kelly said as she eased the paper from the receptionist and read Evelyn's name from the top. "Are you feeling better now?" she said with mock concern.

"Yes, I'm much better. Dr. Dixon is the best."

"Yes, he is." Kelly continued to smile as she tossed her brunette hair in exaggerated enthusiasm.

"Speaking of Dr. Dixon," Evelyn continued with visible excitement. "Did he leave some information with you concerning dinner plans?"

"Ah, yes," Kelly said to Evelyn's elation. "He told me to give you these," she said as she cheerfully handed Evelyn a coupon to see the movie of her choice at Reel Stuff, a local theater, and a gift certificate to Red Lobster. She watched in amusement as Evelyn's smile disappeared and her jaw dropped.

"Oh," Evelyn said.

"You have a pleasant evening," Kelly said as Evelyn slowly walked away, still looking at the coupons in disbelief.

Greg walked into Jessica Charles's room and found her alone. Her television was on but she wasn't watching. Her head was turned and she stared toward the window, not noticing that her doctor had entered the room. There was a bandana wrapped around her head to cover her baldness, yet she was as beautiful as ever. Greg watched quietly for a moment until he noticed a lone tear stream down her face.

"Grace," he said, "are you all right? Are you in any pain?"

She faced him slowly as his voice slightly startled her and interrupted her trance.

"Hi," she said. "If you're looking for your mother, she's with my mother getting coffee."

"You're speaking better," Greg observed.

"I have a good therapist," she said as she wiped a tear.

"Why are you crying?" Greg asked—trying not to appear

overly concerned—as he pulled a stool right beside her bed and sat.

"Long story," she said softly.

"You're the last stop on my rounds," he said. "I've got time to listen."

"My life is so messed up," she said slowly as another tear rolled.

"How so?" Greg asked. He took a Kleenex from the table and wiped her cheeks gingerly.

"The police want to talk to me about the accident, but I don't remember."

"Who told you that the police want to see you?"

"Mama said that they called. But I don't remember what happened."

"Then that's all you have to tell them."

"But a lady is dead and they think I may have caused her death," she said as her tears broke. "I want to say I didn't, but I don't remember."

"Don't cry, Grace," Greg said. Standing from his seated position, he took both of her hands in his. "You don't have to talk to anybody right now. They have to get clearance from me, and I won't let them upset you with a bunch of questions."

"But the lady must have family. They want to know. I have to try and remember so I can give them closure."

"Grace," Greg said as he continued to hold her hands, "you don't have to *try* and remember anything. You just had major surgery a couple weeks ago. My concern right now is your recovery. If the details come back to you as time passes, you can tell them then. Until then, all they have to know and understand is that you don't remember anything."

"You don't understand," she insisted through more tears. "A lady died. She was somebody's loved one and, somehow, I was involved. Somebody cared about her and I have to remember for them."

"Let me tell you something," Greg said while electronically lifting the head of her bed so that he could sit on the stool and she would still face him. "Whatever happened out there was an accident. The police need to know the facts. You can't give them facts until your memory concerning this accident is restored. Don't rush this. Yes, a woman died. I know she had loved ones. People really cared about her. I know that better than you can understand, but you still need to be concerned with your own health right now."

"God has really brought me a long way, hasn't He?" she said.

"Yes, He has. You're progressing better than we ever imagined and we want that progression to continue."

"I know," she said as Greg wiped her tears once more. "So much has happened. It seems like I've lost so much. I've lost parts of my memory, a portion of my mobility, and speech, my hair, my fiancé, my degree."

"Whoa," Greg said. "You have a fiancé?"

"Had," she corrected. "Mama said he moved on while I was still at Saint Mary's. He said he couldn't stand to see me like that and he didn't think I'd pull through, so he called off the engagement. Took the ring right off my finger."

"You haven't lost anything worth keeping," Greg said, feeling anger inside for the hurt that this man had caused her. "Your mobility and speech are already being restored and your hair will grow back with no problem. Your degree certainly isn't a total loss. You only had one semester to complete and you'll do that in the very near future.

"And as far as your fiancé is concerned, any man who will leave a woman because she's in critical condition isn't worth her tears. He was about to vow to love you in sickness and in health and he bailed at the first hint of your health failing."

"I guess you're right."

"I *am* right," Greg said as he began writing on her chart. "For the record," he continued, "I think he was a fool."

"Why do you say that?"

"I've only known you for a short time, I admit that. However, I think your faith in God and your determination to make a full recovery are incredible. I also think you have beautiful brown eyes, a lovely smile, and a very sweet disposition."

"Thank you." Jessica blushed.

"Dr. Dixon," Mattie interrupted as she entered the room. "You finally made it."

"Yes, ma'am."

"Your patient has been kinda down in the dumps today."

"I know, Ms. Mattie," he responded, "but she'll be okay. We just had a long talk. She told me that the police contacted you."

"Yes, they did. Do you know a good attorney? I think we might need one."

"Well, I know an excellent attorney," he said as he thought of Derrick, "but he wouldn't be available if you needed counseling on this matter. I'm sure I can assist in finding a good one though. Meantime, if the police contact you again, tell them to call me."

"Hi, Greg."

"Hi, Mama," Greg greeted her as she walked in the room. "I'm going to leave you three ladies for now. I have a lot of paperwork to complete in my office before my shift ends."

"Okay," his mother said just before she and Mattie began chatting.

"Dr. Dixon," Jessica said, "when can I start physical therapy? I'm so tired of this bed and the wheelchair."

"The therapist penciled you in for next week."

"There's no way I can start sooner?"

"I know you're anxious to get your life back, and that's certainly understandable, but they have schedules with other patients as well. If there's any way I can get you started earlier, I will."

"Thanks," Jessica said in audible relief. "And thanks for the encouragement. You know—the stuff you said earlier."

"I meant it." Greg returned her smile and headed toward the door. "Well," he announced, "I have to go and complete some paperwork in my office. With any luck, the rest of the evening will be quiet and I may even be able to catch a nap while I'm in there. You ladies take care," he said as he passed his mother and Ms. Mattie.

"Thanks for everything, Dr. Dixon," Mattie said.

"Bye, son," Lena said. "I'll see you later."

"Yes, ma'am," he said, closing the door behind him.

The night turned out busier than Greg had planned. He had an emergency surgery to perform, and once again it was successful. As he headed back to his office to prepare to go home, he stopped at room 42 to check one last time on his favorite patient. Jessica was still awake, lying in bed listening to music.

"So you like Donnie McClurkin, huh?" Greg spoke softly so as not to startle her, this time, as he approached her bed.

"Dr. Dixon. Hi," she said.

"Hi. How are you?"

"I'm okay," she said. "I would have thought you were off duty by now. You pull long hours."

"I just got off about fifteen minutes ago," he said with a yawn.

"I guess you didn't get that nap that you had planned."

"In my experience, most things in life don't go as we plan."

"Tell me about it," she agreed.

"I spoke to the therapist and she says she can't fit you in before next Monday."

"Oh . . ." Jessica was visibly disappointed. "Thanks anyway."

"So have you ever seen Donnie in concert?" Greg tried to lift her spirits as he sat on the stool beside the bed.

"No. Have you?"

"Yes. He's quite good, actually. Is he your favorite?"

"One of many."

"I like him too, but I'm a Winans and Take 6 fan."

"I've seen Take 6 in concert," Jessica said. "They were good."

"I've seen them four times," Greg said. "They are *excellent*. The Winans do a good show as well."

A brief silence blanketed the room.

"So, tell me more about you," Greg said.

"Like what?" Jessica asked.

"Favorite color?"

"Red."

"Mine is blue. Favorite television show?"

"*E.R.*"

"Ugh," Greg grunted. "I hate hospital shows. Mine is *Jeopardy.*"

"The game show?"

"Yes." He laughed at her surprised expression. "Favorite movie?"

"I don't know." She thought for a moment. "Something Denzel played in, I'm sure."

"Of course." Greg nodded knowingly. "My favorite movie is *Courage Under Fire.*"

"That's a Denzel movie."

"So it is," he noted. "Favorite actor?"

"Denzel." She laughed.

"Dumb question," he said. "I'm a Tom Hanks fan. Favorite actress?"

"Julia Roberts."

"I'd have to say Angela Bassett. Favorite food?"

"Seafood."

"Me too. Favorite thing to do when you have free time?"

"Play the piano."

"Really?" It was Greg's turn to be surprised.

"Yes," she said. "And sing," she added. "I like to sing."

Greg smiled. "Promise me that I'll get to hear you sing one day."

"Okay."

"Would you like for me to carry out your therapy until next week?" Greg suddenly asked.

"You mean it?"

"Yes. It would be late at night because I could only do it after my shift ends."

"That's fine with me. I'm usually awake until around 2:00 A.M. anyway. I don't sleep well when I'm not in my own bed."

"You want to start tonight?" Greg asked.

"Sure," she agreed with excitement. "You're not gonna get in trouble for this, are you? I don't want you to get into trouble."

"No, I'll inform Dr. Grant tomorrow. I am licensed to do therapy. Physical therapy was my minor in medical school. Tonight I'm just going to give your legs a deep massage."

He helped her turn over to her stomach before beginning the massage. She winced with pain at the onset. Her muscles had tightened due to her legs' inactivity. In an attempt to get her mind off of the discomfort, he began his game again.

"Well, my favorite free-time thing is basketball."

"Why doesn't that surprise me?"

Greg laughed. "Had to do something with all this height."

"Did you play in high school?"

"Yes," Greg answered. "And in college," he added.

"That's nice."

"Favorite car?"

"Jaguar," Jessica said.

Greg beamed. "Mine too."

"I can't afford one," she added, "but one day I'm going to go to a car lot just so I can take one for a test drive."

"I have one."

"You do?" Jessica was impressed. "Do they drive as smoothly as I've always imagined?"

"Like a dream," Greg said. "I'll have to let you take her for a spin one day."

"I'd like that."

"Favorite sport?"

"Tennis." She yawned.

"Well, you already know mine." Greg laughed again. "Sports hero?"

"Michael Jordan," she said as Greg knowingly said it along with her. They shared a laugh.

"I like Muhammad Ali," he said. After a few moments of silence, he continued. "Okay, I have a thought-provoking one for you. If you had a choice of having one person sing you a love song, who would it be?"

"Boyz II Men," Jessica responded with another tired yawn.

"That's four people."

"Okay . . ." She thought, "Brian McKnight. Yeah, definitely— Brian McKnight."

"Okay," Greg said. "I'll give Brian his props, but just because I'd probably rather be serenaded by a woman, I'd choose Halle Berry."

"Can she sing?"

"Probably not," Greg admitted, "but when it's Halle Berry, who cares?"

"That's funny." Jessica laughed sleepily.

Greg massaged her legs in silence for several minutes. Jessica had nice calf muscles and Greg could feel them relaxing as he continued his massage while listening to Donnie McClurkin's live recording of his London concert.

"Favorite flower?" he finally asked.

Jessica didn't respond. She had fallen asleep.

"Now, how am I gonna know what kind of flowers to buy you?" he whispered.

The clock by her bedside read 1:08 A.M. By now, normally, he'd have already been home, taken his shower, and been asleep. He didn't mind though. He enjoyed his time with Jessica. He pulled the covers over her and prepared to leave. Walking quietly, he turned off the CD player and her light and headed home.

CHAPTER 7

"John." Detective Weeks entered Detective Morrison's office after a brief knock on the door.

"Yes, Robert," Detective Morrison looked up from his paperwork. "Please tell me that we have found a match to the composite sketch of last week's bank robber."

"Sorry, sir, but this one might bring you even more peace of mind."

"What you got?"

"New developments in the Madison case."

"The car accident back in January? You're kidding. We've searched that one with a fine-tooth comb. What could we have missed? Did the survivor regain memory?"

"No, sir. Our new development is just that, a *development*. A roll of film taken of the site that had never been developed until now."

"What?"

"Yes, sir." He handed the pictures to Detective Morrison, who began looking through them carefully.

"What are these photos of? The grassy areas? Are these tire tracks?"

"They would appear to be, sir."

"But how could she have gone over there when her car hit the other vehicle and came to a stop right here?"

"My question exactly."

"There was a third car involved here."

"That's what I concluded too, sir."

"Who else has seen these new photos, Robert?"

"Tim Bartow got them developed, but I don't think he really looked them over. He just knew they weren't the film he was intending to develop and he remembered that accident site and gave them to me."

"Fine. You find Detective Bartow and I'll meet the two of you at the original accident site in an hour. We have some work to do."

"Yes, sir."

Jessica sat in her bed listening to her mother and Lena argue about the length of time needed to whip the batter when baking a cream cheese cake. She laughed inside because she realized that her mom had finally met her match.

"Why don't you two just have a bake-off?" Jessica suggested.

"A what?" Lena said.

"A bake-off. Both of you can bake a cake and pick people to taste it. That way, you'll know if the time spent whipping the batter makes a difference."

The two ladies looked at each other in silence for a moment as though giving the idea consideration.

Mattie finally spoke up. "I don't need nobody to tell me I'm right. I know I'm right 'cause my cakes have always been the big hit at family functions and stuff."

"Yeah, well, I've had people ask me to bake cakes for weddings," Lena added. "Now that's when you know your cakes are good."

Dr. Grant entered Jessica's room and interrupted the argument. "Good morning."

"Hi, Dr. Grant," Jessica said.

"I hear you've been getting some therapy from Dr. Dixon for the past week," he continued while approaching her bedside. "How's that going?"

"Fine. He helped me walk around for a little while last night. I couldn't walk long, but it felt good to be on my feet."

"That's good." Dr. Grant nodded. "I just wanted to let you know that we're moving you to the third floor today."

"Why?"

"Because we no longer characterize you as an intensive care patient. You're doing extremely well."

"Thank you." Jessica smiled.

Mattie jumped in. "Is Dr. Dixon still gonna be her doctor?"

"Yes, ma'am," Dr. Grant said, easing her tension. "Dr. Dixon's office is on this floor because this is the unit that needs him most, but he has patients on every floor of this hospital."

"That's my baby." Lena beamed. "They just need him everywhere, don't they?"

"He's a great doctor," Dr. Grant agreed with a smile. "The good part about being on the third floor is that you'll be closer to your appointed physical therapist. Dr. Young is one of the best. She has several patients on that floor so she's there all the time."

"Can I keep Dr. Dixon?" Jessica suddenly asked.

"He'll still be your doctor," Dr. Grant told her.

"No—I mean as my therapist?"

Mattie and Lena exchanged glances and then looked toward Dr. Grant for his answer.

"Well, Dr. Dixon isn't on our staff as a therapist. I admit, I kind of bent the rules by letting him fill in as one. Since he told me it was only for a week until Dr. Young was ready, I allowed it. Aside from that, he was donating that time. When his rounds finish at 11:00 P.M., he's off our clock. He wasn't getting paid for the hour of therapy afterward."

"Oh," Jessica said. "I didn't know."

"It's always hard to change physicians once you get comfortable with one, but I promise you, Dr. Young is excellent in her field of expertise."

"I'm sure she'll like her too," Mattie said. "I'm just glad Dr. Dixon will stay on as her regular physician."

"Yes, he will," Dr. Grant assured her as he prepared to leave. "I'm going to have Dr. Dixon complete your papers to have you changed to the third floor and then we'll get you situated in your new room."

"Thank you, Dr. Grant," Jessica said.

"Well, praise the Lord," Lena said. "You 'bout to get put in a regular room. That means God is sho 'nuff blessing."

"Yes, He is," Mattie agreed as she kissed her daughter's forehead. "You been in here for about a month, right?" she continued. "In that time, you done had the surgery that Saint Mary's couldn't give you, you regained consciousness well before the time that the doctors thought, your stitches are out, you done started talking clearer, you walked for the first time yesterday, and now you're going to a regular room."

"Ain't God good?" Lena nodded.

"Oh, yes," Mattie said.

"You want to know the even bigger miracle?" Jessica asked.

"What?" both ladies asked.

"The two of you just agreed on something." Jessica laughed.

"Well, it's hard not to agree on the goodness of God," Lena said.

"Hello, ladies." Greg walked into the room with his clipboard in hand.

"Hello," they all responded as Greg bent down to kiss his mother's cheek.

"Well, don't I get one of them?" Mattie asked as he passed her.

"I'm sorry," Greg apologized. He stopped to kiss her as well.

"Don't be giving away my kisses," Lena said. "You got a child." She faced Mattie and pointed toward Jessica. "You want a kiss, get it from her."

"They've been at it like this all morning," Jessica told Greg.

"I can imagine," Greg said.

"We wouldn't have this problem if your mama was more like you," Mattie said to Greg.

"Or if *your* mama was more like you," Lena told Jessica.

"It's just love," Greg told his patient. "They love each other to death."

"Umph!" Mattie grunted and returned to her seat.

"Speaking of love," Lena said, reopening the previous discussion, "ain't my cakes delicious, Greg?"

"Huh?" Greg looked at her in confusion.

"Here we go again," Jessica said.

"My cream cheese pound cakes," Lena clarified. "Ain't they delicious?"

"Yes, Mama. They're the best."

"You only think hers are the best 'cause you ain't never tasted mine," Mattie chimed in.

"I'm sure yours are delicious too, Ms. Mattie."

"But not like your mama's. Right?" Lena said with a look of warning.

Greg bailed himself out by facing a giggling Jessica. "So, how are *you* doing this morning?"

"I'm fine," she said.

"You were still awake when I left last night. Did you sleep well?"

"I must have fallen asleep right after you left," Jessica answered.

"Well, she slept good then," Mattie said, " 'cause she was still asleep when I got here at 10:00 this morning."

"Good," Greg said as he wrote in her chart. "Dr. Grant told me that he already informed you of your move to floor three."

"Yes."

"Dr. Young is prepared to start your therapy later this afternoon."

"Yeah," Jessica said. "He told me that too."

"Well, don't sound so glum." Greg smiled. "This is what you've been asking for, right?"

"Yeah." Jessica forced a smile.

"She wants you," Mattie said.

"Mama," Jessica started.

"What?" Greg was confused.

"For her therapist," Mattie explained. "She don't want this Dr. Young person. She wants you to keep doing it. That's why she don't sound too happy."

Greg's heart fluttered on the inside, but he tried to stay calm and professional. He pulled up the stool and sat by Jessica's bed.

"Is that true?" he asked. "Do you want me to remain your therapist?"

"I did," Jessica admitted, "but Dr. Grant said that he couldn't allow it."

"I'm not on staff as a therapist."

"But you're licensed and you got a degree," Lena pointed out.

"That's not what they look at," Greg explained. "If I had a degree that allowed me to pursue a career as a doctor, but I decided that I only wanted to be an orderly, they wouldn't let me practice medicine if a patient came in, knew me, and just wanted me to care for him. Hospitals have to be concerned with liability."

"It's okay," Jessica said. "I understand. I'm sure Dr. Young will be fine."

"She will," Greg said. "She's the best. But thank you for thinking enough of my abilities to request me."

"No," she said. "Thank *you*. I had no idea that you were volunteering that time. I wouldn't have agreed to have you do it if I'd known you weren't getting paid."

"I assumed as much. That's why I didn't tell you," he said as he stood and prepared to leave. "Kelly will be in shortly to get you in your wheelchair and have you relocated. I'll check on you again later once you're settled."

"Thanks," Jessica said as he left the room.

"You got a good boy there," Mattie complimented.

"I know," Lena responded.

"Wonder where he got it from," Mattie added.

"Okay, Mama," Jessica warned. "I agree, Ms. Lena," she continued. "I was blessed with a wonderful doctor."

Lena corrected her. "You were blessed with the best."

"A man who sticks with you through sickness," Mattie added. "That's the kind of man you need in your life. Not like that ol' Leroy Jackson."

"Mama, you liked Leroy," Jessica reminded her.

"Yeah, I did," she mumbled. The disappointment was visible on her face. "Old sorry scoundrel," she added. "He really let me down."

"Well, you ought to have better character discernment," Lena said. "Especially when it comes to who dates your daughter."

"Do you scan all your son's dates with a magnifying glass?" Mattie asked.

"I would if he ever had a date," Lena said.

"You trying to say Dr. Dixon don't date?"

"If he does, he don't never bring a girl home for me to meet."

"Well, can you blame him?"

"Mama," Jessica warned.

"Well, look at how she goes on. That man probably got dates lined up every night from now till Christmas. He just don't tell *her* about them."

"Well, as much time as he spends here at the hospital," Jessica said, hoping she was right, "I wouldn't be surprised if he didn't date much. When would he have the time?"

"Exactly," Lena said. "Now, how did you get such a smart child?"

"Okay, Miss Charles," Kelly said as she entered the room with two orderlies and a wheelchair, "we're ready to go."

Lena and Mattie gathered their belongings and followed as

Jessica was wheeled into the elevator and taken to the third floor. Her new room was much like her old one. With the assistance of the orderlies, Jessica climbed onto the firm mattress of her new bed.

"Now you let us know if you need anything," Kelly said. "Dr. Dixon has given strict instructions that the staff on this floor takes care of you as well as the fourth-floor staff did."

"Really?" Jessica tried not to blush, but failed. Mattie and Lena exchanged smiles.

"He sure did," Kelly said. "But according to this chart information, he'll still be your attending physician, so I'm sure he'll follow up to make sure his orders are being carried out.

"Dr. Young will be in within an hour to start your therapy," Kelly continued. "Meantime, we're just a button push away if you need anything."

"Thank you," Jessica said just before Kelly disappeared into the hallway.

"Now, that there's a nice lil' white girl," Lena remarked. Mattie nodded in agreement.

As the women waited for Dr. Young's appearance, Kelly took the short walk down the hall to check in with Greg to let him know that Jessica had settled into her new room. Shortly after Kelly left, another knock on his door took his attention from his paperwork once more.

"Come in," Greg said without looking up.

"Hi."

"Sherry, what are you doing here?" Setting his paperwork aside, Greg got up from his desk and walked around to greet her at the door.

"We missed you at church yesterday," she said, "so Dee and I decided to drop by and pay you a visit."

"Well, I'm happy to see both of you," he said while taking a wiggling Denise from her arms. "I started to leave to drop in on services, but my load was way too heavy this weekend."

"Ms. Lena told me that you were hard at work."

"How's Rick?"

"I'm not sure, Greg." Sherry shook her head as she spoke. "Physically, he's fine. Mentally, I'm just not sure. He's so preoccupied with his mother's death. He's got a major case right now, so at least it's helped to get his mind on other things, and it's keeping him away from the police station for now. I know the detectives appreciate that."

"He's still checking in?"

"*At least* once a week—sometimes twice. I think that Detective Morrison is going to totally lose it one of these days and I can't say that I'd blame him, Greg. I mean, I know he means well, but his interest in solving this mystery has turned into an obsession."

"Well, the police have been here once to speak with Grace, but I was there to monitor the questioning. It didn't go all that well. The fact is, she can't help them out much right now."

"Yeah, Ricky told me about that. He said that Jessica 'claims'—as he put it—not to remember any details surrounding the collision."

"I've spoken to her, Sherry," Greg said. "I believe her when she says she doesn't remember. I know, better than anybody, how detailed and fragile her surgery was, and I know that the probability of her not remembering is very good.

"I've spoken to her mom, too," he continued. "There are other important details of her life that are either gone or cloudy. It was a couple of weeks before she even remembered that she was engaged. Be that as it may, I do believe that all of her memory will come back to her at some point."

"Wait a minute," Sherry said. "Are you okay?"

"I'm fine. Why do you ask?"

"You just told me that your dream girl is engaged."

"Oh, that. Well, he called off the engagement while she was in a coma at Saint Mary's. She was pretty heartbroken about it at first, but she realizes that she's better off without a man who would leave her and then move on so effortlessly."

"Well, good for her. And good for you too, I guess."

"That's right," Greg readily agreed. "That's very good for

me. And if she hasn't totally come to the realization that it's good for her—I have plans to show her that."

"Listen to you." Sherry laughed. "It's so funny to hear you talking like that. You've never shown this much interest in a girl before."

"I know," he agreed. "And you know what? Me and Grace—it just feels right."

"She must be something special."

"You want to meet her?"

"Oh, Greg. Could I really? I mean, I'd love to, but how would I be introduced? Have you already told her about your being Ms. Julia's godson?"

"No, not yet, but I will soon. She knows about me and the church and how we prayed for her during the time of her surgery. So, you'll be introduced as my best friend's wife. It's the truth. You are. Whether he sees me as his best friend right now or not, I am."

"Can I meet her soon?"

"How about now?"

Sherry walked nervously behind Greg as they got on the elevator and took it one floor down. Denise laughed at her godfather as he made silly faces at her while walking to room 33.

With both their mothers gone, the room was quiet as they entered, with the exception of the television that Jessica didn't seem to be watching.

"Hi," Jessica said. She turned down the volume upon their entrance. "I wasn't expecting you until later."

"I know. I have someone I want you to meet. This is my favorite little girl, Denise, and this is her mother, Sherry."

Jessica did a quick double take when she turned her eyes toward Sherry. Briefly looking back at the television screen at an old episode of *Living Single,* she found the likeness fascinating between her and the show's star.

"Sherry?" She felt foolish repeating the name as though she'd misheard it the first time. Sherry laughed as she greeted her with a warm handshake.

"Yes—Sherry," she assured her. "I'm so happy to finally meet you. Greg has told me so much about you. You know what?" Sherry added. "Has anyone ever told you that you look like Chanté Moore?"

"Chanté Moore," Greg said with a snap of his fingers. "That's who you remind me of. I've been trying to think for weeks."

"Chanté Moore?" Jessica said with a laugh. "No . . . no one has ever told me that, but I'll certainly accept it as a compliment." She continued, "Has anyone ever told you that you favor Queen Latifah?"

"My whole life through." Sherry laughed. "I may need to look into it. Perhaps we're related."

"Sherry is my best friend's wife, and Dee here is my goddaughter."

"Oh," Jessica said, hoping that she didn't appear as relieved as she felt at finally understanding Sherry's role in Greg's life. "Well, any friend of Dr. Dixon's is a friend of mine." She smiled.

"I missed church yesterday and Sherry stopped by to check up on me," Greg said.

"It's not like him not to break away for a couple of hours to stop in on Sunday services."

"Where's Mom and Ms. Mattie?" Greg asked as he looked around.

"I'm not sure," Jessica said. "Dr. Young came in and said that she'd be back for the therapy session, and Mama and Ms. Lena said they were going to let us have some privacy. I'm not certain which way they went, but Dr. Young should be back any minute."

Greg handed Denise back to Sherry as his pager beeped.

"Sorry, ladies," he said. "Duty calls. You know your way back, right?" he asked Sherry.

"Yes. I'll only be a minute."

"I'll check in on you later, Grace," he said as he left the room.

"What a pretty baby," Jessica remarked as Sherry sat.

"Thank you," Sherry said.

"How old is she?"

"Four months."

"Wow. She's so alert."

"Okay, I'm sorry for the delay," Dr. Young said as she walked into the room—cutting their chatter short. "Oh, I'm sorry," she remarked after seeing Sherry.

"Oh, no," Sherry said. "You go ahead and do your work, I can leave."

"Well, you don't have to leave," Dr. Young said.

"You can stay if you like," Jessica said. "I could use the company."

"Okay." Sherry returned to her seat and pulled out a bottle for Denise.

She watched as Dr. Young took Jessica through a series of exercises with her legs. She could tell from her expression that some of the moves were uncomfortable, but Jessica was determined to get through them. Her final exercise was to walk while pushing a wheelchair. Dr. Young helped her off of her bed and stood close behind her as she slowly put one foot in front of the other and pushed the chair from the bed to the door and back.

"Very good," Dr. Young praised her as she made her final walk back to the bed. "You're going to be walking on your own in no time. Was there any discomfort with the walking?"

"Not discomfort, really," Jessica explained as she got back into bed with her therapist's help. "It just feels like I don't have complete control of my muscles in my legs as I walk."

"Muscles feel a bit shaky?" Dr. Young asked as she wrote the details on her chart.

"Yes. Just a little. But I don't want to stop," Jessica quickly added. "I want to walk as much as possible."

"That's good to hear. Many of my patients are afraid of falling and don't want to get up the next time. I'm glad you're not like that."

"Are we going to do the therapy every day?"

"Yes, we will."

"Good," Jessica said as she lay back on the bed.

"Well, that's your hour for today." Dr. Young got up and prepared to leave. "I will see you again tomorrow at the same time," she concluded, pushing the wheelchair out as she left.

"That was really good," Sherry said as she draped a baby blanket over Denise, who was now sleeping on a makeshift bed that she had made out of the extra blanket that was in the closet.

"I want to get out of this bed so badly," Jessica said. "My birthday is less than a month away and I don't want to spend it in this bed."

"Do you tell God that when you pray?" Sherry asked.

"Well, not specifically," Jessica began.

"You should."

"But He knows without me saying those exact words."

"I know, but sometimes I think He pays special attention to those things that we want badly enough to ask for directly."

"I never thought of it like that."

"I'm not saying that He won't do it otherwise," Sherry clarified. "I'm just speaking from my own experiences."

"I understand. Thanks."

"You're welcome."

"So, how long have you known Dr. Dixon?" Jessica asked while trying not to sound as though she was taking a personal interest in her physician.

"Since middle school," Sherry answered. "We were like best friends throughout middle school. Well, I guess I was his best *female* friend. His best male friend was my husband."

"Did the two of you ever date?"

"Greg and me?" She laughed. "No. We've always just been good friends. In fact, my husband and I never dated until our senior year. We went to the prom together. Before that time, we were all just friends."

"That's nice," Jessica observed. "I went to high school in Maryland. Several of the people I went to school with live here now. I even attend college with a few of them, but I was never popular in school, so I can't say I ever had a best friend. There were people who were nice to me, but I guess I was sort of a nerd. I was really shy and spent all of my free time studying. I still do that now."

"Greg was like that in high school, too," Sherry said. "I always wondered what attracted him to my husband, who was always a loud one. Me and Ricky maintained a B average, but Greg was like a whiz kid or something. He was the top honor student in our senior class and even got to say a speech at graduation. Then he went to college on a full scholarship."

"Somehow, I can't see him not being popular in high school. He's so popular around this hospital."

"Oh, he was popular in high school." Sherry laughed. "Especially with the girls. He never had a steady girlfriend, although he took Ebony Simmons to the prom. It was funny because several of the popular girls asked him. Ebony wasn't the most attractive girl and she wasn't popular, but I think he went with her because she didn't ask him. They'd never dated before the prom and they didn't go out together again afterward, but for one night of her life, Ebony was the envy of most of the girls in our senior class."

"Well, she has a nice story to tell her kids." Jessica smiled.

"Speaking of kids," Sherry said as she stood, "I need to go home and put mine to bed. Plus Ricky is probably wondering where I am. He should be home from work by now."

"Thank you for stopping by, Sherry. It was really nice meeting you."

"Same here," Sherry said as she put the blanket away and gathered Denise and her baby bag. "You're just as sweet as Greg described," she added while standing at the door. "I'll try and stop by again soon."

"I'd like that."

Once again, Jessica's room was quiet. Knowing that her doctor had made the nice comment about her brought a smile to her face. Quietly reaching for the Bible on her nightstand, she began reading.

A nurse interrupted her briefly when she walked in to give her the appropriate medications and left. As soon as she'd finished her Scripture reading, her mother and Ms. Lena returned.

"Where have you two been?" Jessica asked.

"We went over to that restaurant down the street and got something to eat," her mother answered.

"Eddie's Steak House?" Jessica asked. "I heard one of the doctors talking about it the other day."

"Yeah, that's the one," Mattie said.

"Worst service in the world," Lena added.

"Really?" Jessica said. "I heard that they were good."

"The food is good," her mother said, "but it took forever to get it."

"Yeah," Lena chimed in. "I was so hungry by the time the food came, I was just about ready to eat the sugar from the packets on the table."

"Well, if you had've listened to me in the first place, we could've just got some sandwiches and a Coke from that nice little sandwich shop."

"I didn't want no sandwich. I wanted some *real* food."

"Well, at least we wouldn't have gotten two years older while waiting to eat."

"The important thing is you had a chance to eat," Jessica said.

"Anyway," Lena said after a brief pause, "how did your therapy go? Do you like the new lady?"

"It went fine. She thinks I'm doing well. I still would rather have had Dr. Dixon, but I like her."

"Well," Mattie said, "I'm glad of that. If you got to have a new doctor, it's best that you at least like her."

"Mama, you look tired. You've been spending late evenings here. Why don't you go home and get some rest? I'll see you again tomorrow."

"Well, I *am* kind of tired," Mattie admitted. "I just hate to leave you here by yourself. It's bad enough that you got to be away from home."

"I'll be okay."

"Are you sure?"

"Yes, ma'am. You go home too, Ms. Lena. You spend about as much time out here as Mama."

"Well, somebody's got to make sure your mama behaves herself while you're off your feet."

"And I appreciate that," Jessica said with a laugh.

The two women kissed her cheek and left the room. Shortly thereafter, and with her Bible still in hand, Jessica drifted off to sleep.

CHAPTER 8

For the first time since the day of the deadly accident, Detective Morrison didn't rinse down two Alka-Seltzer tablets with water at the knowledge of an oncoming visit from his least favorite lawyer. Maintaining a professional demeanor in Derrick's presence had been a tough battle that had gotten tougher over the weeks, but somehow he'd managed.

"I received a message at my office that you wanted to see me," Derrick said as he anxiously entered Detective Morrison's office without knocking. "Have you solved this case?"

"Do come in, Mr. Madison," the detective responded sarcastically. Standing, he shook Derrick's hand and walked around his desk to close the door that had been left open. "Please have a seat."

"Thank you," Derrick said.

"I would have called you a few days ago, Mr. Madison, but I just figured that I'd see you soon anyway. It's been almost two weeks since I saw you last. That's odd."

"Well, believe me, it wasn't by choice. I've been prosecuting attorney in a case that, with any luck, will end this week."

"I wasn't complaining," the detective assured him with a half-hearted laugh. His jabs were intentional, but not hard enough to ruffle Derrick's feathers. "My reason for contacting your office was to give you both good and bad news."

"Please tell me that you have solved this case."

"Somewhat, but not exactly," Detective Morrison said. "We've solved one very important aspect of it, but that closure actually opened another door."

"I don't follow you."

"We have determined that Miss Charles didn't cause the accident that killed your mother, Mr. Madison."

"What!" Derrick blurted as he stood in anger. "How can you come to that decision?"

"Calm down, Mr. Madison, and let me finish."

"Oh, you'd just love that, wouldn't you?" Derrick accused. "You'd just love for me to sit back and take whatever crap you dish out. Well, it ain't happening," he continued. "What? Did the family pay you off or something? Does her family belong to some type of crime group that threatened you into this crazy conclusion? What?"

"*Sit down*, Mr. Madison." The officer's patience had run its course.

"Not until I get a sensible explanation!"

"You'll get one after you sit down!" Detective Morrison yelled.

"Fine," Derrick said as he slowly sat in his seat and rubbed his chin.

"Thank you," Detective Morrison said as he quickly calmed himself. "Now, as I was saying, we found new evidence, in a previously overlooked set of pictures, that Miss Charles didn't cause the accident. Now it was indeed the impact of her car with your mother's car that led to the injuries that caused your mother's death, but the accident was probably unavoidable."

"So what are you saying? Someone else caused the accident?" Derrick tried to remain calm.

"That's exactly what I'm saying. We have determined that a third car was involved that somehow left the scene. We found tire marks in the grassy area across the street from the impact that didn't match the tires of the cars driven by Miss Charles or Ms. Madison. We've concluded that a third car slammed into Miss Charles's car, which caused it to cross into the oncoming lane of traffic and hit Ms. Madison's car head-on. The damage to the right side of Ms. Charles's car coincides with this conclusion."

"So where is this third driver?" Derrick asked.

"That's the new mystery," Detective Morrison said. "We're checking with local hospitals now to see if any of them treated anyone with injuries that could be related to a car accident in the days following this particular incident. We're focusing on the county hospitals both here and in Maryland right now. In our experience, people like this go to the hospitals where their injuries will kind of mesh with other injuries treated there on a normal basis."

"So what you want me to believe is that you've been investigating the wrong person all this while, and now all of a sudden a magic lightbulb has gone off and you can see clearly that she didn't do it—but you don't know who did. Is that what you're telling me?" Derrick asked.

"No, Mr. Madison. We haven't been investigating the wrong person. You have been investigating the wrong person. We've been investigating an accident scene and yes, new developments came forth, and yes, they conclude that Miss Charles was not the cause of this tragedy. However, we were never investigating Miss Charles. I believe that was your self-made job, Mr. Madison."

Derrick became angry again. "Well, I wouldn't have had to do it if you and your men were doing your jobs."

"We were and still are doing our jobs," Detective Morrison defended. "That's why we've come across this added information. If you were doing our jobs as you think you were, you wouldn't have been so dead set on accusing this woman, because you would have been able to step back from the situation and look at the details. That's called investigation, Mr. Madison."

"My mama is dead, Detective." Derrick pounded a fist on the desk in front of him. "Do you understand what I'm saying? My mama is dead because of this accident, and you're no closer to solving this case than you were three months ago. The only person who we know for sure was a part of that accident is in Robinson Memorial right now getting the best possible care from a top-notch doctor who *used* to be my best friend.

"She's right there and nothing has been done because she *said* she couldn't remember. Now I see that nothing will *ever* be done, because now you are going to write a report that clears her name. Way to go, Detective. Thanks for nothing!" Derrick said as he stormed from the office and slammed the door.

"So much for being proud of progress made," Detective Morrison said as he dropped his folder onto his desk and reached for the Alka-Seltzer that he'd thought was unnecessary.

"If you want a job done right, sometimes you have to do it yourself," Derrick mumbled as he got into his car and headed toward Robinson Memorial.

Not wanting to spend time looking for a free parking spot, he parked in the paid parking area directly across the street.

"Hi." Creshondria smiled as he approached her desk.

"Can you tell me what room Jessica Charles is in?"

"Room thirty-three," she said after checking the records.

"Thank you." Derrick got on the half-full elevator and got off at the third floor. He found the room with no problem and pushed the door open without knocking.

Jessica turned to see the strange man entering her room. Because his face appeared to be unfriendly, she immediately became fearful.

"Hello," she said cautiously.

"Are you Jessica?" he asked.

"Yes."

"Good," he said as he moved the call button from her reach and sat down on the doctor's stool.

"Who . . . who are you?" she asked. "What do you want?"

"I want answers," Derrick began. "Answers that only you

can give and I don't plan to leave without them. It's as simple as that."

"What answers?" Jessica tried not to appear afraid but her heart pounded within her chest. "Who are you?"

"I'm Derrick Madison. Julia Madison was my mother. You killed her in a car wreck back in January and I want to know what happened."

"I don't know what happened," Jessica said as tears began to stream down her cheeks. "I've already talked to the police. I told them I didn't know."

"Yeah, I know about your little talk with the police. Maybe the police bought your amnesia story, but I don't."

"I've been trying to remember, but I don't."

"Try harder."

"Please leave."

"You think I wanna be here? Do you know how sick it's making me just to look at your face?" Derrick said. "I will *gladly* leave—but not until you tell me what happened. How is it that you can't remember? Why is it that all of a sudden the police think a third car was involved? Did you strike some kind of deal with the cops?"

"What?"

Derrick continued his interrogation. "What is it? Is your family rich? You paid them off? Tell me. Huh?"

"I don't know what you're talking about, now get out of my room." Jessica's voice level rose as panic began to take over.

"Do you have a mama, Jessica?" Derrick showed no signs of obeying her order.

"Yes."

"Put yourself in my place, put me in yours, and put your mama in my mama's. You wouldn't like me very much right now, would you? Well, that's how I feel. I don't like you very much right now and all I'm asking for is an explanation."

"I don't know."

"Were you drunk?"

"I don't drink."

"How do you know that you don't drink? Huh? Maybe you just don't *remember* that you're a sloppy drunk who likes to get behind the wheel of a car when you get plastered. Did you fall asleep at the wheel? Maybe you sneezed and just lost control of the wheel for a moment. Is it possible that you just weren't paying attention to the road?"

"I don't know!"

"Wrong answer!" he said as he stood over her with his face close to hers. "Try again!"

"I don't know! I don't know!" Jessica screamed.

"Rick!" Greg rushed into the room after hearing Jessica's cries. "What are you doing?"

"Don't talk to me, Greg. She owes me answers and I'm here to cash in."

"Have you completely lost your mind?" Greg said as he snatched Derrick from the bedside where he still stood, hovering over Jessica's trembling body.

"Get away from me!" Derrick ordered.

"Get out of here, Rick. Get out of here right now!"

"Get your hands off of me!" Derrick said as he pushed Greg away and pointed at Jessica. "You're the only one who knows the truth, now talk to me!"

"I'm sorry! I'm *so* sorry!" Jessica wailed.

"I don't want your 'sorry'!" Derrick banged the wall with his elbow.

"Stop it, Rick. I'm not gonna let you treat her this way. Now for the last time, get out of here!"

"You're not going to let *me* treat *her* this way? What are you now? Her Superman? Mama's dead, Greg. Remember Mama? When did the laws change? Since when do criminals get all the protection? First the police, now you! Why is everybody covering for this murderer?"

"That's it, Rick," Greg said as he grabbed his arm and led him toward the door.

"Turn me loose!" Derrick snatched his arm away.

"You remember when you wanted to fight me last month?" Greg asked angrily as he grabbed Derrick's collar and pressed his back against the wall. "Remember when I said I wasn't going to fight you? Well, all bets are off. You're on my turf now and this is my patient. I will *not* allow you to come in here and start throwing around threats and upsetting her. You wanna fight?" Greg's teeth were clenched as he spoke. "Come on," he said as he stepped back and motioned for Derrick to step forward.

"Are you threatening me?" Derrick asked angrily.

"Do you *feel* threatened?" Greg echoed the words Derrick had said to him weeks earlier.

"Dr. Dixon," Dr. Grant said as he entered with three security guards and several other hospital employees who followed to see what all the commotion was about, "I don't think you want to do that. He's not worth it."

One of the security officers stepped between the two of them. "Do you want us to arrest him?" he asked Greg.

"No," Greg said as he stepped back and calmed himself. He looked at Jessica for confirmation. She shook her head, declining to press charges. "He was just leaving," Greg added. "Please escort him to the parking lot."

Derrick looked emotionlessly at Greg as he turned and quietly walked away with the security guards without further incident. The crowd slowly dispersed as Greg assured Dr. Grant that he and his patient were all right. Greg closed the room door after the last person left and hurried to Jessica's bedside as she was drying the last of her tears with a tissue.

"I'm sorry, Grace," he said as he sat on the stool. "I don't know what else to say. You certainly didn't deserve that."

"I was so scared," she said while fighting the flood of more tears. "I didn't know what he was going to do."

"I know," Greg said. He took the wadded tissues from her hand and gave her fresh ones. "I'm sorry, but I honestly don't believe he would have hurt you. He's just very upset right now and has been for several months. I know I can't convince you of this, but he really isn't a bad person—just a misguided one right now."

"How do you know him?"

Greg stood and took several moments to collect his thoughts. He hadn't been prepared to give Jessica the news today, and finding out this way wasn't going to make her happy. Turning back to face her, he finally spoke.

"Maybe I should have told you this a long time ago. I'm not sure why I didn't, but I just thought it wasn't the best thing to do given the circumstances. I mean, with me being your doctor and all. I know I don't deserve to ask any favors right now, but please don't be angry when I tell you this."

"I'll try."

"Rick was—I mean Rick is—my best friend."

"What?" The look on her face was a mixture of disbelief and disgust.

"Wait," Greg pleaded. "It's a long story, so give me a minute. Rick and I went to day care, grade school, high school, and college together. His mother was my godmother and she and my mother were best friends. Rick and I were virtually inseparable until a couple of months ago. He found out that I was your physician and had performed your surgery and he lost it. He's been blaming you for the death of his mother since the accident first happened.

"Well, once he found out that I had done the surgery and that the surgery was a success, he was livid. We'd never physically fought before, but when he found out about your being my patient, we got into a scuffle. He hasn't spoken to me since.

"Today is the first time I've even seen him since then. He made it very clear that I wasn't welcome at his house, and he even stopped attending our church so he wouldn't have to see me. He was also angry with our pastor for praying for your operation's success. It's been real hard for me. I've missed his friendship."

"Oh, God. I had no idea."

"I know you didn't, Grace. That's the way I wanted it to be until I felt the time was right."

"When would that have been?"

"I don't know. But I do know that I never meant for you to find out like this. I never would have expected him to show up here. I'm truly sorry. Please don't be angry."

"I'm not angry," Jessica said tearfully. "I'm just sorry that I've caused you so much trouble."

"It's not your fault that he chose to handle his grief like this. I don't know why, but he insists on harboring this animosity. I've never known him to be as angry as he has been about this. He and his mother were close, but this is just so unlike his character. I guess it's the not knowing that's getting to him."

"He mentioned that the police think a third car was involved."

"Really?"

"Yes, but he apparently thinks it's a cover-up. He believes I killed his mother. Oh, God. I wish I could remember."

"You'll remember in God's own time, Grace. I hadn't heard about a third car. That must be a new development, but whether a third vehicle was involved or not, you're not a murderer. The collision was an accident."

"Wait a minute," Jessica suddenly said. "Is this Rick the same as Ricky? Sherry's husband, Ricky?"

"Yes."

"But she came to see me and she was so nice. She even called me this morning to see how I was doing and said she was going to stop by again this week sometime. I never would have known that she thought I killed her mother-in-law. How am I ever going to face her again?"

"That's because she doesn't see it as you killing her mother-in-law. She sees it as an accident, just like I do. She doesn't feel the same way Rick does. Sherry's a great person and a wonderful friend. Don't push her away, Grace."

"You know," Jessica began as Greg handed her another tissue, "I was reading a Scripture this morning in Romans that said that all the things that happen to us work out for our good if we love Jesus. I know God's word is true, Dr. Dixon," she continued as her tears broke once more, "but I don't see any good in this."

Greg moved closer and sat on the corner of Jessica's bed. He cradled her in his arms and allowed her to cry on his shoulder. Although she still wore a bandana on her head, he could feel through the scarf that her hair was growing back. He smiled in spite of the situation at hand.

"Listen to me," he said as he pulled away and held Jessica's face close to his. "I know it doesn't look the brightest right now, but good has come of this. First of all, this accident has brought you and your mother closer together and it's brought both of you closer to God. Secondly, my mother lost her best friend in that accident but through the same accident, whether she realizes it yet or not, God has given her a new best friend in Ms. Mattie. Thirdly," he continued, "Sherry told me that you said you'd never had a best friend in your life. This accident gave you one in Sherry. The two of you could be very close if you allow it to happen. I happen to know that she thinks the world of you.

"Fourth blessing, prior to this accident, you were going to marry a man who wasn't for you. This accident proved that when he left you on your death bed. That may not have made you happy, but it was a blessing. And last but not least," he said as he continued to hold her face in his hands, "you met me. If it weren't for this accident, you never would have ended up here, in my hospital, under my care. You never would have met me. And, Grace, your meeting me was a very good thing."

Before Jessica could respond, the room door opened.

"What the police doing outside your room door asking for my ID?" Mattie said as she and Lena entered the room.

"Are we interrupting something?" Lena added as she watched her son continuously stare into the eyes of his patient.

"No, Mama," Greg said softly. He finally released Jessica's face and stood slowly to face the two women. "You all come on in."

"Why do y'all have police outside this door?" Lena repeated Mattie's earlier question.

"And why don't we believe you when you say we weren't interrupting something?" Mattie added.

"Mama," Jessica said.

"No, it's okay." Greg smiled. "But I can only answer one question at a time and think I should answer yours first, Ms. Mattie. Before the two of you came in I was telling Grace how blessed she was regardless of all the negative things surrounding her accident." He continued, "And if you hadn't walked in when you did, I think that somewhere in my speech I was going to ask her to accompany me on a date."

"Oh, yeah?" Mattie smiled with obvious approval.

"Yes, ma'am, but since you all have such bad timing, I'll have to ask her later."

"Don't let us stop you," Lena said as she grabbed her purse. "Go 'head. You want us to leave?"

"No, Mama."

"Yes," Jessica said.

"What?" Mattie said.

"*You* want us to leave?" Lena asked.

"Oh, no, ma'am." Jessica held up her hand to stop the mothers who were all too willing to give them their privacy if that's what they wanted. "I was talking to Dr. Dixon."

"I'm sorry?" Greg said in confusion.

"Yes, I'll go out with you," she said as the mothers exchanged smiles.

"You will?" Greg said in an almost shy, boyish manner.

"Yes."

"Thank you," he said with a smile.

"You're welcome." She returned his smile.

Mattie cleared her throat to break the silence of Greg's and Jessica's lingering gazes.

"Oh," Greg said as his trance broke. "What was I saying?"

"Well," Lena said, "since you saw fit to answer Mattie's question before your own mama's, I guess now is when you were going to explain to us why them police folks are outside the door here."

"Oh, yeah." Greg's face turned solemn. "Rick was here."

"Derrick Madison was here?" his mother said in surprise.

"Who's Derrick Madison?" Mattie asked.

"What did he do?" Lena asked. "Did he come to see Jessica? He didn't do nothing stupid, did he?"

"Who?" Mattie asked again, looking from Lena to Greg. "Who is he?"

"Okay, okay, ladies." Greg held up his hands. "Both of you just calm down and I'll explain everything," he said as he pulled the stool in front of them and sat. "Derrick Madison is the son of the woman killed in the car accident that Grace was involved in," Greg told Mattie.

"What was he doing here? Was he mad? What? Did he hurt you, baby?"

"No, Mama. Take it easy," Jessica said. "I'm fine."

"What was he doing here?" she asked again.

"From what I could gather," Greg explained, "he had been to the police station and was told by the investigating officer that there is now suspicion that a third driver was involved that actually caused the accident. I suppose they believe he or she left the scene of the accident before police and medical personnel arrived. Rick became angry because he thinks that the police are covering for Grace for some reason. He doesn't believe that a third person was involved and he doesn't believe that Grace doesn't remember the details. He thinks she's saying that so as not to be held responsible."

"So he came here to threaten her?" Mattie asked.

"Ms. Mattie, I'm not sure what he hoped to accomplish by coming here and I'm not sure *he* even knows. Let me also tell you this. I've never told you this before and I just told Grace a few minutes ago. I know Rick. He's been my best friend since birth, basically."

"You know the son of the woman killed in the accident?"

"Yes, ma'am."

"When you agreed to take Jessie as a patient and performed her surgery, did you know she was the survivor of the same accident?"

"Yes, ma'am. I knew from the beginning. I knew it even before she was transferred here."

"And you knew your friend's mother?"

"Yes. Julia Madison was my godmother."

"And she was my best friend," Lena added.

"So, the dead lady was your godmother," Mattie said as though needing clarification.

"Yes, ma'am."

She turned to Lena. "And she was your best friend."

"That's right," Lena responded.

She turned again to Greg. "And her son is your best friend?"

"Yes, ma'am."

"So if these people are so close to you, why you taking the time to take such good care of Jessie and why would you"—she turned to Lena—"take the time to sit with me through all of this?"

"I'm a doctor, Ms. Mattie," Greg said. "I take good care of all of my patients. I took Grace as a patient because, as I've said before, I believe this to have been an honest accident. I wasn't seeing her as the woman who killed my godmother. I saw her as a dying woman whose one chance at survival was a surgery that I believed God was able to help me perform successfully.

"In the short time I've been practicing, I've taken care of murderers, drug dealers, rapists, and bank robbers who got injured in police shoot-outs. I cared for them *knowing* that they had maliciously killed or hurt other people. I have to. It's my job. Grace doesn't fall into any of those categories. I didn't necessarily *have* to take her as a patient. If I had told Dr. Grant of the details surrounding my involvement with the Madisons, he would have given the case to someone else.

"I wanted this case. I'm not bragging, but I know I'm the

best surgeon at Robinson Memorial. Grace didn't just need a doctor—she needed *me*. She's a decent woman with a beautiful heart, and in a moment of time she, for some reason, lost control of her car and hit Ms. Julia almost head-on. I miss my godmother. God knows I do, and I hate what her death has done to Rick. But I can't hold that against Grace. If I had handled any of this with a heart full of resentment, I never would have been blessed to get to know two of the nicest women I've run across in quite some time."

"Thank you, Dr. Dixon," Mattie said, standing to hug him.

"Well, that's nice of him to say and all," Lena said, breaking the mood, "but for the record let me just say, I just hang out with you 'cause I feel sorry for you. I mean, if I don't, who will? Don't nobody else want to fool with you."

"Mama," Greg warned as Jessica burst into laughter.

"Excuse me, Dr. Dixon," Dr. Young said as she opened the door to the room.

"Come on in, Sarah," Greg said.

"I understand that you've had some trauma this afternoon," Dr. Young told Jessica. "Do you want to go ahead with your therapy, or would you like to wait until tomorrow?"

"Why don't you wait, baby?" Mattie suggested.

"No," Jessica said. "I want to do it. Today we're supposed to hit the treadmill and I can hardly wait. I want to do as much walking as I can."

"The treadmill?" Greg said in surprise. "That's wonderful progress."

"This girl has determination that's unmatched by any of my present patients," Dr. Young said. "Most of the ones in her same predicament are afraid of the pain or of falling, but not Jessica here. She fell quite a bit a few nights ago, but she got back up and wanted to continue."

"I didn't fall yesterday," Jessica bragged.

"No, you sure didn't." Dr. Young smiled. "Nor the day before."

"That's good to know," Greg said, smiling, "because she's

got a dinner obligation to fulfill in a few weeks. You think it's possible that she'll be able to go home in the next two to three weeks?"

"Are you kidding—this trooper?" Dr. Young said. "She'll be ready."

CHAPTER 9

Mother's Day, May 13

When Denise was born in December, Sherry dreamed of her
first Mother's Day and how great it would be. She imagined her
and Derrick taking Dee to church and then they'd all go out to
her favorite restaurant afterward.

Instead, she spent Mother's Day at her church and he went
to his. After service, he said that he was going to visit his
mother's grave. Sherry could certainly understand that, but she
wanted to feel special on this day as well.

She had initially planned to travel to New Jersey to see her
own mother, but decided to spend the day with her daughter instead. She had spoken to both her parents by telephone and
they understood what she was going through and told her that
they would be continuing to pray for her and for Derrick.

After church services, she stopped by the hospital briefly to
visit Jessica, who was in the middle of her therapy. She was
doing very well and Sherry was truly proud of her and her determination to make a full recovery. Jessica was almost in tears
as Sherry presented her with a get-well card that her second-
grade class had made for her. She and Dee stayed for a little

while, watching Jessica walk the treadmill and perform leg presses, but left shortly after the therapy ended.

As she was driving home, Sherry found herself turning onto Apple Street. She parked her car in front of her late mother-in-law's house and used the key she still had, to go inside. Everything was still in place. Derrick had insisted that they not pack up any of Julia's things. He said they'd do it in time, but for now he wanted everything to remain the way it had been when she lived there.

Sherry put Dee, who had fallen asleep in the car, in the crib that they had set up in Julia's spare bedroom. Julia insisted that they set up a room at her house for the baby because she planned to keep her every chance she could. Had she lived, Julia Madison would have been a wonderful grandmother.

Dust had begun to settle on the coffee tables and book-shelves. Sherry found a feather duster and began cleaning. She wasn't dressed for the task that she had given herself, but she didn't mind. She just didn't want to go home and be alone.

Sherry smiled when she looked through the large number of pictures displayed on the shelves in the living room. Julia was proud of her son and his accomplishments. She had photos of him playing basketball games in high school, pictures of his graduations from high school and college, and pictures of his and Sherry's wedding.

There were also several photos of Derrick and Greg together that covered their lives from childhood through adulthood. If pictures were worth a thousand words, then the friendship of the two men spoke volumes. Sherry knew that the no-nonsense woman wouldn't be pleased to know her only child had all but detached himself from the rest of the world.

Turning her attention from the shelf to the telephone, she felt more memories surfacing. It was an old-fashioned rotary phone that Julia had loved. Sherry remembered how she and Derrick had tried for years to get her to let them purchase an updated one. She'd said the one she had served her well and she didn't want to change. Pressing the eject button on the answering machine, Sherry caught the partially used cassette as it popped out. She put it back in and rewound it. She pressed the play button and went back to her dusting.

There were several days of calls on the tape. Sherry laughed as she heard Lena's voice come on the machine. She and Julia had just seemed to love a good argument. This call, Lena was fussing because Julia wasn't home to take her third call.

"I don't know what you doing and where you are," her voice was saying. "This morning you claimed your leg was hurting. Well, unless you in a wheelchair or something, your leg must be doing better." She continued, "Don't even worry about calling me back, 'cause I'm fixing to take a nap. I mean it. Don't wake me up. I'll just talk to you later."

The next call was Greg, calling just to see how Julia was doing. It was a call he made on a regular basis.

"Hi, Ms. Julia," he said. "I didn't want anything in particular, I just wanted to see how you were doing. Since you're not at home, I guess you're doing okay. I'll probably stop by later today since I have a rare day off. Take care and call me on my cell phone if you want me to bring anything when I come. I love you. Bye."

There were several calls following, everything from different church members calling to find out what dish she was bringing to the women's meeting, to Evelyn Cobb asking if she knew Greg's home number because she had a "medical question."

"Yeah, right." Sherry laughed.

Lena's voice came back again. "Julia Madison, I know you *didn't* tell my Greg to add vanilla flavoring to the cake recipe that I gave him. That recipe was just fine without that vanilla mess. You call me when you get home so I can tell you off firsthand."

Derrick's voice came on several calls later. "Hey, Mama, it's 8:30 A.M. I knew you were checking out yard sales with Ms. Lena, but I thought I'd call and leave you a message. I hope you're bundled up, by the way. It's cold out there. Anyway, the reason I'm calling is that I didn't want you to be looking for me later. Listen, I know I told you that I would drive you to the store this afternoon, but as it turns out I'm going to ride to Maryland with Greg. He has a nine-hour medical conference to attend there. I figured I'd get some business taken care of over there while he was doing that.

"We'll be back late tonight, but I know I won't feel like going to the store that late, so I'll take you sometime tomorrow. I know you really wanted to pick up some of that juice that you love to drink before bed, but it can wait, I'm sure. I don't necessarily want you driving, especially since your hip has been giving you trouble, but if you just have to have the juice tonight, then it won't kill you to drive yourself. If you go, just get the juice and come on home. Then, if you still need some extra stuff, I'll take you again tomorrow after church. Love you, Mama. Don't be mad. I'll make it up to you. Bye."

Sherry put the duster down and turned the machine off. She picked up the telephone and began dialing.

"Hello," Greg answered.

"Hey. Where are you?"

"Sherry?"

"Yes. I'm sorry. It's me. Where are you?"

"I'm heading to the ATM. What's up?"

"Can you come by Mama's house when you're done, or do you have to go back to the hospital?"

"You mean Ms. Julia's?"

"Yes."

"Is something wrong, Sherry? Why are you at Ms. Julia's?"

"I came by to . . ." she started. "Can you just come over? I'll explain it then."

"Sure. I'm not too far away. Give me fifteen minutes."

Sherry listened to the message several more times while she waited for Greg. When she heard his car pull into the driveway, she walked to the door and let him in.

"Hi," he said as he embraced her warmly. "Are you okay?"

"Oh, Greg," she started as she headed toward the phone. "Listen to this."

She played the message again for Greg to hear it. When the message finished, Greg sat slowly on the sofa and firmly wiped over his face with his hands.

"She was on her way to the store when she had the accident," he said. "That's it. That's why he's so angry and bitter. He knew that."

"He's blaming Jessica so he won't blame himself," Sherry said. "You know," she added, "when I found out about how he barged into the hospital that day and scared Jessica, I was totally blown away. That was just so out of character for him. I started thinking that maybe he needed some type of counseling. But now . . ."

"I *still* think he needs counseling," Greg said. "Even if we've found out the reason for his anger, he has to face it head-on. He has to admit that the reason he's so tormented over Ms. Julia's death is that he chose not to go to the store for her."

"He'll see himself as a murderer, like he sees Jessica," Sherry worried.

"He *already* sees himself as a murderer, Sherry. That's the problem. He thinks he killed his mama. He's probably never really seen Grace as a murderer. He's just using her to keep the focus off of himself. With counseling, he'll come to understand that he's not a murderer either. True, he should have taken his mother to the store instead of riding with me to the conference, and if I'd known that she wanted him to, I would have insisted that he did.

"Ms. Julia had been having problems with her hip and maybe her reflexes were slow and maybe that played a part in her not being able to avoid the crash. But who's to say that with him driving, the accident still wouldn't have happened? He needs to know that there really is no one to blame for the accident. Unless, of course, there really was a third person involved. I think counseling is certainly needed."

"So, what do we do now? I mean, what do I do? Do I let him know that I heard the message?"

"No. Not right now anyway. Let me think about this for a little bit," Greg said. "I'll get back with you."

"Thanks, Greg."

"I told you before, Sherry. I am here when you need me, and whether he wants it or not, I'm here for Rick as well. We're not supposed to know about this, so let's leave it alone until we can get a plan together. Rick has proven that his mental stability can be very fragile where this situation is concerned. I don't know how to handle this right now. We're gonna need some insight from the man upstairs."

"That's for sure," Sherry agreed.

"I need to get to the hospital," Greg said as he stood. "Where's Dee?"

"She's asleep in the baby room."

Greg walked softly into the room and leaned over the crib. Denise was still sleeping peacefully. Lowering the side railing, he kissed her gently on the forehead.

"Uncle Greg has to figure out a way to help your daddy," he whispered. "I need to spend more time with my goddaughter, and the only way I can do that is to help your daddy through this."

He walked out of the room and found Sherry still sitting on the sofa. He pulled her to a standing position and hugged her tightly.

"I want my Ricky back, Greg," she said.

"I know," he said. "And we're going to get him back. I promise," he continued as he headed for the door to leave.

"What did you do with Ms. Lena today?" Sherry asked as she walked him to the door. "I know you did something for Mother's Day."

"Yeah." Greg nodded. "I took both Ms. Mattie and her to dinner today. Ms. Mattie is so much like Ms. Julia it's scary. She and Mama fuss all the time just like Mama and Ms. Julia used to do."

"Really?" Sherry smiled.

"Yeah. I'm telling you, it's weird. But there is one subject matter that they totally agree on and they let me know it every chance they get."

"What's that?"

"Grace." Greg gave a short laugh. "They both think the two of us are perfect for each other. We haven't even gone out yet, and they've made a love connection with the two of us."

"So, when is the big date?"

"Her birthday is this coming Saturday. I'm going to take her to see *The Brothers.*"

"The new movie with all the fine men?" Sherry asked. "You sure you want to do that?"

"Yes, I do. I think it will be fun to see her reaction when the likes of Morris Chestnut and Shemar Moore appear on-screen."

"D.L. Hughley and Bill Bellamy ain't bad either," Sherry said as Greg laughed.

"Yeah, well, we'll see how I compare to the competition."

"That's cool and all," Sherry said, "but I'm telling you now, if Ricky wants to receive any attention from me at the movies, *The Brothers* would not be a good choice to take me to—okay? Now, what else you got planned?" she asked as he continued to laugh.

"Well, then we have reservations for dinner at The Sax. You know—the new restaurant on Virginia Avenue."

"Wow." Sherry grinned. "I'm impressed. I hear it's a very ritzy place. Me and Ricky tried to get in the weekend that it opened and it was booked."

"I know. I made our reservation over a week ago and barely got a table."

"Evelyn is gonna be so crushed if things work out for you and Jessica. She so has her heart set on roping you in."

"I thought she'd step back after I dissed her at the hospital several weeks ago."

"She took a step back all right," Sherry said, "and then she took two steps forward."

"Well, she'll find out about Grace soon enough. I plan to invite her to church with me very soon."

"So, I guess this means you have a date set to release her from the hospital."

"Yep." He smiled brightly. "In fact, I'm releasing her tomorrow. Dr. Young gave the okay on Friday. I watched her therapy on yesterday and she walked with no problem. She did fall once, but that's because she thought she felt strong enough to jog. Almost busted her behind in the therapy room." He laughed.

"You didn't laugh at her, did you?" Sherry playfully hit his arm.

"Yeah, but she didn't see me. She didn't even know I was watching."

"Are you nervous about the date?"

"Nervous? No. Excited? Yes."

"I'm happy for you, Greg." Sherry smiled. "I hope things work out for you and Jessica. She seems like such a sweet girl."

"Sherry," Greg said as he stood on the top step, "I know this hasn't been easy for you. You've been trying to be supportive to Rick and his situation and at the same time be supportive of Grace and me. You've somehow made time to spend with Grace and become someone she considers a friend. I can't tell you how much that means to her. Therefore it means a lot to me. I try to be there for her," he continued, "but I'm sure there are times when she wants to talk to a woman."

"We've talked about you, you know," Sherry said.

"Oh, really?"

"Yes, really."

"Good things?"

"Let's just say that these feelings that you have for her aren't one-sided. She's pretty fond of you too, Greg."

"She said that?" Greg was visibly pleased.

"Not in those words," Sherry admitted, "but she made it pretty clear that she thinks highly of you. She thinks you're the perfect guy. And she loves the fact that you call her Grace. And those were her words."

"I'm glad to know that," Greg said. "I'm pleased she's doing better and that Ms. Mattie will finally be able to take her home, but I must admit I'm going to miss having her there at the hospital all day."

"Well, it's not like you won't be able to see her once she checks out."

"I know, but the way it is now, I can see her any time I want. After tomorrow, I'll have to actually make time to see her. You know how hectic and full my schedule is at the hospital."

"I know."

"Speaking of the hospital," Greg said as he walked down the steps of the porch and to his car, "let me go. I'll call you once I figure out how to handle this new information."

"Okay. Thanks again."

Greg drove to the hospital with his mind flooded with thoughts. The message that Derrick had left his mother the day of her death shed a whole new light on things.

"No wonder you're so angry, my friend," Greg said, thinking of how Derrick must have felt upon learning of his mother's accident. His own words, "it won't kill you to drive yourself," must haunt him over and over. He needed to find someone to blame so he wouldn't feel so responsible.

"Dr. Dixon," Creshondria said in her usual "I'm too sexy for my job" voice, "you're back. Love that suit."

"Thank you, Shon," he responded as he headed toward the stairs.

"You got it right," she said gleefully.

"And I'll probably regret it for the rest of my life," he mumbled as he climbed the stairs to the fourth floor.

"Dixon," Dr. Merrill said as he stopped him in the hall.

"Good afternoon, Dr. Merrill."

"For those of us who keep our schedules and stay at work, it's a *tired* afternoon," Dr. Merrill said.

"Is there something you're trying to say, Merrill?"

"Don't try and get cocky with me, young man," he said to

Greg's amusement. "You think nobody notices that you sneak out for a couple of hours just about every Sunday to attend church services on your job time?"

"I don't sneak out, Dr. Merrill. I get permission. And when I leave, I'm on call if I'm needed."

"When I was a young doctor," he lectured, "nothing was more important than the well-being of my patients. I made sure that their doctor was on hand when they needed me."

"Then I guess we have something in common," Greg said, smiling sarcastically, "because I do the same thing."

Dr. Merrill frowned. "Give you people a degree and you get beside yourselves."

Greg had always known that Dr. Merrill was quite prejudiced and had never approved of his position at the hospital. It disappointed the gray-haired doctor even more that none of the other surgeons, who were all white, shared his feelings.

"When you say 'you people,' " Greg continued to tease, "you mean tall people? Maybe people with low haircuts? Or people whose favorite color is blue? No, wait a minute." He put his finger under his chin as if to think deeply. "People with their own teeth?"

"Let me tell you something, young man," Dr. Merrill said as he pointed a trembling finger at Greg. "This hospital had better be grateful for doctors like me instead of you. Because if they were all like you, every time we turned around, one of them would be in some church, sitting on cushioned pews, listening to preachers. Why? Because they're all just a bunch of kids, so young and naive that they feel they need some unknown higher power to direct them."

"No, Merrill, let me tell *you* something," Greg said. "This hospital had better be grateful for doctors like *me* instead of *you*. Because if they were all like you, every time we turned around, one of them would be in some church, lying in front of the altar, *unable* to listen to the preacher. Why? Because they're all dead in caskets—because they were all too old and senile to have seen a need to serve the Higher Power, which is Christ Jesus. You have a nice day, Dr. Merrill."

"Who are you calling old and senile? Don't you walk away from me, you young whippersnapper," Dr. Merrill said as Greg walked past him and headed down the hall. "Didn't your mama teach you to respect your elders?" he called.

I'd better keep walking, 'cause if he messes around and says something derogatory about Mama, I'm going to have to move into the church for God to forgive me of what I'll end up doing to him.

"Would you like help getting out of that suit, Doctor?" a female doctor said as he turned to go into his office to change clothes.

"Now, Dr. Evans, I think if I had asked you that question, you'd say that it was sexual harassment."

"No, Dr. Dixon," she corrected as she walked away. "If you had asked me that question, I'd have said yes."

"Oh, God," he said aloud as he changed into his work clothes. "What has happened to all the decent women? If this is what I have to look forward to, what will my sons and grandsons have to deal with? Is there a real lady in the house?" he mumbled as a knock came to his door. "Come in," he called as he hung his suit in the closet.

"Hi."

He turned as he heard the voice.

"Grace," he acknowledged in surprise. "Aren't you in therapy right now?"

"I just finished. Dr. Young said it was okay for me to keep walking around as long as it felt comfortable."

"Does she know you took the elevator and are no longer on your floor?"

"No," Jessica admitted. "Guess I should go back, huh?"

"No," Greg said. "Have a seat."

Jessica sat as Greg reached for his desk phone, dialed a few numbers, and hung up.

"So how have you been today?" he asked her as he stood by the side of his desk with his arms folded.

"Fine," she said. "I hardly have any pain during therapy now and it's just such a blessing to be able to get around."

"You're doing wonderfully," Greg admitted. "Don't overdo it though. Remember to take it a day at a time."

"I know. The other day I tried to trot a little. I'm not going to tell you what happened."

"I can imagine." Greg smiled knowingly as he remembered seeing her take the fall as she tried to jog during therapy.

"Hello?" he said as he picked up his ringing telephone. Jessica quickly realized that he was talking to Dr. Young.

"Thanks for calling me back, Sarah," he said. "I just wanted to let you know that Ms. Charles is in my office on the fourth floor. She got a little excited with the walking thing." He paused. "Yes, she's fine. I'll see to it that she gets back to her room safely. Thanks. Bye."

"Was she upset?" Jessica asked.

"No. Not at all," Greg assured her. "So, to what do I owe this honorable visit?"

"I just stopped by to say hello." Jessica shrugged. "I wasn't even sure that you were in today."

"I guess that means I hadn't checked in on you today."

"No, I didn't mean it like that. I just meant I hadn't seen you. I don't want to make it sound like you're obligated to stop by my room every day."

"But I am," Greg said as he rounded his desk and picked up his schedule. "See?" He brought the clipboard to her and pointed to her name.

"Well, that's why I hadn't seen you. I'm last on the list today."

"You're last on my list every day."

"I am?" She tried not to look disappointed.

"You know how, especially as a kid, you were required to eat dinner first? You had to eat all your meat and vegetables before you could have the thing that you really wanted, which was dessert?"

Jessica laughed. "Yeah, I remember those days."

"Well, that's kind of like my schedule," Greg explained. "Meat and veggies are good for you. All my patients are good," he continued as Jessica began to get his point. "All of these right here are my meat, potatoes, green beans, and mac and cheese," he continued. "Then after I'm done with all of that, I get to end my shift with pineapple upside-down cake."

"Oh," Jessica said.

"Or in this case," he said, laughing as she blushed uncontrollably, "red velvet cake."

"I'm sorry," she said as she covered her face with both hands as another knock came to Greg's door.

"Come on in," he said while opening the door for Lena and Mattie.

"That therapist lady told us that Jessica was up here," Lena said.

"Hi, Ms. Lena. Hi, Mama," Jessica said.

"You're just walking all over the place now, ain't you?" Mattie said as she hugged her daughter.

"And it feels great," Jessica said with a smile.

"I'm glad you're all here. Now I'll only have to make this speech once," Greg said as yet another knock came to his door. "I'm a popular guy today," he joked as he headed back to the door.

"Hi," Sherry said as she walked in with Denise. "Oh, my, you have a full office."

Greg motioned to a chair. "Join the fun."

"Hi there, Sherry," Lena said as she stood and hugged her.

"Hi, Ms. Lena. Hi, Jessica. You must be Ms. Mattie."

"I am."

"Ms. Mattie," Greg said cautiously, "this is Sherry Madison."

"You're the wife of the man who walked into my Jessie's room the other day," Mattie said.

"Yes, ma'am," Sherry said softly.

"Well, don't just stand there," Mattie said as Greg and Jessica exchanged smiles of relief. "Come on over here and give me a hug and let me take a look at this baby that everybody talks about."

"Okay," Greg said as they all settled down. Sherry pulled a chair next to Jessica and handed her the sleeping baby. "As I said earlier," Greg continued. "I'm glad you're all here. In my hands I have papers that will allow Grace to be released tomorrow."

The room came alive with joyous chatter as the women all excitedly hugged Jessica and then one another.

"This is wonderful," Mattie said. "I get to take my baby home? Is it for good? She don't have to come back for therapy or nothing?"

"No, ma'am," Greg said. "Her therapy is signed as completed after today and she will be free to go. Now I will give you the number of a doctor for her to get checkups from as a precautionary measure. We're not expecting any setbacks, but should any concerns arise, I'm here."

"And if I have to come back, you'll be my doctor?" Jessica asked.

"I'll insist."

"Dr. Dixon," Mattie said as she walked around his desk. He stood as she approached. "You are the most wonderful doctor I have ever met. I declare, if I was a few years younger and you was a few years older, I'd snatch you up myself."

"Thank you." He beamed as he welcomed her embrace.

"Oh, I don't think so," Lena said to Jessica's and Sherry's amusement. "I wouldn't dare let you nowhere near my son. I don't care how young you were."

"Like you could stop me," Mattie said.

"Oh, I could stop you," Lena assured her.

"Ladies, ladies, ladies," Greg said as he shook his head.

"Sorry," they both mumbled.

"Thank you," Greg said. "Now I'm going to have some paperwork sent to your room later today," he told Jessica. "You and Ms. Mattie look it over and sign the appropriate spaces."

"Okay." Jessica smiled.

"You sho do look good holding that baby, Jessie," Lena said as Greg dropped his head into his hand.

"Sho 'nuff do now," Mattie agreed.

"Ladies," Greg said, "could you perchance be any more transparent?"

"Well, she do," Lena said. "Don't she, Sherry?"

"Uh . . ." Sherry hesitated as she looked at Greg, who was giving her a look of warning. "Well, she kinda does, Greg," she finally said. She turned to Jessica, who was blushing heavily. "You kinda do," Sherry said almost apologetically as she smiled.

"There now," Mattie said as though Sherry's agreement made it binding. "See?"

"I tell you what," Greg said as he rounded his desk and took Dee from Jessica's arms and kissed her cheek while she continued to sleep. "Why don't you take your daughter and our parents and wait for Grace in her room? I need to speak with her privately and we'll join you in a couple of minutes. How's that?"

"Okay," Sherry said.

"I'm sorry," he apologized to Jessica once the ladies had left the room. "My mom can be so openly obvious sometimes."

"*Your* mom?" Jessica laughed. "My mama can be downright direct."

"Two peas in a pod."

"Tell me about it," Jessica said. "I thought God had created a one-of-a-kind when he molded Mama, but I see there are two of them."

He laughed. "Scary, isn't it?"

"Yeah."

"Okay, I'm not going to keep you long," he started. "I just wanted to tell you what a joy it has been to have you as a patient and how remarkable and rewarding it has been to watch the hand of God snatch you away from death and bring you to this point."

"It's felt pretty remarkable, too," she said. "He had a good vessel to work through."

"Thank you." Greg paused with a smile. "Remember that date we talked about a few weeks ago?" he finally asked.

"Yes."

"How's Saturday night?"

"My birthday is Saturday."

"I know."

"Oh."

"Do you have other plans for your birthday?"

"No."

"Will you spend it with me?"

"I'd love to."

"I'll pick you up at 6:00."

CHAPTER 10

"Happy birthday, girl," Sherry said as she walked past Jessica into the living room and placed her bags and hair dryer on the table. "I think I have everything I need."

"Thanks. And thanks for coming and helping me with this," Jessica said. "I just don't know what I'm gonna do with my hair. I don't have a whole lot to work with right now, you know."

"What are you wearing?" Sherry asked.

"Well, when Dr. Dixon—I mean Greg—called me last night, he said I need to wear something dressy but casual to the movies, so I have these gray silk pants and this black top."

"Okay, that's cute," Sherry approved.

"Then we're going to stop by here and change clothes on the way to the restaurant, because he says it's formal dining."

"Yes, it is and you're gonna love it. It's so chic and it gets rave reviews."

"What restaurant is it?"

"Well, if he didn't tell you, *I'm* certainly not gonna spoil the surprise," Sherry told her. "What are you wearing to the restaurant?"

"This navy blue gown," she said as she rushed into her bedroom and brought out the dress for Sherry to see.

"Oh, Jessica, that's beautiful. Not too fancy, yet very elegant. I love it," Sherry said while admiring the V-neckline and the rhinestone pattern that graced the sleeveless straps.

"You think he'll like it? You don't think it's too much, do you?"

"Are you kidding? Greg is going to *love* this. You're gonna look really nice in that, Jessie. You make me sick with your skinny self."

"Oh, here are my shoes." Jessica laughed at the frown on Sherry's face.

"Girl, you're a fashion genius," Sherry said, holding up the silver shoes that brought out the sparkle in the straps of the dress.

"Yeah, well, I may have the clothes together, but the hair needs your professional attention."

"I absolutely love doing hair," Sherry said. "I really started to miss doing it when I began teaching. Occasions like this give me an excuse and an opportunity to do what I love best. Okay, take off the scarf so I can see what I have to work with here."

"Well, I'm not good at styling hair," Jessica said as she slowly slid the cloth off of her head, "so you can do mine any time you like." Aside from her mother, no one had seen her hair since the stitches had been removed several weeks earlier. Sherry walked up to her and carefully ran her fingers through the short locks. Because she had been wearing the scarf, her hair lay curly but flat on her head.

"Girl, you've got plenty to work with here. Have you ever had a perm or do you just wear it natural?"

"I had a perm at the time of the wreck. When it's natural, sometimes it's too curly to do anything with. At the length that it is right now, I'd go around looking like Sophia on *The Golden Girls* if I tried to wear it natural. I'd rather have it permed."

"Good. I brought a mild perm here for you and once I get this hair straightened out, I'm gonna hook you up. Apparently, he has a thing for short hair. His favorite Hollywood girl has it, you know."

"Halle?"

"Yep. And I think you've got just about as much hair as she does."

"You think so?" Jessica asked as she sat in the chair that Sherry placed in the middle of the floor for her.

"Well, maybe not quite, but plenty enough to give a sharp style to. You haven't been scratching your scalp, have you?"

"No, but do you think it's okay to put chemical on my scalp after the operation I had?"

"That's been weeks and weeks, Jessie. But just to be on the safe side, I did get the okay from Greg, to make sure. He said as long as it was comfortable for you, there was no medical reason why I couldn't do it."

"Then let's do it," Jessica said. "Where's Denise?"

"I dropped her off at Ms. Lena's. She and your mother were at her house when I stopped by and they wanted to keep her. So I put her car seat in Ms. Lena's car and left her with them. They're supposed to come by here after going to the store, they said."

Jessica sat in silence for several minutes while Sherry worked on her hair. Sherry began humming as she worked. Styling hair seemed to make her happy. Jessica recognized the popular new Donnie McClurkin tune. She had listened to the CD endlessly during her hospital stay.

It was one of her favorite cuts from his CD and she began singing softly as Sherry hummed. Sherry stopped humming and listened in awe as Jessica continued singing the lyrics of "We Fall Down."

"Oh, my gosh, Jessie. You can *really* sing."

"She sho can," Lena said in admiration as the two girls turned to see her and Mattie standing in the doorway.

"Hey," Sherry said. "We didn't see you standing there."

"I ain't heard Jessie sing in a long time," Mattie said. She put her bags on the sofa and walked closer to her daughter, placing a kiss on her cheek. "It's a wonderful sound, baby," she said.

"Thanks, Mama."

"We gonna get out of y'all's way," Lena said. "It's three o'clock now, so you don't have but a couple of hours to get finished. We want you to be all ready when my son gets here."

"Yes, ma'am." Jessica smiled as the two women walked out of the room.

"I'm just gonna lay Dee in here on the bed, Sherry," Lena called over her shoulder. "She'll be fine."

"Okay," Sherry called back. "I'm so happy that Ms. Lena has found another friend," she told Jessica.

"I know you miss her, Sherry," Jessica said, referring to Julia Madison.

"I do," Sherry readily admitted. "I couldn't have asked for a nicer mother-in-law."

"I know that maybe I shouldn't ask this," Jessica said, "but how is your husband? Is he doing any better?"

Sherry sighed deeply. "No. He's not himself at all these days. We used to be so close and loving. Now, it's like he's drifting away. It's like he's sinking into this hole of depression. Every time I try to reach out to him, he just pushes me away."

"I'm sorry, Sherry."

"It's not your fault, Jessie. I never have blamed you for any of this—and certainly not Ricky's mood. It's between him and God. Greg keeps saying that everything is gonna work out, but my faith gets shaky sometimes. Ricky seems to be getting worse with time, not better."

"Does he know that you're here? Does he even know that you know me?"

"No."

"Aren't you afraid he'll find out somehow?"

"No, not anymore. If he finds out, I'll handle it at that time. I can't live my life in a shell, shutting everyone out like he's doing right now."

"I wish I could help."

"I wish I could help too, Jessie," Sherry said, "but until he opens his heart and mind to what's really going on inside him, we can't. Even God can't help him if he doesn't allow Him to."

"I know."

"Come on, let's rinse your hair."

"Are we in your way again?" Mattie asked, stepping aside so that they had a clear path to the sink.

"No, ma'am," Sherry said. "You're fine. This will only take a minute."

She rinsed the chemical from Jessica's hair, followed that with a deep conditioner, and then rinsed again. Satisfied that her client's hair was rinsed well, Sherry towel-dried it and fluffed her now straight hairs with her fingers.

"Now look at all the hair you been hiding underneath that rag," Lena commented.

Jessica smiled as she and Sherry went back into the living room. Sherry rubbed another conditioner into her hair and sat her under the dryer. Jessica looked at the clock and began getting nervous. It was 4:15 P.M. She wondered what Greg was doing and hoped that he wouldn't be called in to the hospital.

Greg was hoping the same thing as he walked into Pastor Baldwin's office for a scheduled meeting. A call from the hospital right now would be a devastating blow to his plans.

Pastor Baldwin stood and extended his hand. "Brother Greg, unlike most of my appointments, you actually show up on time. God bless you, son."

"Well, I know your time is as valuable as the rest of ours."

"You're looking mighty spiffy for a Saturday afternoon," the pastor observed.

"If you think *this* looks good," Greg teased, "you should see the new suit that's hanging in the back of my car."

"You have plans?"

"I have a date."

"With your patient?" Pastor Baldwin asked.

"My *former* patient," Greg corrected. "Yes, I have a date with Grace."

"Well, congratulations."

Greg beamed. "Thank you."

"Is she the subject of our meeting today?" Pastor Baldwin asked as he reached for his pad and pen and motioned for Greg to sit in the empty chair across from his desk.

"Not directly, no. It's about Rick."

"I was praying about him earlier today when I was preparing to come here to the church to meet you. For some reason, he weighed heavily on my heart. How is he?"

"Not good, I'm sorry to report. That's why I'm here. I was hoping that somehow you could help. I don't know where else to turn at this point."

"This is probably why he was on my heart so much this morning," Pastor Baldwin said. "What is it that you need me to do?"

"I can't get within a mile of him. Sometimes I think he feels so betrayed by me that he literally hates the sight of me. I think that anything that I say will just sound like I'm protecting Grace.

"Sherry uncovered some new information and shared it with me some days ago. We think it's the missing link in the puzzle of why Rick is so angry, but we hadn't figured out how to talk to him."

"New information? About the accident? Maybe you should talk to the police first," Pastor Baldwin suggested.

"It's not a police matter," Greg assured him. "This is personal. The police have ruled that Grace wasn't the cause of the accident. They've concluded that a third car that left the scene was involved. That third car forced Grace's car into the opposite lane of traffic and that's when she hit Ms. Julia's car."

"Have they found the third person?"

"Not yet. Meanwhile, Rick doesn't believe that theory. Between the two of us, he came to the hospital a few weeks ago and threatened Grace. He straight-out told her that she was lying about her amnesia and that all of us—including the police—were covering for her. I don't know if I've ever been angrier in my life than I was when I walked in on him yelling at her. I'm getting angry right now, just thinking about what he did."

"That's understandable," Pastor Baldwin said. "How did you handle it?"

"Not well, I must admit. I threatened to beat his butt—and I meant it. The doctors and security stopped it from going any further."

"While I understand your anger," Pastor Baldwin said, "I don't think you handled the situation as you should have."

"You're right, and I'll ask his forgiveness if I can ever get close enough to him to do it, but at the time it seemed appropriate. He was threatening the woman I . . ."

"Love?" his pastor offered.

"Wouldn't you do that for Mother Baldwin?"

"I'm sure I would," the pastor confessed, "but I'm not afraid to say that I love Clara."

"I'm not afraid," Greg said. "I just think I should be absolutely sure before I say those words."

"I see." Pastor Baldwin smiled knowingly. "So share the newfound information with me."

"Oh, yeah. I'm sorry, I got off track."

"Don't apologize."

For the next few minutes, Pastor Baldwin sat silently and listened intensely while Greg told him the story of the message that he and Sherry had heard on the answering machine at Ms. Julia's house. There was a moment of silence in the room when Greg finished the day's account. Pastor Baldwin appeared to be deep in thought.

"No wonder he's so distraught," he finally said while shaking his head.

"Yeah," Greg agreed. "Can you imagine the guilt that he's been keeping locked up inside him—afraid to share with anyone how he really feels?"

Pastor Baldwin nodded and then spoke. "Do I recall correctly that his mother wouldn't even have been living in this city had he not vowed to take care of her every need?"

"That's right," Greg said. "Me and Sherry concluded that the reason he's shutting everybody out and has so much anger with Grace, the police, and the rest of the world is that he's really angry at himself and is looking for someone else to blame."

"If he stops seeing himself as a bad son, he'll find out that none of us see him as one either."

"Exactly," Greg said. "Can you help? Can you find a way to get through to him?"

"Your concern for Brother Derrick is highly commendable with all that you've endured from him in the past several months. What I want is for you to go and get ready to meet your date. I am going to stay here awhile and pray about this and I'm sure God will give me an answer on how to handle it. It's going to take His guidance because Brother Derrick is quite fragile and even I am not his favorite person right now."

"Thank you, Pastor," Greg said.

"Have fun on your date. Maybe Mother Dixon will get those grandbabies yet."

"Well, right now I just want to work on getting her a daughter-in-law."

"Moving kind of fast there, aren't you, son?"

"Well," Greg said as he got up and shook his pastor's hand once more, "it's kind of like that message that you preached a few Sundays ago. Remember when you talked about how Peter and the other disciples dropped their fishing nets and immediately followed Jesus when He called them? I believe you said something like 'when you know that you know that you know that it's right, why wait?' Well, that's kind of how I feel. I mean, I'm not gonna propose tonight or anything, but I have very little doubt she's the one."

"I like your confidence and faith. You take care of your future bride, and I'll take care of Brother Derrick."

"Thanks," Greg said again as he left the office and headed for his car. He glanced at his watch. It was 5:20 P.M.

"Okay, nerves," he said to himself as he felt the fluttering in his stomach, "don't start on me now."

Jessica was fighting nervous jitters of her own. She repositioned herself in her chair for the fourth time in fifteen minutes.

"Sit still, Jessie, before you make me burn you with this curling iron," Sherry warned as she turned the final curls in her friend's hair.

"I'm sorry," Jessica said as she took slow, deep breaths. "Can I look in a mirror?"

"When I'm done, you can," Sherry said. "Now be still so I can curl this last one. It's almost 5:30. Greg will be here in a little bit."

"You're not helping, Sherry."

Sherry laughed. "I know. Here, hold this," she said as she handed her a makeup pouch. "I'm only going to put on some eye liner, a little lipstick, and a little powder to stop any shine. You don't need anything else."

"Okay," Jessica said as she sat as still as possible while Sherry quickly applied her makeup.

"Do you two know what time it is?" Lena said as she entered the living room. "Sherry, you know Greg believes in being on time."

"I know, Ms. Lena. I'm done with the hard part. I just need to comb through her curls and she can get dressed," Sherry said. She picked up the comb and began styling. She switched the comb for the brush and then went back to the comb. "You're gonna love this," she told Jessica.

"Can I look in the mirror now?"

"Oh, baby, you look so nice," Mattie said as she stood back and watched Sherry put the final touches on her daughter's hair.

"Okay," Lena added. "Anybody know CPR? 'Cause my boy's gonna need it when he sees you with your hair all fancy and stuff."

Sherry laughed. "I know. And he thought you were a knockout before all this."

Jessica couldn't take it anymore. "Okay, give me a mirror."

"Eat your heart out, Ms. Halle Berry. Bam!" Sherry exclaimed as she flashed the mirror in front of Jessica's face.

"Oh, my," Jessica gasped. "I have hair."

"Oh, come on," Sherry said as she grabbed a Kleenex from her bag. "Don't start with the tears. This looks too perfect to mess up."

"That's right," Mattie said, "and you ain't got time nohow. Now go on and get your clothes on. Dr. Dixon will be here any minute."

"Go on, now," Lena said as she turned from the window. "He's driving up now."

"Oh, my goodness," Jessica said, grabbing her outfit and scampering into the room.

Sherry hung the dinner gown back in the closet just as Lena opened the door.

"Well, hello, son," she said, smiling, as she took his suit bag.

"Mama, I guess I should have known you'd be here waiting," he said as he hugged her. "Hi, Ms. Mattie," he said.

"Hey, Dr. Dixon," Mattie said. "You looking as handsome as ever."

"Thank you," he said as he looked around at all the hair products that were lying around. "Looks like a beauty salon in here," he remarked.

"Here, sit down," Sherry said as she moved the products out of his way and bagged them into her carrying case. "Jessie should be out any minute."

"No, thanks," he said while rubbing his palms together nervously. "I'll stand."

"Suit yourself." Sherry smiled before disappearing into the room with Lena and Mattie to check on Jessica.

"Come on, Greg," Greg said softly to himself, "you're a man. You're not supposed to be this nervous. It's not like it's your first date. Granted, it is your first date with a woman you care for this much. Pull yourself together, man."

"Hi."

He slowly turned at the sound of Jessica's voice.

"Hi," he said. All of the fluttering in his stomach disappeared as he approached her. "You're beautiful," he remarked as he reached for her hand.

"Thank you," she said, blushing. "I have hair," she pointed out with a smile.

"And it's quite lovely," he said. "Are you ready?"

"Yes," she said as she grabbed her purse from the sofa with her free hand.

"Wait a minute." Lena emerged from the room with a camera in her hand.

"Aw, Ma."

"Boy, you better stand up there and take this picture," she said to Jessica and Sherry's amusement.

"This is not the prom, Mama."

"Are you mouthing back at me? Don't let your lil' girlfriend see you get a whipping, hear?" Lena warned as the girls continued to laugh.

"Just come stand here and take the picture," Greg said to Jessica.

"I'm sorry," she said while trying to control her laughter.

Finally, after taking several photos and having his tie adjusted by his mother, Greg was able to leave the house with Jessica's arm linked in his. The ride to the theater was fairly quiet. Greg kept glancing at Jessica in the passenger seat and could tell from her expression that she really liked his Jaguar.

"What movie are we going to see?" she finally asked.

"The Brothers."

"Oh, good." She smiled in approval as Greg maneuvered the car into an available space. "I saw the commercials. I wanted to see that."

"Uh-huh," Greg said. "I'll bet you did. Who's your favorite of the four guys?"

"Probably Morris."

"Not Shemar?" Greg was surprised. Her answer was different than the favorite of the women he'd heard talk about the popular film.

"He's okay," Jessica said, "but I like Morris better."

"I see," he replied.

Helping her from the car, Greg admired the way her silk pants flowed in the gentle breeze. They walked hand in hand as he led her around the long line of ticket buyers and to the entrance area where he handed his prepurchased tickets to the female attendant—who in return shamelessly flirted when giving him the stubs back.

"We get bolder every year, don't we?" Jessica remarked.

"Oh, God, yes," Greg said.

They took two seats on the end of the aisle—about midway in the theater.

"I'll be right back," Greg said.

Jessica sat alone and watched the movie preview. She placed her right hand over her stomach and took in a deep breath. Maybe she could kill the butterflies if she held her breath. Losing the battle, she released a lungful of air and proceeded to try and moisten her parched mouth with her equally dry tongue.

She smiled in relief when Greg returned with two cups of lemonade in his hands. He handed one to her and reclaimed his seat.

"Thank you," Jessica said as she took hers and immediately began drinking.

"I didn't want to get any snacks since we'll be eating afterward," he whispered as the lights lowered and the movie began. This movie about friendship made him think of Derrick and he wondered if Pastor Baldwin had decided on what to do about his situation. As much as he tried to accept the fact that his and Derrick's brotherhood relationship could possibly be shattered forever, he couldn't deny the void that remained in his heart.

The vibrating of his pager broke his thoughts. "Oh, no," he whispered despondently. "Not tonight."

"What's the matter?" Jessica asked.

"It's my pager," he said as he took it from his hip and checked the number. "It's the hospital," he said, to Jessica's disappointment. "I'm sorry. You sit here. I need to make this call. I'll be right back."

Walking out of the theater and into the lobby, Greg pulled out his cell phone and quickly dialed Dr. Grant's office number. The thought of having to end his date so abruptly made him cringe inside.

"Dixon?" Dr. Grant said when he picked up the phone.

"Yes, Dr. Grant."

"Hold on for a minute," he said as he placed Greg on hold.

Greg sighed heavily and impatiently watched the minutes tick away on the clock on the wall as he waited for Dr. Grant to return to the phone.

"I'm sorry," Grant said as he finally picked up again. "It's been crazy around here tonight and I didn't expect you to call back so soon. It's amazing how you always call right back when you're paged. Some of these other docs around here wait twenty or thirty minutes to call back. You relaxing at home tonight?"

"No, actually, I'm on a date. Please tell me this isn't an emergency call-in. Tonight has been a long time coming."

"Relax, Dixon. It's not an emergency, but I do want you to come by the hospital tomorrow morning, if that's at all possible. I know you had requested the day off."

"What's the matter?" Greg asked.

"The police were here a little while ago about that accident patient of yours."

"Jessica Charles?"

"Yes. We're next on the list to search files for the third injured party in the accident. Apparently, he or she didn't get treated at any of the other hospitals that they checked so far. It's our turn. With the severity of the accident, they are finding it hard to believe that he didn't need professional medical care."

"Will I have to work a full shift?"

"Possibly."

"Will I at least be able to leave for a couple of hours for church?"

"Hey," Dr. Grant said, "I ain't about to stand in the way of your duties to God. You can take your normal hallelujah break."

"Then I'll be there at 7:00 A.M."

"Thanks, Dixon."

"Do we have to go?" Jessica whispered as he rejoined her in the theater.

"No," he said to her relief.

"Really?"

"Really," he assured her. "I have to go in tomorrow morning. I was supposed to be off, but something came up that I have to take care of."

"Okay," she said.

"Is it good so far?" Greg asked. "Have I missed much?"

"I can't even tell you," Jessica responded. "I was so worried that you'd have to leave that I haven't been paying much attention."

Now that's what I'm talking about! Too concerned with me to focus on the heartthrobs on the screen. Greg couldn't hold back his smile upon hearing her words. He slipped his hand on top of hers and settled back to watch the all-star cast on the screen in front of him.

"Good movie," Greg remarked as they were leaving the theater, still holding hands.

"Yeah," Jessica agreed, "I enjoyed it too."

"Good choice of actors, huh?" Greg said while holding the car door open for her.

"Good choice of company," she said as she got in.

"Thanks." He smiled as he closed her door.

Greg, two, Morris, zip! Greg thought as they listened to music on the radio during the drive back to Ms. Mattie's house. His mother's car was still there, and both ladies welcomed them at the door.

"How was the movie?" Lena asked.

"It was nice, Mama," Greg said.

"Yes," Jessica agreed, "it was nice."

"Your dress is in your room, Jessie," Mattie said, "and your suit is in my room," she told Greg.

The two of them disappeared behind the closed doors. Mattie and Lena stood in the living room and smiled proudly.

"I think this is gonna work," Lena said. "What you think?"

"I think your son would be crazy not to snatch up a jewel like my Jessie."

"Well, I think *your* daughter ought to be glad that a wonderful man like my son takes interest in her."

"Well, if he didn't, there sho would be some other wonderful man out there who did."

"Maybe so, but how many other men out there would put up with her mama?"

"*Her* mama? What about you?"

"My son tells me all the time that I'm the greatest mother in the world."

"My daughter says the same."

"Well, she ain't but twenty-one, she don't know no better, yet."

"She's twenty-*two*."

"Same difference."

"Mama. Ms. Mattie." Greg put an end to the argument when he joined them in the living room.

"Oooooooweee, look at my baby," Lena boasted as he entered. "Don't he look handsome?"

"He sho do," Mattie agreed. "I done told you if I was a few years younger—"

"And I done told you to back off, you old cradle-robbing pedophile," Lena said.

"Mama," Greg said as he attempted to hold back his laughter.

"She started it," Lena accused.

"*You* started it," Mattie said.

"I did not," Lena said as Greg brushed past her and walked slowly toward Jessica, who had emerged elegantly from her room. "All I said," she continued, "was my child looked good. You the one who started lusting."

"Child, ain't nobody lusting after your son. *However,*" Mattie emphasized, "sometimes I do wonder if he was switched at birth."

"Greg, you hear this crazy woman?" Lena said. "Greg?" she said.

Both women turned to see Greg and Jessica facing one another and staring into each other's eyes as they held hands in silence. With the back of his hand, Greg touched her cheek affectionately.

"God, you're beautiful," he said softly.

"Get the camera," Mattie whispered. Lena retrieved the camera from a nearby shelf and snapped a photo.

"Ma," Greg said upon seeing the flash.

"Oh," Lena said, totally breaking the mood. "Evelyn called for you on my cell phone."

"That couldn't have waited?" Mattie asked.

"Why was she calling me on your cell?" Greg asked.

"She said that she had done already tried calling the hospital, my house, and your house. I guess she was getting desperate. I think she got wind of your date when she called the hospital and was trying to see if there was any truth to it.

"Can you believe that dummy was trying to get me to give her your cell number? If it wasn't for Julia, she'd never have gotten your home number. I told her that she must be out of her raggedy mind if she thought I was going to give her anything."

"You weren't mean, were you, Mama?"

"As a matter of fact, yes, I was," Lena said proudly. "I told her yeah, you were on a date and you didn't want to be bothered."

"Well, that's true," Greg said.

"Y'all ready to go?" Mattie asked.

"Not quite yet," Greg said as he looked at his watch.

"I thought reservations were for 10:00 P.M.," Lena said. "It's a quarter till now."

"I know," Greg began. A knock at the door interrupted his thought. "Okay," he said, walking to the door, "I think we're ready now."

"Hey," Nelson greeted from the porch where he stood.

"Hey, Nelson. I was just about to worry about you."

"I know," he said. "I'm sorry, dog, but one of the other guys took the limo, not knowing that I had already been approved to use it for tonight. I had to run him down and get him to bring it back."

"Mama, you remember Nelson from Ms. Julia's funeral, don't you?" Greg said.

"Oh, yeah," she said. "I knew you looked familiar."

"We'll see you ladies later," Greg said as he once again took Jessica's hand.

"Is Nelson going with y'all?" Lena asked.

"He's driving us," Greg said. He stepped out onto the porch and pointed toward the street.

Jessica gasped.

"Y'all going in a limousine?" Mattie said as they all stepped out onto the porch too for a closer look.

"Yes, ma'am," Greg said. Nelson put on his driver's hat, walked down to the freshly detailed white limo, and opened the door for the couple. "We're going in style," Greg added. With a wave of his hand, he led his date down the steps and to the car.

"These are beautiful," Jessica said as Greg handed her a bouquet of gardenias that were lying on the seat.

"I'm glad you like them," he said. "I had to guess. I never found out what kind of flowers were your favorites."

"I don't know that I have a favorite. I just love beautiful flowers."

"You know, blue is my favorite color," he said.

"I know. You told me."

"So, then, are you wearing this color by chance or by choice?"

"By choice," she said to Greg's delight.

"Thank you," he answered. *Greg, three. Morris, zip. Game over, Morris—go home.*

The scenery of Washington, D.C., at night had never been more captivating. Greg and Jessica stared out of the limousine windows and watched the trees and homes whisk by before entering the business district of Virginia Avenue. The limo came to a slow stop in front of the eye-catching busy restaurant.

Nelson hopped out and opened the door for them once more after he parked in front of the restaurant's entrance. Several waiting patrons stared in admiration as the well-dressed couple stepped out of the limo, arms linked, and walked to the front of the line.

"Reservation for two," Greg said.

"Name, sir?" the host said as he stared, seemingly uncontrollably, at Jessica.

"Gregory Dixon," Greg answered. "*Dr.* Gregory Dixon."

"Right this way, sir," he said as he led them to a secluded table in the corner where the view of the stage was excellent. A live band played music as the waiters and waitresses served the guests.

"She's beautiful, isn't she?" Greg said. The host continued to find it hard to take his eyes off of Jessica as he placed their menus on the table.

"Sir?" he said nervously. "I mean, yes, sir. I'm sorry." He was clearly embarrassed.

"Don't be." Greg smiled. "I'm having a hard time turning away too."

"Yes, sir," he said as Jessica blushed. "May I get you something to drink? A white wine, perhaps?"

"No wine, thank you," Greg said as he looked to Jessica to order first.

"I'd like a raspberry ginger ale," she said.

"Make it two," Greg said.

"I'll bring those soft drinks right out. Is it okay that we pour those in wine-style glasses?"

"That would be fine," Greg said.

"I'll be back shortly. By the way, my name is Spencer," he said.

"Thank you, Spencer."

"This is such a nice restaurant," Jessica said. "I've never heard of it before."

"I'm glad you like it," Greg said. "It just opened up shortly before Christmas."

"Have you been here before?"

"No."

"May I ask you a question?" Jessica asked hesitantly.

"Anything."

"Who's Evelyn?" Jessica asked the question that had been on her mind since Lena brought up the phone call earlier.

"Evelyn is Evelyn Cobb," Greg began as he reached across the table to take her hand. "She's a sales clerk at Sofia's. She's also a member of my church who, with the encouragement of her mother, has been after me for quite a long time. A couple of years at least."

"Is she an ex-girlfriend?"

"I don't mean this in a degrading way, but simply put, Evelyn is nobody. I have never dated her. I've never called her. I've not so much as looked at her intentionally, unless she was speaking to me. I try to avoid her at all costs because any attention that I give her would be taken the wrong way."

"Are you ready to order or would you like more time?" the host asked as he returned with their drinks and placed them on the table.

"Are you ready?" Greg asked her.

"Yes," Jessica said as she quickly scanned the menu. Her eyes wandered to the seafood listing. "I'll have the grilled red snapper plate."

"And you, sir?"

"Give me the Sax seafood platter."

"Good choices," Spencer approved. "I'll get those out to you as soon as possible."

"Thank you," Greg said.

For several uninterrupted minutes, the two of them held hands in silence as the band played soft music. Her skin felt soft beneath the caress of Greg's thumb. The atmosphere in the restaurant was unmistakably romantic. Some couples had left their tables and were out on the floor dancing as the music played.

"When I came to pick you up for the movies," Greg suddenly said, "I wondered to myself if you could get any more beautiful. Now this," he said as he looked at her in total approval. "Have I told you that you're beautiful?"

The look in his eyes was one of genuine sincerity. There wasn't a man on earth that Jessica would rather be sitting across from at the moment than the one whose eyes burned into her soul.

"Yes," she whispered.

"Well, it bears repeating," Greg said as the waiter brought their food to the table.

"Thank you." Jessica blushed. As much as she was enjoying the way he looked at her, she was thankful for the break that the waiter's appearance gave her. Another minute and she was sure she would have passed out from lack of oxygen, due to the nerves that were closing her throat.

Nelson was waiting as they exited the restaurant following the completion of their meals. Jessica hated for the evening to end, but she knew that her prince had to make an early morning appearance at his job. Greg handed Nelson some cash and thanked him as he drove away after returning them to Mattie Charles's house.

"Thank you for going out with me tonight," Greg said as he walked her to the door.

"Thank you for asking me," Jessica said. "I had a wonderful time."

"I'm glad," Greg said. "A girl only turns twenty-two once, you know."

"How old are you, Greg?"

"Twenty-six," he answered. "I'll be twenty-seven in a few months. Am I too old a guy for you to hang out with?"

"No. Twenty-six isn't old at all."

"So, would you like to hang out again tomorrow?"

"Sure." Jessica brightened. "But I thought you had to work."

"I'm going to leave for a couple of hours to go to church. I'd like you to come with me if you can break away from your own services."

"I'd love to go to church with you."

"Great. I'll pick you up at 11:00 A.M."

"Okay."

"Happy birthday," he said as he stepped closer and kissed her cheek softly.

"Thank you," she said as her heart pounded in her chest. She unlocked the door and stepped inside.

"See you in the morning," Greg said as he backed slowly down the stairs, not once taking his eyes away from Jessica.

"I think you should watch where you're going." She smiled.

"Why?"

"Because if you don't, you may fall."

"Thanks for the warning," Greg said as he returned her smile, "but I think you're too late to stop me."

"Stop you what?"

"From falling."

"Why? You haven't fallen yet."

Greg smiled knowingly and turned and walked quietly to his car. He waved as he backed out of the driveway and drove away.

"Oh," Jessica whispered as the realization of his words settled in.

CHAPTER 11

Greg rubbed his tired eyes as he listened to Detective Morrison go through the information that they were looking for in their attempts to narrow the search for the person or persons who had caused the deadly accident. The meeting had started at 8:30 and had gone on for just over two hours. Greg glanced at his watch. His colleagues seemed to have so many questions and the detectives were all too eager to answer each and every one of them.

"The exact date of the accident," Detective Morrison was saying as he began gathering his notes, "was January thirteenth. It's likely that the third driver didn't receive care on the date that the injuries occurred. It's very possible that he or she waited several days before seeking care. Generally, in cases like this, seeking professional care is the last-ditch effort after home remedies don't seem to work."

"Is it possible that he or she didn't get injured enough to need professional attention?" Dr. Grant asked.

"That's possible," Morrison admitted, "but it's not probable. With both the other victims sustaining such serious injuries, it's hard to believe that the third driver didn't at least acquire *some* injuries that needed professional medical attention."

"Wouldn't it make sense to believe that he wouldn't have

gone to a hospital in this city or maybe not even in this state?" Greg asked, hoping they had already thought of that and his question wouldn't add another hour to the meeting. "Isn't it a pretty good guess," he continued, "to say that this person drove out of state so he couldn't be so easily traced?"

"That's a very good question, Doc," Detective Morrison said. "We actually played with the thought of that, and you're right—it made for a good theory. But due to new information, we dismissed that possibility," he said as he nodded toward one of his men.

"We've done some extensive investigating," Detective Weeks interjected, "and we believe that we've found the third car that was involved. A car was found near Third Street. It appeared to have been pushed down an embankment, most likely so it wouldn't be found. The paint and damage match that of the car we believe to have been involved in this accident. The license plate had been removed, but we believe we have sufficient evidence to prove our speculations."

"Well, on our end," Dr. Grant said, "we have several IT people working on downloading all the records from the days following the accident. We'll contact you as soon as we know whether or not we can be of any assistance."

"We really would appreciate any help you can offer us," Detective Morrison said as he and his detective team shook Dr. Grant's hand and began leaving.

The doctors dispersed and went back to work. Relieved that it was finally over, and with only a few minutes to spare, Greg disappeared into his office and quickly changed into his suit.

"Dixon," Dr. Grant called as he spotted him walking toward the elevator.

"Yes?" Greg tried not to sound annoyed.

"How'd your date go last night?" he asked. "I was quite amused when you told me you were out on a date. That's something I don't think I've ever heard you say before."

"I assure you, Dr. Grant," Greg said, laughing, "last night wasn't my first time dating."

"So, how'd it go?"

"It was wonderful actually."

"Oh, yeah? Who's the lady? One of our staff members here, perhaps?"

"Not hardly."

"Do I know her?"

"You've met her," Greg said, "but I'm not revealing her identity quite yet."

"Why all the secrets?" Dr. Grant pressed. "This can only mean one or two things," he continued. "Either she's ugly or she's fat."

"*Or,*" Greg said, feeling a bit offended, "it could just mean that I don't want to tell you who she is until I'm good and ready."

"That's another option, I suppose." Dr. Grant laughed, finding Greg's sarcasm more amusing than insulting.

"I'll tell you this much," Greg added as he stopped at the elevator door. "She's sweet, talented, and smart all rolled up into one beautiful package. And, I'm late picking her up for church."

"In other words, are you trying to tell me to leave you alone and let you leave?"

"No, Grant, not in other words. In those *exact* words."

"Go with God, Dixon."

"Thank you." Greg smiled as he stepped onto the elevator and headed for his car.

For a brief moment, Greg was confused when he pulled into the driveway and found Mattie's car missing. He found relief when the door opened upon his first knock.

"You're here," Jessica said in an almost whimsical tone.

"*You're* beautiful," Greg commented while admiring her red dress.

"Thank you." She smiled. "You look pretty good yourself," she added just before picking up her purse and Bible and walking with him to his car.

"Where's Ms. Mattie this morning?" Greg asked during the drive.

"With Ms. Lena," Jessica said. "They should already be at the church."

"Oh, Ms. Mattie is going to be at church today, too?" Greg was pleased.

"Yes. Apparently your mother invited her at some point while she was over here last night."

"That was nice of her," Greg said as he parked his car and walked around to open the door for Jessica.

"Thank you." She smiled pleasantly and allowed him to take her hand and help her get out.

"You don't have to thank me. I was just looking for an excuse to hold your hand."

"You don't need an excuse to hold my hand."

Her words had Greg beaming as they walked hand in hand toward the front door of the church. He felt proud with Jessica by his side when they walked through the double-glass doors that led to the sanctuary.

Service had already begun and the couple followed the usher who showed them to an empty area on a pew next to Sherry. It was the space where Greg sat every Sunday. Mattie and Lena smiled as they saw their children walk in and sit together.

Evelyn had a different reaction. Her jaw dropped as she watched Greg and Jessica standing together clapping during praise and worship service, and she squirmed in her seat while watching their heads stay so close together as they shared a Bible during Pastor Baldwin's sermon.

"Before we go any further," the pastor said as he closed his Bible and ended his sermon, "I must say that we are so pleased that each of you chose to assemble with us today. Once again, we want to welcome all of our visitors and we certainly hope that today won't be the last time we have you here to worship with us."

He continued, "Shortly before service, I was introduced to a woman with a beautiful spirit and a kind heart. We have in our midst Sister Mattie Charles, a new but dear friend of the Dixon family."

"Leave it to Mama to get her own personal welcome," Jessica whispered to Greg.

"Sister Charles told me that her miracle child would be in service with us today and I see that she is here," Pastor Baldwin continued.

Jessica suddenly felt the attention focusing on her.

"You're blushing," Greg whispered with a smile.

"He's not going to call me up, is he?" she asked.

"Sister Jessica Charles," the pastor continued, "will you please come forward?"

"Oh, my God," Jessica whispered.

"Go on, sweetie," Greg coached. "It's okay."

The congregation, with the exception of Evelyn, applauded as Jessica nervously made her way to the front of the church and took Pastor Baldwin's extended hand.

"Several months ago," the minister said, "we held a special prayer here following one of our services. Do you all remember that? Brother Greg was performing a life-or-death surgery on an accident victim. Most of the doctors didn't give her much of a chance of survival, but Dr. Dixon said he had the faith that with the prayers of God's people and his medical expertise, this young lady would live."

The congregation started responding with words of worship to God as they began to realize who Jessica was. Jessica smiled, still slightly nervous, as Pastor Baldwin handed her the microphone and asked her to give her testimony of her brush with death.

"I wish I could remember it all," she began slowly. "I may not know all the details, but I do know who delivered me," she said to the applause of the crowd.

"I just remember leaving class and driving toward home. The roads were a little bit wet from the rain earlier, but the traffic was light." Jessica began to get a faraway look in her eyes as she spoke. "The traffic was *very* light. There were only three or four cars that I could see."

"What's the matter?" Sherry whispered to Greg.

"I'm not sure," he responded.

"There was one car that had just passed me," Jessica continued slowly. "Then there was a red-and-white car that pulled up beside me. There was a man inside. He blew his horn and when I looked at him, he started winking and waving at me," she said.

The congregation had gotten quiet and had begun listening attentively as Jessica continued. Her eyes were directed toward the ceiling and she scanned the tiles as though she were watching the accident as it happened. Pastor Baldwin's head was bowed in silent prayer.

"She's remembering," Sherry whispered.

Greg felt a sudden rush of emotions as he nodded in agreement and watched carefully as his former patient got her memory back right before his eyes and the eyes of all the people who had prayed for her.

"I turned away and kept driving," she continued. "He started yelling out of his window—asking for my name and number. Then I saw this car driving in the opposite lane of oncoming traffic. I was trying to ignore him and pass him, but he kept driving beside me. He'd speed up when I sped up and slow down when I slowed down." Jessica's breaths seemed to come quicker, her voice trembled, and tears streamed down her face as she reminisced.

"Then I'm not sure what happened next. He was speeding up to try and keep up with me, and I think he hit some standing water or something and he lost control of his car. It started spinning in the road and I tried to get out of the way, but he hit me and I lost control of my car and I hit the car in the oncoming lane of traffic."

By this time, several of the congregation's members were sharing in her tears. Sherry reached over and grabbed Greg's left hand as he wiped his eyes with a handkerchief that he retrieved from his suit pocket. It pained him to imagine Jessica's fear and the fear of his godmother in the moments before the horrendous impact.

"I just want to say," Jessica began again, now looking at her audience, "that I thank God for my life. Life is something that is so easily taken for granted," she said as the congregation agreed with amens and nods.

"I want to thank you all for your prayers," she continued. "I'm so thankful for my mama, who stood by me when others who claimed to love me walked away. I thank God for her because I know there were days that looked dim, but God knew she'd need someone to lean on so He brought Ms. Lena into her life and I'm grateful for that too."

Lena looked at Mattie and smiled through her tears. Mattie nodded to let Lena know that she agreed with her daughter's sentiment.

"I'm so glad that God is all-knowing," Jessica continued as she wiped her tears with the tissue that one of the ushers had handed her, "because He knew that just any old doctor wouldn't be able to handle my case. That's why He placed me in your care," she said as she looked at Greg, "and I'll spend the rest of my life thanking Him for that."

Greg's smiled lovingly as his eyes met Jessica's. Whatever doubts he may have had concerning his feelings for Jessica Grace Charles were totally erased at that moment.

"And last but never least," she concluded, "I want to thank God for just being God. I know I didn't do anything that merited the love He extended to me when He gave me another chance at life, but I thank Him." Her voice broke at the end.

"I know I've been up here awhile and I'm generally not a long talker," she said as a few chuckles went around the room, "but I want to sing just a little bit of this praise to God. Not only because He spared my life, but because I think He just gave me back my total memory."

"Amen." Greg nodded.

"You go on and sing," Sherry said aloud, followed by words of agreement from other parishioners.

After a pause to wipe the tears that continued to flow, Jessica held her head up and closed her eyes as if in prayer.

She began singing the once-popular Andraé Crouch song "To

God Be the Glory." As she began singing the verse for the sec-
ond time, the choir stood and began singing softly behind her.
They sounded heavenly. The congregation stood in worship as
Jessica and the choir continued.

The hairs on Greg's arms seemed to stand up and chills ran
up his spine as he listened. She'd told him that she could sing,
but he had no idea that his Grace had such a strong and beautiful singing voice. Even after Jessica ended her lead vocals and
handed the microphone back to Pastor Baldwin, the choir and
congregation continued to sing the chorus of the song as she
walked back to her seat and into Greg's embrace.

"He's *mine!*" Jessica heard the voice over her shoulder as she
walked beside Greg's car carrying Denise following the services.

Sherry had to attend a brief women's meeting and Greg was
inside speaking with his pastor regarding Pastor Baldwin's
plans to meet with Derrick.

"I'm sorry?" Jessica said as she turned to look into the unfa-
miliar face.

"I said, he's mine," Evelyn repeated. "I am *not* going to
stand back and let the devil steal away from me what I know is
mine."

"What are you talking about?" Jessica asked in confusion.
"Do I know you?"

"I'm Evelyn Cobb and Greg is the husband that God has
chosen for me. I claim that in the name of Jesus," she said as she
raised her right hand as a sign of worship, "and I rebuke you
and your attempt to bring evil into the midst of God's goodness.
That's *my* husband."

"If he's yours, then don't worry about me getting in the
way," Jessica said as she turned to walk away.

"He *is* mine," Evelyn insisted as she stepped in front of Jessica
to stop her from walking off. "There are no ifs about it. I've prayed
about this for a long time now and I know that God is working
it all out. I know you don't understand, but the devil is using
you as a tool to disrupt the work of God. He knows what God

has for me and Greg and he's even using your miracle to try and throw a wrench in God's plan," Evelyn said in a preaching tone.

Sherry was on her way out of the church and saw Evelyn's confrontation with Jessica. She slipped back into the church to find Greg.

"I'm sorry if you feel that I'm being used by the devil," Jessica said, "but I'm not going to argue with you. It would be silly to stand here after such a beautiful service and argue over a man."

"Greg's not just *any* man," Evelyn said. "Sometimes you have to fight for what's yours. Our pastor preached a message the other Sunday that was titled 'Taking Back What the Devil Stole,' " she said, "and I'm taking it back." Evelyn reached into the air and mimicked the movement of snatching something away. "Give it back, Satan!" she ordered. "I'm not going to let you steal my blessing."

"Is there a problem here?" Greg said as he and Sherry walked up to the women.

Both women, surprised by his sudden appearance, stood silently for a moment. Jessica held Denise closely to her chest as if to protect her from the woman who, in her opinion, was exemplifying unstable behavior.

"No, Greg." Evelyn broke the silence and smiled sweetly. "There's no problem."

"Grace?" He looked to her for an answer.

"It's okay, Greg."

He turned back to Evelyn. "What did you say to her?"

"We were just discussing God's goodness," Evelyn lied.

"Didn't sound like God's goodness to me," Sherry said as Lena and Mattie joined them.

"What did she say to you?" Greg lifted Jessica's chin and looked her directly in her eyes. "I need to know."

"She said that God had put the two of you together and the devil was using me to try and stop God's plan, and she wasn't going to allow it to happen."

"Girl, you must done lost your mind," Mattie said to Evelyn as Greg held up his hand to stop her.

"I'm only gonna say this once in *this* tone of voice," Greg said as he removed his hand from Jessica's chin and slowly faced Evelyn. His tone was calm, but firm.

"Uh-oh," Lena said as she stepped back and pulled Mattie with her.

"As long as you live," he continued, "don't *ever* step to Grace again. Do you understand me?"

"But—" Evelyn began.

"No buts, Evelyn," he said. "I've been very patient with you over the past couple of years. *Very* patient. I'm not stupid—I know you want to hook up with me. The weekly dinner invitations that I never accept, the midday pages that I never return, the fake illnesses and sicknesses that I never treat—it wouldn't take a genius to figure it out, but it shouldn't take a genius to get the picture either. It's not happening, Evelyn.

"Personally, I think you can be a nice girl and you have the potential to make somebody a good girlfriend and maybe even a good wife. However, that somebody isn't me. Contrary to your belief, God has not now, nor will He *ever,* put us together. It's not meant to be. I don't have those types of feelings for you and I never will. I've tried to be nice about it and not hurt your feelings, hoping you'd get the message and back off. Today, you crossed the line. Don't *ever,*" he repeated, "step to Grace again. Do I make myself clear?"

"Yes," she said in a near whisper as she brokenheartedly walked away.

"I did *not* want to do that." Greg sighed heavily as he watched her walk away. "I never wanted to have to hurt her feelings."

"I told you, son," Lena said. "Sometimes you have to. She'll get over it."

"Sure she will," Sherry said.

He turned to Jessica. "I'm sorry. I never thought she'd approach you about this. I wasn't prepared for this to happen and I'm sure you were even less prepared. I'm sorry," he repeated.

"It's okay, Greg," she said as she touched his arm.

"We need to go ahead and leave," he said. He reached for Denise and kissed her. "Uncle Greg has to go back to work for a little while," he said, placing a kiss on her cheek between every few words that he spoke.

"Are you working all day?" Lena asked. "Do you think you'll be able to come by the house for dinner?"

"I'm not sure, Mama. I would certainly love to be able to come by and eat, but we're searching our records for some information today. It could take a while. I don't know if Dr. Grant is going to want me to pull a complete shift tonight or not," he concluded as he opened the car door for Jessica.

"Okay," Lena said, "but if you can, there's plenty."

"Thanks, Mama," he said, kissing her and then Mattie as she stood with her face cocked to the side. "I'll see you all later," he said with a wave at Sherry and Denise.

The drive from church was awkwardly silent for several minutes. Greg wondered what Jessica thought of him at the moment. He'd told her about Evelyn, but he had downplayed her pursuit of him. Though he was angry at Evelyn for her shameless display, he was also disappointed in himself for not seeing it coming.

"I'm really very sorry, Grace," he finally said.

"Stop apologizing, Greg," she said. "It's really okay."

"It never should have happened," he remarked. "I take all the blame for it and I promise I'll make it up to you."

Grace smiled. "I really enjoyed the service," she said to change the subject.

"I'm glad." He nodded. He was glad for the opportunity to talk about more pleasant things. "I had no idea you could sing like that. You could give your twin sister a run for her money."

"What twin sister?"

"Chanté," he said.

"Oh, her." She laughed. "To have my voice compared to hers is definitely a compliment. Thanks."

"I'm serious," Greg insisted. "You have a true talent in that voice box of yours. You ever thought of doing it professionally? You could be another CeCe Winans or Yolanda Adams."

"There was a time when I thought about it," she admitted. "I was much younger then. Now I think I want to teach voice training instead."

"That would be nice," Greg said. "I'll bet you'd be really good at that."

"I think it would be rewarding," she agreed. "It would be my way of helping people—kind of like you do at the hospital—but with a smaller paycheck."

Greg laughed at her analogy. "I wish I didn't have to go back in." He sighed as he pulled up to Jessica's house.

"Important surgery today?"

"No. Actually, we're going through our records for January and February on all the injury cases that came in that could be accident related."

"Why?"

"Well, I guess it's okay for me to tell you the details." He thought for a moment. "We're trying to find the person who caused your accident with Ms. Julia. At least now I can let them know that the person was male. Until your sudden memory recall today, we weren't even sure of that. The police are assuming he was hurt enough to need medical care."

"Oh, he definitely was," Jessica said with a nod of her head.

"He was?" Greg said as he turned down the volume on his radio. "How do you know? Did you get a look at his injuries?"

"I remember shortly before I passed out, right after the collision, he came running to our cars to see if we were okay. I remember him reaching through my broken window and shaking my shoulder."

"You remember that?"

"Yes. I remember barely being able to open my eyes. His face was already starting to swell and there was blood on it. He was nursing his left arm like he could barely move it without a lot of pain. I was trying to respond to his calls, but I couldn't. I think seeing Ms. Julia and me so bloodied scared him. He just ran off."

"Do you remember what he looked like?" Greg asked.

Jessica thought. "No, not really. I know he was black and very young looking, but that's about it."

"Grace," Greg said, "I need you to come to the hospital with me. I want to call Detective Morrison and let him take a statement from you. I'll be there with you and I won't allow them to upset you. That would also allow you to be on hand if we need to ask any questions. Okay?"

"Sure. I'm not worried about being upset by the questioning. I've prayed so long to be able to remember so I could help. Now's my chance."

"Why don't you go and change into some more comfortable clothes? I'll wait for you out here," Greg said as he got out and opened the door for Jessica.

"Okay. I'll be right back."

Greg sat in his car and waited. He wanted to get closure on this matter as badly as Jessica did. Maybe, somehow, finding the third person in this matter would bring Derrick peace of mind. Just maybe he'd be able to forgive himself for not being there when his mother needed him. Greg prayed that this new information, coupled with Pastor Baldwin's planned visit, would cause a miracle to take place in Derrick's heart.

"Good afternoon, Brother Madison."

"Reverend Baldwin," Derrick said as he opened his door to the pastor's knocks, "what are you doing here?"

"May I come in and have a word with you?"

"I don't mean no disrespect, Pastor, but there's really nothing that I have to say."

"Then don't talk," Pastor Baldwin said. "Let me do the talking and you lend me your ears for just a few minutes."

"There's nothing for you to say either," Derrick said.

"Oh, there is a lot that I have to say."

"Okay, then." The little patience that Derrick had had ran

out quickly. "Let's just be real," he continued. "Frankly, Pastor Baldwin, whatever you have to say, I don't want to hear. All I've listened to over the past few months is people trying to tell me how wrong I am. Well, I'm sick and tired of it and I'm not hearing it anymore."

"I think you should listen for a change, Brother Madison."

"What for? Do you have anything new to say that ain't been said already? Are you going to come from a different approach? You got a new attention grabber for me?"

"As a matter of fact, I do," Pastor Baldwin said in a stern voice. "How about this one? Shut up!"

"What?"

"I said, *shut* up," he repeated. "Has anyone come from that angle, Derrick?" the pastor asked—dropping Sunday morning titles. "Has anybody just told you to shut up? Well, that's what I'm doing. Now, let me in."

Derrick stood surprised and speechless for a moment.

"By the way," Pastor Baldwin continued calmly as Derrick quietly stepped aside to let him into his house, "your lovely wife asked me to let you know that she'd be home later. She wanted to give us some time alone to speak."

"Did she ask you to come by here?"

"No, she didn't." Pastor Baldwin sat and crossed his legs. "In fact, I guess you could say it was the other way around. I told her that I was coming over to speak with you and she volunteered to make herself scarce."

"I'll bet she did," Derrick said. "Seems like I don't see much of her or Denise anymore."

"Is that her doing?"

"Well, it ain't all my fault, if that's what you're getting at," Derrick defended.

"Lose the attitude, Derrick," Pastor Baldwin said in a fatherly tone. "Nobody's pointing any fingers. Now, why don't you tell me why the two of you aren't seeing much of each other anymore? The Derrick and Sherry I knew just a few months ago could barely keep their hands off one another. You think I didn't know why you all were late for service all those Sunday mornings?"

Derrick couldn't help but smile at the comment. "Yeah, well, those days are long gone," he said soberly.

"Why?"

"Things happen."

"Such as?"

"First of all," Derrick said, "I'm not stupid. I know she still sees Greg. For all I know, maybe *he's* keeping her satisfied these days."

"You know that's not true."

"How do I know that? It wouldn't be the first time he stabbed me in the back."

"How did Greg stab you in the back?"

"*You* know, Pastor Baldwin. All of you stabbed me in the back. My mama was a good godmother to Greg and she was a faithful church mother in your congregation. She thought the world of you."

"And I thought the world of her."

"No, you didn't!" Derrick shot back. "If you did, you wouldn't have been praying for the survival of her killer."

"Derrick," Pastor Baldwin said, "listen to yourself. You, for months, have insisted on calling that child a killer and a murderer. Deep in your heart, you know that's not true."

"How is it—" Derrick started. He stopped his sentence as Pastor Baldwin held his hand up to silence him.

"Accidents happen on the highway every day of the week," the pastor continued. "Every day, when we watch the news, we find out that somebody lost his life in some incident on the road. Prior to Mother Madison's death, did you see all those people who unintentionally caused the accidents as murderers?" He held his hand up to silence Derrick again as he was about to speak.

"You haven't been in service with us for I don't know how many weeks now, but you know what I remember? I remember back around Thanksgiving when a group of us brothers went to visit the men's shelter. Do you remember that?" he asked and then continued before Derrick could answer.

"I remember you speaking to and having prayer with a man who was the lone survivor of a house fire that killed his wife and sister. He had been all upset because there was suspicion that someone had deliberately set the fire. Then he found out that a cigarette that he had dropped in the garbage right before bed had been the cause. He was upset because he lived and would have to carry the fact that he couldn't save his wife and sister from a fire that he had caused."

"What are you trying to say?" Derrick stood with angry tears in his eyes at his pastor's analogy. "What are you trying to say?" he repeated.

"I am trying to say the same thing to you that you said to that young man," Pastor Baldwin said. "I'm trying to say that sometimes in life we falter and make bad choices. When that happens and repercussions follow, sometimes we want to find someone else to blame when the truth is, it was human error. There was no wrong intent on that young man's part. True, he should not have been smoking, but he didn't drop a lighted cigarette in the garbage intentionally.

"That girl didn't kill your mama, Derrick. We know the details. We know that your mama had asked you to take her to the store and you put her off. We know that your mother was driving at that time because she wanted to drink some warm apple cider before she went to bed. Apple cider that *you* were supposed to take her to get."

Heavy tears broke free as Derrick sank back down on the sofa with his face buried in his hands.

"But what we also know," Pastor Baldwin continued as he moved to the sofa with Derrick and placed his hand on his back, "is that you didn't kill your mama any more than Sister Jessica did. You didn't send her out there and set the accident up to happen. You made a bad choice, yes. But even in that, you don't know that the accident wouldn't have happened with you in the car with her. Maybe both of you would have been killed."

"That would have been so much better," Derrick said through his tears. "Oh, God, that would have been so much better. I promised my whole family that I'd take good care of Mama. If it weren't for me, she wouldn't have even been in this city, let alone on that street."

"You did take good care of your mother, son," Pastor Baldwin said, to comfort him. "Your mother was happy here. She was happiest around you and Sherry. I'd hate to think how miserable she would have been living down South with the sisters who she herself referred to as heathens."

"At least there she would have been living," Derrick said.

"I think that where Mother Madison is right now, she wouldn't trade for anywhere down here," Pastor Baldwin said.

Derrick got up and walked into the restroom and came back with tissue in his hand. He sat back on the sofa in silence for a moment.

"I just don't feel like nothing should be done about her causing that accident. Maybe she's not a murderer. Maybe I was wrong for confronting her and taking my anger out on Greg, but something should be done. I don't think she should just be able to say she doesn't remember and it becomes a closed case blamed on a third unknown person."

"It's not a closed case, Brother Derrick," Pastor Baldwin said, reverting to his pastoral role. "Sister Jessica was in service today."

"What?"

"Yes. We were graced with the presence of both her and her mother."

"What were they doing there?"

"Worshipping with us. Her mother was invited by Mother Dixon and she was invited by Brother Greg."

"Greg invited her to church?"

"There's a whole world of things happening out there that

you're missing out on because you've shut the world out.
Brother Greg has become very fond of his former patient."

"What are you saying? Greg is *dating* this girl now?"

"Actually they only had their first date last evening, but
there is definitely a spark between the two of them and I think
it's a beautiful thing."

"I don't understand this," Derrick said as he shook his head.
"How could he do this? Does Sherry know about this?"

"You see how bad this has gotten, Brother Derrick? *You're*
asking *me* if your wife knows about something. Shouldn't you
know if she knows? There is no reason for you to have driven
this wedge between you and the woman you love. Yes, she
knows about it, but this is not the point I'm getting at. May I
finish?"

"Sorry. Go ahead."

"I called Sister Jessica up today to share her overcoming
story. While she was up talking to the congregation, God restored her memory of the accident. She told the whole story.
Contrary to your belief, there *was* a third person involved, and
Jessica's probably somewhere right now letting the police know
what she recalls. This is not a closed case, Brother Derrick.
Nobody has forgotten your mother or the tragedy itself. It's just
important that we find the right person."

Derrick leaned forward and stared at his own hands. He
took a deep sigh, unsure of how to respond. His pastor was
right—he'd made a mess of everything. Losing his mother was
out of his control, but losing his family and friends was definitely his own doing.

Pastor Baldwin finally broke the silence. "I'm going to tell
you something else, and if you lash out at Sherry because of
what I say, I'm going to pray that God gives *you* a lashing that
you'll never forget. I can do that, you know. That's one of the
advantages of being a preacher."

"Tell me what?" Derrick said as he sat up straight, totally
missing the humor in what the preacher had just said.

"Sherry has befriended Jessica."

"I thought so," he said to Pastor Baldwin's surprise. "I was hoping that it wasn't true, but I figured that it was."

"Oh?"

"Yeah. I'm not exactly proud of myself, but I followed her one day. We had an argument here two or three weeks ago and she took Dee and left. I thought she was headed to Greg's house because I knew he was off that day. I knew because I had just passed his condo a few minutes earlier on my way home from work. Anyway, I followed her and she didn't turn onto his street. Then I started thinking that maybe there was some other guy, so I kept following her. She pulled into the hospital parking lot. I figured then that she was going to see the girl."

"You never confronted her. Why?"

"Didn't have the energy."

"Is that the real reason?"

"That and the fact that I was just relieved that she wasn't running to Greg for comfort."

"You didn't really think that he would have an affair with your wife, did you?"

"Well, I haven't been doing my own job, so it was possible. I mean, I don't have to tell you how close they are."

"Their closeness never bothered you before."

"That's because our marriage was solid."

"You see how the forces of evil have eaten away at you, Brother Derrick? You've been so overcome by grief and guilt for your mother's death that you haven't been able to see anything for what it really is. This didn't happen to you overnight. This didn't happen to your marriage overnight. There have been a couple of Sundays since Mother Madison's death that you and your wife have been late for services, so I know this didn't happen overnight. Little by little your grief was turned into hatred and insecurity.

"The Derrick Madison I knew just a few months ago would *never* have barged into a hospital room and threatened a sick woman who couldn't even get out of bed to defend herself. Nor would he have punched his best friend in the mouth or raised his voice at his godmother and threatened her only child to her face. Yes, I've heard all the terrible details," he said as Derrick looked at him in a surprised manner.

"I guess I owe some apologies," he said quietly.

"Yes, you do," Pastor Baldwin agreed. "However, as I said, things didn't get this bad overnight, so don't expect them to heal overnight. It may take some time. I suggest you start with your wife and work your way down."

"I miss my mama," Derrick said tearfully. "I spent all day on Mother's Day sitting at her grave and talking to her—hoping she could hear me."

"Meanwhile, your wife and the mother of your daughter spent the day alone, trying to keep herself busy so as not to think about how alone she was."

"I know." Derrick wiped a lone tear.

"I miss your mama, too, Brother Derrick. Everybody who knew and loved her misses her. The difference between you and everybody else is that the rest of us have decided to let her rest in the arms of God. If she could see you and your actions since her departure, would she be pleased?"

"Oh, I don't even want to think about that," Derrick said. "Do you think she's been watching me?" he suddenly asked.

"Only God knows, brother. I think it's more important that we should fear how *He* sees us more than any other," Pastor Baldwin concluded as he stood to leave, "and I think it's safe to say that He has definitely been watching you."

"Will you pray with me?" Derrick asked.

"I thought you'd never ask."

CHAPTER 12

"We really appreciate this additional information, Miss Charles," Detective Morrison said as he continued to write in his notepad. "This narrows the gap quite a bit. We can now rule out female suspects and white suspects of either gender."

"Plus," Detective Weeks added, "we can also narrow down the injury possibilities."

The meeting only consisted of Detective Morrison, Detective Weeks, Dr. Grant, Dr. Lowe, Greg, and Jessica. It was a busy day at the hospital so Dr. Grant instructed the other doctors to work as regularly scheduled.

Greg could see the fatigue on Jessica's face. They had been questioning her for well over an hour. Detectives Morrison and Weeks were finally closing their notes.

"You did good, Grace," Greg said as he reached out and squeezed her hand.

She smiled. "Thank you."

"So," Dr. Lowe said, "what we're basically looking for now is any patient that we saw that may have had head and/or face trauma."

"And a possible sprained or broken arm," Dr. Grant added.

"I suggest you check over your January patients very closely," Detective Morrison said. "From what Miss Charles has told us,

I doubt very seriously that he could have gone into February with these injuries without treatment.

"Of course," he continued, "it's always possible that he could have been treating himself until the pain just got the best of him. With bruises and a sprain, he could have actually made an attempt at doing that."

"But if the arm was broken, I think the pain would have been too severe for lengthy self-treatment," Dr. Grant said.

"I've got it," Greg suddenly said, almost as though talking to himself.

"What?" several in the room said at once.

"I got it," he repeated. "I think—no, I'm almost sure I know who this guy is."

"What?" Dr. Grant said. "Just like that? What? You got that sweat towel in here somewhere?"

"Sweat towel?" several said again.

"Never mind," Dr. Grant said. "Who do you think it is?" he asked Greg.

"I'm sure I saw him in January," Greg began, as he started pacing the floor excitedly.

"Slow down, Dr. Dixon," Detective Morrison said as he re-opened his book. "What do you think you remember?"

"I remember treating a guy with facial bruises and a broken arm," Greg said.

"Which arm?" Detective Morrison asked.

"Left."

"That's the one he was cradling according to Miss Charles's statement," Detective Weeks pointed out.

"Keep talking," Detective Morrison said.

"I'm not sure of the date," Greg said, "but this guy came in and he had some pretty bad bruises on his face, and after the X-ray we found out that his arm was broken. He told me that he had gotten into a fight with a friend because he had slept with the friend's wife and had gotten caught."

"And you're fairly sure that this was in January," Dr. Grant said.

"Yes. Dr. Pridgen met him as well. As a matter of fact, he's the one who stitched his head. I believe he needed eight stitches."

"Have the front desk page Dr. Pridgen," Dr. Grant told Dr. Lowe.

"Did you cast his arm?" Detective Weeks asked.

"Yes."

"Did he come back to have the cast removed?"

"No. At least, not to my knowledge. I didn't remove the cast."

"How likely is it that he removed the cast himself?" Detective Morrison asked.

"It's more likely that he went somewhere else to have it removed," Greg said as Dr. Grant nodded in agreement.

"Yes?" Dr. Pridgen said as he slipped into the room with the others.

"Dr. Pridgen," Detective Morrison said, "do you by chance remember giving stitches to a head injury back in January?"

"You're kidding, right?" Dr. Pridgen said with a laugh. "I've done so many head stitches that I couldn't say that I remember any one case in particular."

"Pridgen," Greg said, "remember the young dude that came in back in January that told us he had gotten into a fight with his friend and had gotten pushed down the steps and that's how he broke his arm and got those cuts and bruises?"

"Oh, yeah," Dr. Pridgen remembered with a laugh. "Mr. Lover-boy. The one who was getting it on with his friend's wife and got caught."

"This is great," Detective Weeks said. "Do either of you remember what he looked like?"

"Yeah," Dr. Pridgen said. "Like he had been hit by a truck."

"Never mind that," Detective Morrison said. "What we need is to find his information so we can get an address."

"What are the chances that he gave us his real address?" Dr. Grant asked.

"Unless he's really stupid, the chances are very slim," Detective Morrison admitted.

"He was pretty stupid," Greg said.

"How about we check back with you all tomorrow and see if you have any new information for us?" Detective Morrison suggested. "You can pull that record as well. We'll need to see his paperwork."

"All right, then," Dr. Grant agreed.

The doctors and detectives all mingled for a few minutes before they finally dispersed. Dr. Grant walked curiously around Greg's desk before heading for the door.

"What?" Greg said.

"Nothing. I was just looking for that towel."

"Good-bye, Grant."

"I'm leaving. Was service good?" he asked as he stood in the doorway.

"It was."

"Did you pray for me?"

"I did."

"Thanks," he said as he closed the door.

"Anytime."

"What towel?" Jessica asked once they were alone.

"It's a long story," he said as he reached for her to stand. "I'm proud of you, Grace. You did a good job in here today. I know you're exhausted, but your information really helped out."

"I'm glad," she said.

"I wish I didn't have to work," he continued. "I wish I could spend some time with you later this evening."

"There'll be other evenings."

"You know," he said as he held her hands in his, "my life gets hectic sometimes. A lot of people need me."

"I know."

"I guess you do, huh? You used to be one of those people."

"I'm *still* one of those people," Jessica said, correcting him.

Greg beamed. "Oh, yeah?"

"Yeah."

"I guess what I'm trying to say is," Greg said as his eyes

turned serious, "that I'd love to pursue and establish a relationship with you. I hope you share in my feelings."

"Yes," she assured him.

"My schedule is crazy," he said, "but I promise that I will find a way to make more time for you. Until now, I've never really had a reason not to work long hours, so I'll have to make some adjustments. But I want you to know that you mean a lot to me. I'll do what I have to, to make it work."

"I understand your job, Greg. I wouldn't ask you to jeopardize it in any way."

"I'm not talking about jeopardizing," Greg said, "I'm talking about prioritizing, Grace. I have to make time for you. I'm not doing that because I think you'd demand it; I'm doing it because I know that you'd desire it, and so do I."

"Okay," she said as the phone interrupted their moment.

"Hello?" Greg answered. "Okay, good. No, you're right on time. Thanks, sweetie. Talk to you later. Bye."

"Duty calling?" Jessica asked.

"No. That was Sherry. I had asked her to come by and pick you up. She's waiting out front by the newspaper racks, she said."

"Okay," Jessica said as she picked up her purse. "Try not to work too hard."

"I'll try," Greg said as he walked her to the door.

Once they were at his office door, he stepped in front of the closed door and pulled her close to him.

"May I?" he asked as he lifted her chin.

Jessica's heart skipped a beat. "Yes," she said.

Greg cupped her face in his hands and kissed her lips softly.

"What time do you turn in for the night?" he asked, still holding her face close to his.

"It varies," she answered, feeling weak in the knees from his kiss.

"I'd like to stop by after work for just a few minutes. It'll be around 11:30 or so."

"I'll wait up."

"Thank you," Greg said as he kissed her once more and stepped aside, holding the door open for her.

"I'll see you later," she said.

"I will be counting the hours," he said.

The walk from Greg's office to the exit doors seemed longer than at any time before. Jessica prayed that her knees would hold up long enough for her to make it to Sherry's car. She was relieved to see the Town Car pull up to the front doors upon her exit.

"You're smiling," Sherry observed when Jessica got into her car. "The questioning must have gone well."

"It did," Jessica said. "Once they got all the information and started discussing it, Greg and another doctor, whose name I can't recall, actually remembered treating someone with the injuries that I described. So, the police are out looking for him now."

"Well, that sounds promising," Sherry said. "No wonder you're smiling."

"Greg kissed me," Jessica said, unable to hold it any longer.

"He what?" Sherry said. "So, *that's* why you're smiling."

"It was just a little kiss, but it was nice."

"Yeah," Sherry said. "I remember when I used to get kisses."

"I'm sorry, Sherry," Jessica said.

"No, girl. Don't stop smiling. You deserve to be happy."

"So do you."

"Thanks," Sherry said. "So what are you doing with the rest of your evening?" she said, to change the subject.

"Well, I hope you all left some dinner for me, because that's the first thing on my list of things to do."

"Oh, there's plenty left. Ms. Lena cooked like she was feeding a half dozen men. She told Ms. Mattie to fix you a plate for later," Sherry said as she pulled into the driveway of Jessica's home.

"You want to come in and stay over here awhile?" Jessica offered. "I'll be up late tonight. Greg wanted to stop by after work and I told him I'd wait for him."

"It'll be at least another five or six hours before he comes by," Sherry said. "You go ahead and eat your dinner and get a nap or something. I'll be fine. I need to get little sleepyhead back there a bath and into bed, but thanks for the offer. I really do appreciate it."

"Are you sure?" Jessica asked.

"Yes, I'm sure. I really am very happy for you and Greg. I think the two of you make a very beautiful couple."

"Thank you."

"You'd better be good to him, too," Sherry said. "He really took his time finding the right girl. Don't break his heart, Jessie."

"I'd never do that," Jessica promised. "You know, Leroy and I dated for almost two years. We got along great most of the time and I really did love him. But he was nothing like Greg. With Greg, I'm always surprised by something. Just little things, you know. He's so romantic. From the way he's chosen to call me Grace, to the soft, almost barely a kiss that he gave me today. It was just so romantic. Am I making sense?"

"Yeah," Sherry said. "Greg has always been a romantic guy. He's just never had anyone to share it with before now. He really cares deeply for you. I've really only known one girl in his life prior to you that he referred to as his girlfriend. When we were at Georgetown, he dated a girl named Tonya Byrd for about a month. I think he really liked her, but he geared so much time to his studies that he didn't spend as much time with her as she needed him to. He was pretty hurt when she broke up with him, but he recovered rather quickly."

"That's what he was talking about," Jessica said thoughtfully.

"What?"

"When I was getting ready to leave the hospital today, he said that he needed to change his work schedule so he could spend more time with me. He was so insistent upon it. I told him that it wasn't necessary, but he kept saying that it was something he had to do."

"Yeah," Sherry said, "I'm sure that's what his mind was thinking of at the time. He doesn't want to chance losing you."

"But I honestly don't mind his work schedule."

"Tonya may have told him the same thing about his class load. Maybe he thinks that you will eventually have a problem with it. You'll have a pretty hard time convincing him that it's not going to become an issue."

"Are you sure you don't want to come in?" Jessica asked as she opened her door to get out.

"Yes, girl. Now go on," Sherry said, laughing.

"Okay. Thanks for the listening ear."

"Anytime," Sherry said as she watched Jessica walk up the steps to the home she shared with her mother.

It was just after 6:00 P.M. when Sherry parked her car in front of her condo. Derrick's parking space was empty.

"I guess Daddy's out visiting the police station again," Sherry told Denise as she got her out of her car seat. "Or, maybe he's visiting Grandma's grave."

With Denise in one arm and her baby bag in the other, Sherry finally got the door unlocked and walked in. To her surprise, there was a vase with a dozen arranged roses sitting on the coffee table in the living room. Beside the roses were two beautifully wrapped gifts and two cards attached. Sherry smiled as her heart raced. She put Denise in her playpen in the corner and picked up the first card with the envelope marked *mommy*. The front of the card had a picture of red roses. Derrick had written on the blank inside in mock childhood penmanship.

Roses are red, violets are blue, but neither is more stunning than the beauty of you. Thanks for being such a wonderful mommy.

                              Love, Denise.
P.S., please forgive Daddy for waiting so long to give you this.

Sherry laughed tearfully as she picked up the second card. On the front was a picture of praying hands with the caption

YOU ARE ALWAYS IN MY PRAYERS. She opened the card. It too had been blank inside and Derrick had handwritten her a note.

Hi, Sweetie.

This card was the closest thing that I could find to what I wanted to say. I guess with Mother's Day being last weekend, occasion cards were no longer in demand. I chose this one with the praying hands because I needed to beg your forgiveness. I've been a terrible husband and father lately and I beg of you to forgive my senselessness. This past weekend was your first Mother's Day, and I allowed myself to be so overcome by other things that I didn't even take the time to thank you for being a loving wife and for giving me such a precious daughter.

Sherry, I love you with all my heart and I hope you still know that. You and Dee are the best gifts a man could have. I spoke to Pastor Baldwin today. He didn't say anything that I didn't already know, but I guess I just needed to shut up for once and listen to somebody else. He told me that you knew about the phone call to Mama—and I'm okay with that. I'm glad you know. Keeping it from you was killing me anyway. He also told me about your friendship with Jessica. That one took a minute, but I need you to know that I'm okay with that as well. You and Greg were right all along; she's not a murderer, and I'm glad she lived to tell the story.

I have a lot of other people to ask forgiveness from, but it was only right to start with you. Please find it in your heart to give me a chance to make it up to you. In the boxes, you'll find one gift for you and one for Denise. Please put them to use and I'll be home shortly to take my two favorite girls out to dinner. Reservations are at 8:00. I love you, Sherry.

Your husband, and your baby's daddy, Ricky.

Tears flowed from Sherry's eyes as she dropped to her knees and said a prayer of thanks to God. After drying her tears, she immediately reached for the small box with Denise's name on it. Inside was a beautiful olive-green-and-white dress. Green was Derrick's favorite color. Under the dress were a pair of white socks and white shoes.

"Look what Daddy bought you, Dee Dee," she said as she held the dress up for Denise to see.

She placed Denise's dress on the arm of the sofa and anxiously reached for her own gift. There was definitely a color scheme here. She pulled out an olive-green skirt suit with gold buttons down the front of the top. It was very nice. He had even bought her a pair of panty hose and olive dress pumps. Still tearful, Sherry took both outfits into her bedroom and turned on the shower to take her bath. Before dressing herself, she gave Denise a bath and dressed her.

"Aren't you beautiful?" she told Denise as she kicked and laughed.

She placed a bib around Denise's neck and proceeded to quickly dress herself. The suit was a perfect fit.

"Do you think Mommy should wear these earrings or these?" she said as she flashed both pairs in front of Dee's face.

"How about these?" Startled, she jumped and turned to face Derrick.

He was standing in the doorway of the bedroom dressed in an olive-green suit and holding a small box in his open hand. He walked slowly toward Sherry and handed her the box.

"Thank you," Sherry said softly.

She opened the box and found a heart pendant and diamond earrings to match. Derrick slowly took the necklace from the box and put it around Sherry's neck as she held up her hair for him to attach the hook. Sherry closed her eyes as he softly kissed her neck.

"Hi, precious," he said as he turned to Denise and picked her up from the bed. "Daddy hasn't talked to you in a while," he said as he kissed her cheek and held her close to his chest.

Sherry quietly put on her earrings and shoes and then went into the baby's room to prepare a fresh bag for Denise. From there she went into the kitchen and packed two bottles of milk.

"I'm ready," she said as she stood in the doorway of the bedroom watching Derrick play with their daughter.

"You're beautiful," he said as he walked toward her with Denise in his arms. "Both of you are beautiful."

"Thank you," Sherry said.

It seemed that ages had passed since they all rode in the same car together. Sherry's heart was full of happiness, but she tried not to show it. She knew that Derrick expected her to make him work for his requested forgiveness. She just wanted to play along for a little while.

Derrick pulled into the valet parking line of a restaurant called Maestro. It was known for its Italian cuisine. Pasta was a favorite in the Madison household. Although Sherry had eaten earlier in the day with Lena and Mattie, she searched the menu for her favorite dish. They sat in silence for several moments.

A waiter approached their secluded corner table. "May I take your orders now?"

"I'd like the pasta primavera, please," Sherry said as Derrick nodded for her to order.

"Would you like a different drink with that or is the water sufficient?"

"I'd like a sweetened tea. Also, can you give me a small empty bowl for the baby?"

"Yes, ma'am. And you, sir?"

"Do you serve crow?" Derrick asked to Sherry's amusement.

"I'm sorry, sir?" the waiter said.

"Never mind." Derrick smiled. "I'll take the Italian herb chicken with roasted potatoes and corn, please."

"And your drink?"

"I'll have an iced tea as well. Sweetened, please."

"Very well, sir," the waiter said as he took their menus. "I'll have that out to you as soon as possible."

"Thank you," Derrick and Sherry said.

"Made you laugh," Derrick said after the waiter walked away.

"I see you haven't lost your sense of humor," Sherry said. "I hadn't seen it in a while."

"There are other talents of mine you haven't seen in a while too," he flirted. "I ain't lost those either."

"So you say," Sherry responded. She took a drink from her glass.

"Want proof?" he asked. " 'Cause we can eighty-six this dinner and go straight for dessert."

"I'm not cheap," Sherry flirted right back. "You pay for this dinner and we'll discuss the *possibility* of dessert later."

"You're on," he said as he reached across the table as if desiring to shake hands on the deal.

Sherry placed her hand in his and he turned his wrist and pulled her hand up to his lips. Then, concentrating on each finger separately, he kissed each fingertip softly.

"That's cute and all," Sherry said as she pulled her hand away, trying to pretend his kisses had no effect, "but you're still paying for dinner first."

"Oh, I'll pay for dinner," he said as he opened his wallet. "I'll even pay for dessert if you want," he continued. "How much would you charge for all night?"

"Derrick!" she whispered sternly as she tried not to laugh.

"Come on, baby," he said, "name your price."

"How much you got?"

"Right now," he said as he opened his wallet and scanned his bills, "I have about four hundred dollars."

"That's not enough."

"That's why God made ATMs," he said.

Sherry laughed. "You are *so* silly."

"Yes, I am," Derrick said as he turned serious. "At least I have been. I've been about as stupid as a man can get. Baby, I am so sorry."

"If I say it's no problem, or that everything's okay," Sherry said, "I'd be lying. I've been so alone and so hurt for the past several weeks. I never would have thought you'd put me through anything like this," she continued. "I understand your sadness about Mama—I miss her too. But me and Dee—we didn't deserve this, Ricky."

"I know, sweetie. I've been a fool. I didn't even realize that it had gotten so bad. I didn't even know how much I missed you and Dee until after I spoke to Pastor Baldwin," he confessed. "I didn't know how much I missed Greg until then either."

"We've all missed you too," Sherry said as their food arrived. They sat in silence as the waiter placed their plates and drinks on the table and handed Sherry the empty bowl.

"Greg talks about you all the time," she continued once the waiter left. "He was talking the other week about how he missed playing basketball with you," she said while emptying a small jar of baby food into the bowl.

"So, he hasn't started hating me yet?"

"Nobody hates you, Ricky."

"You think he'll talk to me if I ask him to?"

"As long as you aren't coming to bad-mouth Jessica in any way. That is the one thing that he won't tolerate. Just ask Evelyn."

"You're kidding." Derrick smiled. "He got into it with Evelyn?"

"*Did* he!" Sherry said with a laugh. "He told her in no uncertain terms that she was never to disrespect his Grace again as long as she lived."

"Whoa," Derrick said. "He's got it pretty bad for this girl, huh?"

"Yes, he does. She's a pretty great girl, Ricky. If you're ever gonna have a relationship with Greg again, you'll have to accept Jessica. He's not gonna have it any other way."

"I should have known that he had more than medical concerns for her that day he threatened to go a few rounds with me at the hospital."

"Yeah," Sherry said as she fed Denise.

"Well, what do you know?" Derrick said with a smile. "Dr. Gregory Paul Dixon is in love."

It was almost 11:30 P.M. by the time Greg finished his rounds and was preparing to leave. He turned out the lights in his office and headed for the elevator.

"Dixon," Dr. Grant's voice called behind him, "I'm glad I caught you."

"Yes, Dr. Grant?"

"Detective Morrison called a few minutes ago. They got their man."

"You're kidding." Greg was elated. "Was it the same guy Pridgen and I treated?"

"It was. And here's the funny part," Dr. Grant started with a laugh.

"The address he gave us on the paperwork was actually his," Greg said, finishing the sentence for him.

"Exactly. The detective said he wasn't home when they went by his place, so they had to wait on him. Apparently, he works evenings, so they just sat outside the address until he came home."

"Did he confess to leaving the accident scene and everything? I mean, do they have enough evidence to hold him on it?"

"Yeah. He actually confessed and gave a statement. Stupid kid's only eighteen years old. Probably hadn't been driving too long and was so busy trying to impress Miss Charles that he wasn't watching the road as he should have."

"Grace will be glad to hear that the case is finally closed. I have to stop by her place on the way home. I'll tell her."

"Stopping by her place this late?" Dr. Grant analyzed. "So, is she the woman you're dating? Is she why you've been riding on the clouds lately?"

Greg smiled. "Yes."

"Ah," Dr. Grant said. "She's a pretty girl. Got some nice long legs."

"I know."

"Is it serious?"

"You remember when I left at 4:00 P.M. and told you to page me if you needed me?"

"You took that hour to go by and pick her up?"

"No," Greg said as he reached in his pocket and pulled out a small box. "I took that hour to pick *this* up."

"Well, I'll be," Dr. Grant said as he looked in the opened box. "That's some kind of ring there," he said. "I had no idea. I thought that you had just started seeing this girl."

"Last night was our first official date."

"And you're ready to propose? Look, Dixon, I know you lost your father when you were very young so maybe you never had that man-to-man talk. I'm sure you've heard the saying 'why buy the cow when the milk is free?' There are so many women who'd fight for a chance to get with you. There are at least fifty of them in this hospital alone, including patients and employees. I'm sure Jessica, or Grace as you call her, would do the same. Why would you do something so permanent if it's not necessary?"

"First of all, Dr. Grant," Greg said, "let me say that I respect you to the highest in your profession. However, if you ever compare Grace to a cow again, I'll have to hurt you. Secondly, I'm not giving her this ring out of necessity—I'm doing it out of desire. I want this. I *love* this girl. I don't just want her in my bed. I want her in my life."

"Did you just threaten to hurt me, Dixon?" Dr. Grant said, seeming not to have heard the rest of Greg's speech.

"I'm afraid I did," Greg said after a moment of thought.

"Give her the ring, son. You are definitely in love. Let me know how it goes," he said as he walked away.

"I will," Greg said as he sighed in relief that Dr. Grant hadn't taken his words personally.

Greg constantly glanced at his watch as he tested the speed of his Jaguar on the highway. He could only hope and pray that

Jessica hadn't turned in for the night. He'd waited all afternoon for this moment.

"I'm sorry I'm late," Greg apologized as he stepped inside the door that Jessica held open for him.

"It's all right," she said. "I was just watching a movie."

"Oh?" Greg said as he turned to face the television. "What's on?"

"*The Pelican Brief.*"

"Denzel Washington," Greg observed. "I guess my timing is bad."

"No, it's not," she said, laughing, as she turned the volume down. "I've seen it before anyway—several times. You want something to drink?"

"No, thanks." Greg sat beside her. "I have good news to share with you."

"I have news too." She smiled.

"Okay, you go first," Greg said.

"I had left a message a couple of days ago with the dean at the college. She called me back today and said I can get back in school in a couple of weeks."

"That's *great* news," Greg said. "Do you need a note from me or anything?"

"She didn't mention it, but I guess I could get one just to be sure."

"I'll write it tomorrow."

"And," she said, "if all goes as planned, I'll be able to graduate by September."

"I am so proud of you," Greg said. "I'll be on the front row barking when they call your name."

"Okay." She laughed.

"Well, you ready for my news?"

"Yes."

"The police picked up our guy."

"Did they?"

"Yep. It really was the guy that we treated for the so-called fight with a friend. He lived at the address that he gave us, and when they caught him he confessed to leaving the accident scene."

"Oh, that's wonderful," Jessica exclaimed as she hugged Greg tightly.

"Nice hug," he said as she pulled away. "Let me see what else I can tell you that would bring you such joy."

"If you want a hug from me, all you have to do is ask," Jessica said.

"What about a hand?"

"A hand?"

"Yes," Greg said. "If I wanted a hand from you, could I just ask?"

"I don't know—I guess. I don't think I understand the question."

"Grace . . ." Greg stood and nervously walked to the window and looked out. "We've only known each other for a few months and it's so hard for me to explain to other people how much I care for you." He turned and faced her from across the room.

"When you were placed in my care at Robinson Memorial, taking care of you became a priority for me. Even before I met you—when your case was assigned to me—I knew that I had to take care of you. Are you getting what I'm saying?"

"I'm not sure," she said honestly.

"Just give me a minute," Greg said. "I promise it'll all make sense when I'm done. The first day I laid eyes on you, you only had about a half inch of hair. It was growing back from when they shaved you at Saint Mary's. There was a tube going down your throat and your face was bruised from the accident. Yet, when I looked at you, all I could think of was how beautiful you were."

Jessica smiled as he continued.

"I knew that your chances of surviving another surgery with your injuries weren't real good, but I knew that somehow God had to work a miracle through me. I knew that you had to live and I knew that there was a place in my life that only you could fill, and if you didn't live, there would always be an empty place where you were supposed to be.

"That's why I went to Pastor Baldwin and my church family for prayer—because I knew. And everything just fell into place so nicely. My mother becoming friends with your mother and her approval of you. Your mom's approval of me and Sherry's instant friendship with you. Even when Leroy broke your heart, it was just another part of the plan.

"Oh, sweetheart," he said as he sat by her on the sofa and grabbed her hands, "I'm still not making much sense and I know that. All I'm really trying to say is that ever since you were placed in my care, everything that I've done has been because of what I feel in my heart for you. Do you know what I'm saying?"

"Yes." Grace nodded. "You're trying to say that you love me. I love you too, Greg."

"But that's just it," Greg said. "I already knew you loved me, yet this is the first time you spoke the words. Are you just finding out that I love you?"

"No, I knew."

"I know you did, because somehow that's how our relationship began. There was not one day from the time I met you that I didn't love you, Grace. Not *one* day," he said. "And when you opened your eyes in the hospital that day that they paged me to tell me that you were awake," he continued, "I knew you loved me too. Whether *you* knew it yet or not, Grace, *I* knew that you loved me."

Greg's words were so touching that Jessica almost found them overwhelming. "I guess we've got something really special here," she said with tears in her eyes.

"But that's not what I'm trying to tell you," Greg said. "Don't get me wrong, we do have something special. I do love you, but I knew you already knew that. That's not what I'm rambling on and on about. I don't know quite how to bring this to my point."

"What point, Greg? Just say it."

"Okay," he said. "What are you doing on October sixth?"

"October sixth? I don't know. Nothing that I know of. Why?"

"That's my birthday. I'd like you to spend it with me."

"Sure." Jessica smiled. "I'd like that too. What do you have planned?"

"I want to go to church and I want you by my side."

"I'd love to. Is there a special service that day?"

"Yes," Greg said. "A wedding."

"Really? Who's getting married?"

"Us," Greg said as he took the box out of his pocket and slid to the floor onto one knee.

"Oh, my God!" Jessica gasped and covered her mouth as tears flooded her eyes.

"Jessica Grace Charles," he said as he pulled her left hand down from her face and held it in his, "we've only known each other for a short time, but what we have is right. I know it and I know that you know it. I'm still young and you're even younger, and there are folks who'll say we ought to wait, but I want this and I want it now," he continued. "I know my job takes a lot of my time, and I have a pager attached to my hip all the time because I never know when duty will call. But if you'll marry me, I promise that every day of my life, I'll do whatever I have to do to make time for you. I'll always protect you and I'll never put anything or anyone ahead of you. I love you, Grace. Will you marry me?"

"Greg," she said through the tears, "that was so beautiful, and I know you meant every word of it. But I need you to understand this. I was your patient once. I needed you to be there for me if anything ever went wrong. I don't want you to change that. I know those people need you, because I've been where they are. I don't know what I would have done had you not been able to be there whenever duty called. Yes, I'll marry you," she continued, "but only if you promise that you will be there for them too. I don't want it any other way."

"But I need you to know that you're more important than anything that happens on my job," he said.

"I already know that, Greg," she said. "I'll always know that. Please promise me that you'll be there for them like you were for me."

"I promise," he whispered as he slipped the ring on her finger and stood, pulling her to her feet with him. "Thank you for saying yes," he said as he hugged her closely. "I love you."

"I love you too."

CHAPTER 13

"Maybe I should do this by myself," Derrick said as he tucked his shirt into his pants. "After all, I managed to get things like this on my own."

"No, sweetie," Sherry insisted as she finished getting Denise dressed. "We're doing this as a family. This worked out perfectly. School is out today for teachers' planning, so I'm able to come with you."

"I just don't want it to look like you're coaxing me into doing this."

"It's not gonna look like that. You're going to do all the talking. Besides, I think Ms. Mattie and Jessica would be a bit apprehensive about letting you in their house if you go alone. Keep in mind, they only know one side of you."

"Okay," he agreed. "Here's my visitation order. Tell me if it sounds okay. We'll go to the hospital to see Greg first. Then we'll see Ms. Lena, Ms. Mattie, and then Jessica."

"I think we should see Greg last. I mean, I think his reception will depend a lot on what happens with the other three."

"Okay," he said as he picked up his keys, "Ms. Lena it is."

"Are you nervous?" Sherry asked on the drive to Lena's house.

"Why, do I look nervous?"

"Not really. You're just so quiet."

"Well, I guess I don't have much energy after last night."

She laughed. "Cut it out."

They parked in front of Lena's house and walked up the steps hand in hand. Derrick carried Denise, who was sucking vigorously on a bottle that she had just begun holding by herself.

"Well, good morning," Lena said as she opened the door and welcomed them in. "I ain't had a visit from the three of you in a while, and I ain't seen *you* in a month of Sundays," she said to Derrick as he passed by her.

"Yes, ma'am," he said.

"Have a seat. I was just doing a little housecleaning. Y'all want something to drink?"

"No, Ms. Lena," Sherry said. "Sit down with us for a minute. We need to talk to you."

"All right." She sat down and smoothed out her skirt.

"Ms. Lena," Derrick started. "I owe you an apology and that's why I'm here."

"Last time you was here, you was looking for Greg."

"I know. I'm sorry about that. I was wrong. I never should have come into your house with that tone of voice or with the attitude that I displayed."

"No, you shouldn't have."

"I'm not making excuses, but I was angry and feeling hurt and betrayed that day, and I guess I wasn't thinking straight. I was very disrespectful to you and I'm sorry."

"Derrick," Lena said, "I know you been hurt, son. Losing Julia like that was a blow to all of us. None of us expected that she'd be gone so soon. I understood your pain 'cause I was feeling pain too. What I don't understand is why you took out all your pain on the people who love you the most."

"It's a long story, Ms. Lena," he began.

"Well, then, keep it to yourself," she said as she stood. "I ain't got time for no long stories," she continued as Sherry burst into laughter. "I said I was in the middle of cleaning my house. I'm on a schedule here. You said you're sorry and I forgive you, now give your godmama some sugar before I take a switch to your behind."

"Thanks, Ms. Lena." Derrick smiled as he stood and bent down, kissed her cheek, and hugged her tightly. While still hugging her, he stood up straight, lifting her off the floor in the process.

"Put me down, boy," she said, laughing.

He eased her back to the floor and Sherry stood to hug her as well.

"I don't know what you done to get him back to his old self," she told Sherry, "but keep on doing it."

"I wish I could take the credit," Sherry said, "but this was definitely the Lord's doing. The Lord and Pastor Baldwin, that is."

"Well, thank the Lord and thank *you*, Pastor Baldwin," Lena said as she playfully swatted Derrick's leg with her cleaning cloth.

"We'd love to stay longer, Ms. Lena," Derrick said, "but I have a few more stops to make. Maybe we'll see you later in the week."

"All right," Lena said as she walked them to the door. "It really is good to see all y'all together again," she said as they walked out the door.

"Feels good too," Derrick said as he put his arm around Sherry's waist and kissed Denise.

This time of day, the drive from Lena's home to the house Jessica shared with her mother was about a fifteen-minute ride. The rush hour was long over, so traffic didn't pose any delays. Sherry pointed toward Mattie's house so that Derrick would know where to park.

"Now I'm nervous," Derrick admitted as they started toward her front porch.

"It'll be okay," Sherry assured him as she rang the doorbell.

"Sherry," Mattie said as she opened her front door. Her face sobered as she looked beyond Sherry and saw Derrick approaching with Denise in tow.

"May we come in, Ms. Mattie?" Sherry asked.

"Sure, baby," she said as she opened the door wider and stepped aside.

"Hi," Derrick said as he walked in.

"Hi."

"Ms. Mattie," Sherry said, "this is my husband, Derrick. Derrick, this is Ms. Mattie Charles."

"Nice to meet you, Ms. Mattie," Derrick said as he extended his hand.

Mattie looked at his hand for a moment. "Same here," she said as she placed her hand in his.

"Is Jessie home?" Sherry asked while looking around.

"No, she's not," Mattie said as she motioned for them to have a seat.

"Ms. Mattie," Derrick began after being seated, "I'm here to apologize for my actions. I've behaved pretty badly over the past few months and my behavior affected you in a negative manner. I just want to say I'm truly sorry. I was hoping Jessica was here so I could apologize to her as well."

"Well, I think *she's* the one who needs to hear the apology. I can't say that you did me no wrong, personally—but I think you did a lot of wrong where my Jessie is concerned."

"I agree," Derrick said. "However, I think that I wronged you too. I hurt your daughter and that, however indirectly, hurt you as well."

"Greg begged us not to charge it to your heart. He said that you're really a nice boy."

"He did?"

"Yes, he did," Mattie said. "From what I heard went on in the hospital room, I found it hard to believe. Then I met Sherry and little Dee here. That's when I started thinking that there must be some good in you somewhere in order for you to be blessed with a family like this."

"They are a blessing," Derrick said as he looked lovingly at his wife and daughter. "I don't have legitimate reasons for acting like a fool, Ms. Mattie, but when I lost my mother, it felt like I was going to lose my mind as well."

"Well, you must *have* lost it for a minute, 'cause from what I heard, you acted like some kind of hoodlum up in that hospital room."

"I think that's a fair statement," Derrick said. "Mama meant the world to me. I needed somebody to blame for her death. It wasn't right and I admit that, but Jessica just seemed like the person to blame at the time. I'm sorry."

"Well, if my forgiveness is what you need to move on, then you got it. It takes a big man to admit when he's wrong, so I forgive you."

"Thank you," Derrick said. "I really did need to hear that before my next stop. I'm going to go by the hospital and see Greg. Do you know when Jessica will be home? I would like to apologize to her in person."

"Greg ain't at the hospital," she said. "He came by a couple of hours ago and took Jessie to breakfast. After that, they were going to stop by his place so he could write a letter of release for her to take to them folks at her school so she could complete her enrollment."

"She's getting back in school?" Sherry smiled.

"Yeah," Mattie said proudly. "And she won't have to go but a couple of months before she qualifies for graduation."

"Oh, that's great. I know she's happy."

"Oh, she's got more than one reason to celebrate these days," Mattie said. "They're probably at his house by now, if you want to see them."

"Thanks for taking the time to listen to me," Derrick said as he reached to shake her hand.

"Oh, you can do better than that," Mattie said while spreading her arms for a hug.

"Thank you," he repeated as he hugged her.

"You're welcome."

"See, that wasn't so bad," Sherry commented as they drove away.

"I think everybody is letting me off too easily," Derrick said. "Don't get me wrong, I'm happy that they are forgiving me, because I don't deserve it—but I just kind of thought they'd have to think about it first or something."

"They know you weren't yourself, Ricky."

Greg's car was parked in front of his penthouse and Derrick pulled up right beside it. He almost felt strange getting out at Greg's house. After his spending an average of four days a week visiting his friend's home, it had been nearly four months since he'd been there at all.

"He's still the same old Greg," Sherry said as she noticed his hesitation. "You go ahead. I'll be there in just a minute. I think Dee Dee has dropped a load. I'm going to change her diaper right quick."

Derrick walked up to the door and rang the bell. On the other side of the door, in his office, Greg was busy typing Jessica's letter.

"You mind getting the door, baby?" he called to her as she was getting a glass from the cabinet for a drink of water in the kitchen.

"Not at all," she said. With the empty glass in her hand, she opened the door. The glass shattered as it crashed against the floor.

"Greg!" she called, backing away in terror.

"It's okay," Derrick said as he saw her fear. "I'm not gonna hurt you."

"Grace, what's—" Greg started as he joined her at the door and looked in Derrick's face.

"I'm . . . I'm sorry," Derrick said. "I didn't mean to frighten her."

"Go into my office for a minute, sweetheart," Greg whispered to Jessica as she held his hand tightly. The panic he read in her eyes made him angry. "Go on," he repeated.

"I'm sorry," Derrick repeated as he looked at the broken glass.

Greg didn't respond. He bent down and picked up the large pieces of glass.

"What happened in here?" Sherry asked as she joined Derrick in the doorway.

"Grace answered the door," Greg said as he dropped the broken glass in a trash can near the door.

"Oh, Greg," Sherry said, "I'm sorry."

"It's not your fault," he said as he kissed her cheek and then Dee's.

"Let me help you with that," she offered.

"No," Greg said. "Why don't you check on Grace for me? She's in my office. I'll take care of this."

"Sure," Sherry said as she turned to face Derrick. "Here's the one you're going to have to work for," she whispered before kissing his lips and heading to Greg's office.

Derrick closed the front door as Greg walked from the room and returned with a broom and dustpan. Derrick sat on the couch and watched as Greg quietly swept the glass from the hardwood floor into the dustpan and dumped it in the trash can. He wanted to offer a helping hand, but he could feel Greg's anger with him at the moment. After he put the cleaning supplies away, Greg came back into the living room and sat on the sofa opposite Derrick. Neither of them spoke for a moment.

"Is this a good time for us to talk?" Derrick finally asked.

"Nigga . . ." Greg started in anger. Sitting back in his chair and taking a deep breath to try and compose himself, he began again. "Just the *sight* of you nearly scared Grace to death," he said. "Naw, it ain't a good time to talk—but then again, I don't know that such a time exists."

"Greg, I know you're angry with me. You have every right to be. I've given you a good reason to be."

"Which reason would that be, Rick? Punching me in the mouth? Threatening to hurt me to my mama? Barging into my patient's hospital room and threatening her? Accusing me of stabbing you in the back? Calling me a liar? Which reason have you given me to be angry with you?"

"Listen, Greg—" Derrick began.

"No, *you* listen," Greg interrupted. "Twenty-six years, Derrick. Count them, *twenty-six years*. That's how long we've known each other. At the age of three, I remember crying on your lap at my daddy's funeral. I remember you crying on mine when you found out your daddy wasn't coming home. In second grade, when Tommy Lester and Jarvis what's-his-name ganged up on you, it was me who got my behind beat trying to take up for you. In the sixth grade when our house burned down, it was your bed I slept in every night for the next six months until Mama could find another place to live," Greg said as angry tears threatened his eyes.

"In the tenth grade, when you tried out for basketball and weren't going to make the team if you didn't ace your upcoming math exam, who stayed up late nights tutoring you so you could make the cut? I did. The summer of ninety-one when we were out shooting hoops and I broke my ankle, it was you who helped me hop three blocks to my house because I couldn't walk by myself. That next year, when Sherry kicked your sorry tail to the curb because you told her she had to choose between you and God, who went to bat for you because he was tired of hearing you cry all day and every day about what a fool you were? Me, Rick, that was me.

"On your wedding day, when we were taking our showers and getting dressed an hour before showtime and you noticed that you forgot to bring fresh underwear, who gave you the only pair of underwear that he brought with him? I did. I stood at that altar as your best man, all dressed up in my tux without any drawers on because I gave them to you, Rick.

"Twenty-six years of growing up together and having each other's back, and you could just throw it all away like that because I saved a girl's life who you thought deserved to die. *Yes,* I'm mad. I'm mad because we haven't played a single game of one-on-one this year. I'm mad because you asked me to be Dee Dee's godfather and then you canceled her christening because you didn't want me standing there. I'm mad because for the first time in my life I am totally and completely in love and I couldn't share that with you after twenty-six years of friendship."

Cheers and laughter coming from Sherry and Jessica in his office interrupted Greg's speech. Derrick looked with confusion toward the office door.

"You were supposed to know about that ring even before Grace," Greg added.

"What?"

"I remember going with you to pick out Sherry's engagement ring the weekend before you proposed. I had to pick out Grace's ring by myself."

"You're engaged?" Derrick asked in shock. "I had no idea . . . I had no idea," he repeated. "Sherry didn't tell me that."

"That's because Sherry's just finding out. That's what the commotion is all about, I'm sure. I just proposed last night."

"Wow." Derrick sighed. "I don't know what to say, man— except that I'm sorry. You're right. I've been beyond stupid for the past few months. Twenty-six years is a long time to be friends, and I miss your friendship. There are no valid reasons for my behavior, but I just felt so betrayed and so guilty. I should have been there for Mama, Greg. If she had died in her sleep or of a heart attack, it still would have been painful, but I could have dealt with that. She died 'cause I wasn't there for her and I couldn't handle it. I'm sorry."

"Did you apologize to my mama?" Greg asked.

"Yes. Your mom and your future mother-in-law. I stopped by both their houses before I came here. They were gracious enough to forgive me. I know I can't erase all the damage I've done, Greg. I just want a chance to make it right. If this marriage is what you want, then I'm happy for you. I'm glad that you found the love of your life, but I don't want Jessica to tremble every time she sees me. If she's gonna be your bride, I need a chance for her to know the real me. I need a chance to gain her trust. Please, Greg. I need your forgiveness if there's even a chance for us to get things back to normal."

Greg sat in silence for a moment and then slowly got up and walked to his office. He returned, holding Jessica's hand with Sherry following close behind.

"Grace," he said, "this is Derrick Jerome Madison, Sherry's husband." He paused. "And my best friend. Derrick, this is Jessica Grace Charles, my bride-to-be."

"I'm sorry," Derrick said as he extended his hand to Jessica, who was still apprehensive. "I'm sorry for everything. I promise that nothing like that will ever happen again. Please forgive me."

"Okay," Jessica said softly as she took his hand and shook it gently.

"Rick is gonna be my best man," Greg told her.

"With pleasure." Derrick smiled in spite of his watery eyes. "I sure will."

"He and Sherry are also treating us to dinner tonight," Greg added.

"What a wonderful idea, Ricky," Sherry said.

"Uh, yeah," Derrick said. "Sometimes I surprise myself."

"Well, congratulations, again," Sherry said as she hugged both Greg and Jessica. "I guess we'd better go so we can get some other things done before dinnertime."

"Yeah." Derrick smiled. "We have stuff to do, so we'll meet you all at the restaurant at 6:00 this evening."

"Oh, please," Greg said. "Y'all ain't fooling nobody. Just go on home and get your *stuff* done," he said while making the quotation gestures with his fingers. "Call me around 5:00 and we'll decide on a restaurant."

"Greg." Jessica blushed, playfully punching his arm.

"Thank you," Derrick said as he reached out to shake Greg's hand.

"No—thank *you*," Greg said as they shook hands and embraced. "I was wondering what that new Derrick had done with our old Derrick."

"Well, he's back," Derrick said. "Oh, and by the way," he added in a lowered voice as he and Sherry headed out the door, "that story about the underwear thing? Don't tell nobody else, okay?"

CHAPTER 14

Sunday, May 27

Pastor Baldwin smiled from the pulpit as he saw Sherry and Derrick walk in thirty minutes into the service. Greg and Jessica had gotten there early along with their mothers and had managed to save a space on their pew wide enough for Sherry and Derrick to fit in.

"Had stuff to do this morning?" Greg asked sarcastically as he firmly shook Derrick's extended hand and kissed Sherry's cheek.

"Just wait till you get married," Derrick responded with a laugh. "You'll have stuff to do too."

"Word," Greg said as he laughed.

As the praise and worship service ended, the announcer came to the podium to make the weekly announcements.

"We'd like to once again welcome all of our visitors to our service today," she said. "Whether you are visiting for the first time or you are a repeat guest, we thank you for your presence and hope that you'll come again."

She opened her folder. "Our announcements are as follows. All ushers are asked to meet with Sister Thorpe for a brief meeting immediately following services. There will be a fun day held at the youth center next door tomorrow, which is Memorial Day. Please make plans to attend. There will be activities planned for both adults and children.

"June fourth is our pastor's birthday; please remember him in your own special way. Our pastor will be christening Denise Sherrell Madison following the sermon today. We are asking that parents, grandparents, and godparents of the child assemble around the altar immediately following the close of today's sermon. Last, but not least, Mother Lena Dixon and Sister Mattie Charles asked me to make a special announcement."

Greg leaned across Jessica and said to his mother, "No, you didn't." The frozen smiles on Ms. Mattie's and her face confirmed his suspicion as the announcer continued.

"They would like to proudly announce the engagement of their children, Dr. Gregory Dixon and Miss Jessica Charles."

There were surprise gasps coming from all areas of the congregation. Just before they burst into applause, there was a loud thud midway in the church. Several ushers scampered for that area as the thunderous applause got louder.

"Ms. Lena ain't the one who needs a fan this morning," Lena remarked with a grin as the ushers carried Evelyn's outstretched body out into the foyer.

"Well, praise God," Pastor Baldwin remarked as he took the podium. "God is still good anyhow. One of you nurses, go on back there in case they need some assistance in the rear," he instructed as he opened his Bible.

"That child don't need no nurse," Lena mumbled. "Need Jesus, that's what she need," she said as Mattie agreed with a nod.

"Mama . . ." Greg warned.

"Please turn with me to the book of John, chapter three," Pastor Baldwin began. "Before I bring the sermon for today, I'd like to beg of Sister Jessica to come and bless us with a song."

"Amen!" several people in the crowd agreed.

"Sing, baby." Greg smiled proudly as Jessica got up and

walked to the front of the church and took the microphone from Pastor Baldwin's hand.

After a brief moment of thought, she began singing the deep-meaning, apologetic words of BeBe Winans's song "Coming Back Home."

"Whoa," Derrick said in surprise at the sound of her voice.

Greg's smile indicated that his friend's reaction pleased him.

By the time she and the choir had finished the song, the audience was on their feet in praise and Derrick's face was buried in a handkerchief that he was soaking with tears. Sherry stroked the back of his neck, knowing that the song had expressed what he felt in his heart.

"There are some people who are talented to sing," Pastor Baldwin said as the crowd settled down and returned to their seats. "You, my sister, are *blessed* to sing," he concluded. Greg squeezed Jessica's hand in agreement.

"Let us pray," he continued. "Our Father, our Father, our most righteous Father, we come to you not asking you to fill our pockets with money or to bless us with cars and homes. We come to you to thank you for your mercy and your grace. We have testimonies all around us, God. If you don't do another thing for us, you have already done more than we deserve.

"Thank you for life. Thank you for sparing all of us—but in particular, thank you for breathing life back into our Sister Charles."

"Yes, Lord," Mattie said as she raised her hands in thankful worship.

"And, God, we know that you are the source of all of our strength," he continued, "but we thank you for Deacon Warbuck. The doctor said he'd never walk on that leg again, but, God, you strengthened those old bones and he's walking today because of it."

The congregation clapped in worship for the miracle of the oldest member of their church. Deacon Warbuck was eighty-seven years old.

"Oh, God, you gave us all the mind to want to be here to worship together today, and there are no big *I*s or little *U*s, but we especially thank you for renewing that mind in Brother Madison. Lord, you know he's been through some trying times and the devil took his weakest moment and tried to steal his mind. Thank you for renewing his mind and bringing him back home.

"Thank you for your love that rests in our hearts today. Thank you for giving Brother Dixon a love of his own. Thank you for giving him love *and* Grace. Let your grace and Grace's grace be almost more grace than he can stand."

Greg smiled as his pastor put a twist in his prayer and had a little fun with Jessica's name. He peeked over at Jessica and saw that she was smiling too.

"Bless us all, Lord. We thank you for all you've done so far and all that you have planned to do in the future. We glorify your name and we will love you forever. We pray all these things in Jesus' name. Amen."

"Amen," the congregation responded as they sat and prepared for the sermon.

It was surprisingly short. Pastor Baldwin came from the familiar passage of Scripture, John 3:16. He spoke to his listeners about the deep love that God had for His people—a love, he insisted, that could be compared to no other. This was one of his "tune-up" sermons. He both stood at the pulpit and walked the floor as he preached. By the end of his sermon, the congregation was on its feet, some screaming, some jumping, some just waving their hands.

The usher brought him a glass of water as he closed his Bible and extended his hand toward the Madison family.

"Come on, Jessica," Derrick said as he saw her still standing at her seat as they were walking forward.

"Huh?" Jessica said.

"How you gonna play me like that?" he whispered as he walked back to her. "If you gonna marry Greg, you gotta be Dee's godmother."

She smiled. "Really?"

"Yes," he said as he pulled her by her arm to follow him.

Greg smiled and took her hand as she stood next to him. Sherry's parents had flown in to town for the christening and stood by her side as the maternal grandparents. Derrick looked at the empty space beside him and suddenly found himself fighting intense sadness.

"Come on," Lena said, tugging at Mattie.

"Where we going?" Mattie asked.

"We're going up here to be that baby's grandmothers," Lena said.

Derrick could hear the audience begin clapping, but he didn't know why they were applauding until he saw the two women walk up and stand beside him. His tears broke. Lena and Mattie embraced him together.

"Denise," Pastor Baldwin said as he took her from her mother's arms, "you've got a lot of people here who love you, and that's a blessing. I charge each of you to band together and help raise this child to know the way of the Lord," he said as he anointed each of their heads and Denise's head with blessed oil. Be the father and mother that God would be pleased with. Be the grandparents and surrogate grandparents that God would be pleased with. Be the godparents that God would be pleased with.

"Her soul's salvation depends upon each one of you. This is a cruel world and she'll need the protection and love of all of you as she grows up and becomes a toddler, an adolescent, a teenager, and an adult. God is holding each of you responsible in your respective positions in her life, to give her the guidance that she will need. If one of you falls short, another needs to be there to pick up the slack."

After he finished charging each of them, he said a prayer for all of them and they returned to their seats.

Following services, several members of the congregation congratulated Greg and Jessica as they tried hopelessly to make their way through the crowd and out the door. Greg stopped

218 Kendra Norman-Bellamy

once to introduce Jessica to Sherry's parents and then continued to walk toward the door. Evelyn stood and watched in silence as they passed.

"Finally made it, huh?" Derrick laughed as they joined him and Sherry on the front lawn.

"Yeah," Greg said as he put on his shades to block the sun from his eyes. "Where's Mama?"

"They were ahead of us coming out," Jessica said. "I saw them."

"They're over by Ms. Lena's car," Sherry said.

"This is a rare day off of work for me," Greg said as they all walked toward the parking lot. "How about we all go out and have Sunday dinner?"

"Since my folks are heading back to New Jersey, I don't have any other plans," Sherry said. "You want to go, baby?"

"Sure," Derrick said. "I'm always game for a good meal."

"Mama, what do you and Ms. Mattie have planned for this afternoon?"

"I don't know what Mattie got planned, but I ain't got nothing to do in particular."

"Me either," Mattie said.

"How about we all go out to dinner?" Greg offered.

"That's a good idea, 'cause it was Mattie's Sunday to cook," Lena said.

"So, just what are you trying to say?" Mattie defended.

"I'm *trying* to say that eating out is better."

"And you think your food is better than restaurant cooking?"

"My son says my food is the best."

"He just don't be wanting to hurt your feelings," Mattie told her.

"It's better than your cooking, that's for sure."

"Jessie," Mattie said, "you tell her that my cooking is the best."

"Greg, Derrick, Sherry," Lena said, "y'all tell her who's the best cook in this whole state."

"Grace, you're riding with me, right?" Greg said as he started walking away.

"Yeah," Jessica responded as she grabbed his hand and followed him.

"You all choose the restaurant and we'll follow you," Sherry said as she turned toward their car.

Derrick pointed to Mattie as he followed Sherry. "She's my mother reincarnate."

"See how they avoided your question?" Mattie said as she got into the passenger seat of Lena's car. "Told you they just don't want to hurt your feelings."

"I didn't hear no answer from Jessie either," Lena pointed out.

By the time they arrived at the family-style buffet restaurant, Mattie and Lena had calmed down. They went through the line and pulled two tables together so they could all sit together.

"Greg," Mattie said as they held hands around the table, "you want to say grace?"

"Yes, Ms. Mattie." He smiled and turned to his fiancée. "I just love saying Grace. Grace, Grace, Grace," he said' to the amusement of Derrick and Sherry.

"Boy," Lena warned, "put your mind on the Lord and pray over this food."

"Sorry, Ma," he said as they rejoined hands. "Dear God," he said, "thank you for this food that we are about to receive. Bless the hands that prepared it. If there is anything unclean on our plates, we ask that you purify it and make it nourishing to our bodies. Protect us from any sickness or harm. We thank you and we receive it in your name. Amen."

"Amen," they all responded.

"My goodness," Mattie said as she turned to Lena. "Look how deep that child has to pray. He's used to eating your food, too. Now that tells us all something."

"No, you didn't," Lena said as the rest of them laughed.

"Child got to pray that your hands were clean and that he don't need medical attention after he eats; now, that's a shame," Mattie continued.

"Now tell me this woman ain't just like Julia Madison," Derrick said. "I just love you, Ms. Mattie," he said as the table shared a laugh.

"This," Sherry said as she pointed at Lena and Mattie, "is what you two have to look forward to for a lifetime."

"Bring it on," Greg said as he scooped up a forkful of mashed potatoes from his plate and fed it to Grace. She picked up a piece of chicken and fed it to him, as Sherry and Derrick nudged each other and watched.

"I love you, Grace," Greg said as he kissed her hand. "Love me?" he asked.

"I do," she said in her best "bride" voice.

"You do?"

"I do."

"I do too, sweetheart."

"This wedding may seem like a long way off," Lena lectured, "but October is just around the corner."

"No, actually it doesn't seem like a long way off at all," Greg said. "We've got a lot of work to do in a short period of time."

"Have you decided who all will be in the wedding party?" Mattie asked.

"Y'all please don't have a trillion folks marching up in there," Lena said. "I mean, I know it's your wedding and all, but that's just so unnecessary."

"Mama," Jessica said, "I don't even know a trillion folks. I don't know anybody actually. Not well enough to put in my line. I already asked Sherry to be my matron of honor, but I don't know who else to ask."

"Let Sherry be it." Greg shrugged. "I'll have Rick and you'll have Sherry. That's good enough."

"That's it?" Lena asked.

"That's fine with me," Jessica said.

"We only had three guys and three girls," Sherry said, "and that was including the flower girl and ring bearer."

"I guess we need to get a couple of kids from somewhere," Jessica said to Greg.

"We can if you want," Greg said. "I'm sure Pastor Baldwin's grandkids would do it happily, but I don't think it's necessary. Just let flowers already be dropped down the aisle that you'll come down, and Sherry and Rick can have the rings already in hand."

"That would work," Derrick agreed.

"Unless you just want a bunch of different people walking in and doing things," Greg said to Jessica, "it can be just the four of us and Pastor Baldwin at the altar."

"I don't care who walks in," Jessica said as she kissed her groom-to-be, "as long as I walk out with you."

"Morris Chestnut ain't got nothing on me," Greg bragged, returning her kiss.

"Well now," Sherry said, "I don't know about all that."

"Anyway," Greg said.

"I guess we need to go shopping for a dress," Mattie said. "Oh, I'm just so excited."

"And you get whatever dress your heart desires," Greg added. "It's on me."

"The dress is the bride's responsibility," Jessica said.

"Girl, you shut up and let that man buy your dress," Sherry said. "I'll go with you to pick it out."

"Thank you." Jessica smiled sweetly.

"When you don't know the city all that well, and you don't know a lot of folks," Lena said to Jessica, "it's kind of hard to stick to traditional wedding mumbo jumbo."

"I'll take you to a great florist," Sherry said excitedly, "and you can go with me to pick out my dress."

"Do we get a dress too?" Mattie asked.

Greg jumped in. "Yes, ma'am. Whatever dress your heart desires."

"Ooh," Mattie said. "I'm gonna love you as a son-in-law."

"Mama," Jessica said.

"I *want* to do this, Grace," Greg assured her. "I'll take care of getting the reception catered and getting a person to take pictures and video recording. I'll even take care of getting the musicians and singers together."

"Well, what will I do?" Jessica asked.

"You can do whatever you want, sweetheart, but all you *have* to do is show up at the church."

"Take him up on that, girlfriend," Sherry said. "Take it from me. A wedding can be hectic to plan. If he's offering, you'd better take it."

"Okay," Jessica said. "I have only one request."

"Anything," Greg said.

"I want the color scheme to be blue and white. I want the wedding to be your favorite color."

Greg beamed. "I think I can arrange that."

CHAPTER 15

Fast-forward

Just as sure as Lena Dixon had spoken the words—time passed quickly. And just as sure as Sherry had told her—by the time Jessica had searched endlessly for a gown, she was glad that Greg had volunteered to take care of the bulk of the wedding plans.

She'd seen and tried on several beautiful gowns that she liked, but Jessica wanted a gown that would take her groom's breath away as she walked down the aisle to meet him. None of the ones she tried on had given her that feeling . . . until now.

"Oh, Jessie!" Sherry gasped as Lena and Mattie looked on. *"That's the one."*

Jessica was escorted to a full-length mirror by one of the store's saleswomen so that she, too, could see how the dress looked on her.

"Baby, you look beautiful," Mattie said.

Jessica was speechless as she looked at her own reflection in the mirror. Her big day with the man of her dreams was only a month away.

"Wait till Greg sees you in that!" Lena exclaimed.

Jessica had just begun to think that the dress she was looking for just couldn't be found. This one, however, exceeded her imagination. The beaded bodice and jeweled neckline were sensational. The gown fitted perfectly to Jessica's slim waistline and the bottom filled out into a princess-style skirt. The headpiece that the assistant had chosen added to the majesty of the gown.

"Do you like it, Jessie?" Lena asked after the bride-to-be stood, silently staring for several minutes.

"Yes," she said. "I love it. It's so beautiful."

"Yes, it is," Sherry agreed as she walked around Jessica, carrying Denise, now eight months old, in her arms. "Are you gonna wear your hair hanging or are you going to sweep it up in some type of bun or roll?"

"I'm not sure yet. I'm thinking of cutting it short like it was before it all grew back."

"Girl, let your hair alone," Mattie scolded. "You wanted it to grow back and now you're talking 'bout chopping it all off."

"Not *all* off, Mama," Jessica said, "just to the length it was when we went on our first date."

"The Halle Berry length," Sherry said. "I liked it like that."

"Either way, it'll be pretty," Lena added.

Jessica stood in silence while the ladies each admired the dress. They touched the beading, spreading the train, admired the pearl buttons that closed the back. The verdict was finally in. The dress was a winner.

"Would you like me to prepare it for your purchasing?" the saleslady asked.

"How much is it all total?" Jessica asked.

"Don't answer that," Lena interrupted.

"That's right," Sherry said. "We'll take it. I have the charge card right here."

"But, Sherry—" Jessica said.

"No, Jessie," Sherry insisted. "Now go and take the dress off so we can buy it. Greg wanted you to get what you liked. You *love* this one more than any of the others and you know it."

"I admit I love it, but I don't want to spend an arm and a leg just because he offered to pay. I don't want to take advantage of his generosity."

"Girl, take that dress off and stop yapping 'bout nothing," Lena said.

"But, Ms. Lena," Jessica started.

"Now the only reason I ain't gonna tell you off about talking to my Jessie like that," Mattie told Lena, "is 'cause I agree with you."

"Yeah," Lena said. "That and the fact that you can't do nothing 'bout it no way."

"Don't start, you two," Sherry warned as the clerk, trying to keep a straight face, helped Jessica off of the platform that she was standing on and disappeared into the dressing room.

"Now why don't you two go ahead and pick out your dresses while we're here?" Sherry suggested. "I already know which one I'm getting." She headed for the back of the store and picked out a navy blue gown with white lace. Trying it on and then taking it to the front of the store, she waited patiently for the others.

"I like that," Jessica remarked when she joined Sherry at the front counter and admired her friend's choice.

"Thanks. Now if your mama and mother-in-law would come on, we could get out of here and call it a day."

The mothers were headed to the front of the store as Sherry finished her remark. True to nature, they were busy arguing while carrying their dresses draped over their arms.

"What's wrong now?" Sherry asked.

"Ain't nothing wrong," Mattie said in disgust. "I wanted the dress she got, that's all."

"Well, you should have seen it before me."

"Did they only have one?" Jessica asked.

"No. There's a whole rack of them back there," Mattie said.

"So why don't you get one, too? I think it would be cute for the two of you to be dressed alike."

"She don't want to be dressed like me," Lena said.

"Got that right," Mattie agreed.

"Besides," Lena added, "she don't want to be embarrassed by my dress fitting my shape better than hers."

Sherry laughed. "Ooh, no, you didn't, Ms. Lena."

"What shape?" Mattie placed her hands on her hips. "Now just for that," she continued, "I'm going right back there and getting one. You gonna have to do a whole lot of jumping jacks in the next three weeks for you to look better than I do in that dress, sister."

Silently, Jessica shook her head and sighed. The store clerks, finding the behavior of the women entertaining, laughed at the ladies' conversation. With the final choices made, the tired women prepared to check out.

"That will be $4,940.31," the clerk said as she totaled the dresses. "Will that be cash or credit?"

"*How much?*" Jessica gasped.

"Jeeeeesus!" Mattie said with her hand over her heart.

"Here you go," Sherry said calmly as she handed the card to the clerk.

"How much was that dress?" Jessica repeated the question she'd asked earlier.

"Never mind all that, child," Lena said. "Just let it be."

"She might as well," Sherry said. "It's done now."

"Sherry, how much was the dress?" Jessica insisted.

"Three thousand dollars, Jessie. Okay?"

"*Three thousand dollars?*" Jessica repeated in disbelief. "Put that back," she told the clerk. I can't spend that kind of money. I didn't plan on the *whole* wedding costing much more than that. Put that back."

"Jessie," Lena said, "calm down. It's okay. I know you're worried 'bout how much of Greg's money you're spending, but believe me when I say that he actually expected you to pay more. He told me so."

"He thought I'd spend *more* than three thousand dollars?"

"He sho did," Lena assured her. "His exact words to me were, 'If she wants to buy a five- or six-thousand-dollar gown, let her do it. I want her to have whatever she wants. It's her day and she's only going to do it once as long as I'm living.' "

"See?" Sherry said. "Our total bill for all four dresses was less than what he expected to pay just for your gown."

"And I don't know what kind of wedding you thought you was having that the whole thing wasn't gonna cost more than three thousand dollars," Lena added. "Now, get that dress."

"The dress *is* beautiful, baby," Mattie said.

"I know," Jessica agreed, "but he already bought my dress for graduation tomorrow. It's just too much."

"He bought the dress for your graduation 'cause he wanted to, Jessie," Lena said. "That ain't even got nothing to do with your wedding dress. Greg *wants* to do this. Why don't you let him?"

"He sounds like a winner to me," the clerk commented as she handed Sherry the card back.

"He is," Jessica said with a smile. "Okay," she conceded after a pause, "we'll take it."

"Good thing," Sherry said, "because I had already paid for it."

"Well, it sure is hot today," Mattie mentioned.

Finally finished, the women walked out into the bright sunshine and toward Sherry's car. It was a beautiful day, but the heat was higher than normal this time of year.

"That's why there are so many bugs out," Lena said as she mistakenly ran into a man walking in her direction.

"Excuse me," she said to him.

"Excuse me," he said at the same time.

"Well, well," Mattie said. "Speaking of cockroaches."

"Ms. Charles!" he said, obviously surprised.

"Oh, my God," Jessica mumbled.

"Jessica?" he said in an even more surprised tone.

"Let's go, Mama," Jessica said as she opened the car door.

"Not yet, baby," Mattie said. "I got something I want to say."

"He's not worth your breath, Mama."

"Who is this?" Lena asked.

"This here," Mattie announced, "is Leroy. He was s'posed to be my son-in-law this coming December."

"Oh," Lena said, "so *you're* Leroy. You the one with the magic tricks."

"What?" he asked in confusion.

"Ain't you the one who disappeared into thin air, Mr. Houdini?" Lena asked.

"Can I talk to you for a minute, Jess?" Leroy said, ignoring Lena's sarcasm.

"And what would you have to say, Leroy?" Jessica said. "Whatever it is can be said around my family and friends. Better yet, it can be said to yourself, 'cause I really don't want to hear it."

"Baby, wait a minute."

"I'm not your baby, Leroy."

"Amen to that," Mattie chimed in.

"Look, Jess, I know you're mad, but I was distraught. I didn't want to see you like that. It was too much for me. I didn't even know that you were—"

"Living?" Jessica finished his sentence as she slammed the car door and approached him. "You didn't even know I pulled through, did you, Leroy. You didn't even bother to check up on me after you took the ring off of my finger, did you?"

"I couldn't, baby," he said. "I couldn't bear to hear them say you had died. I'm sorry. I made a mistake. Let me make it up to you, boo."

"Boo?" Mattie said. "Lena, hold my dress so I can knock the little bit of sense he got left out of him."

"No, Mama," Jessica said. "Let *me* handle this."

"Jess, I made a mistake," Leroy repeated. "Everybody is entitled to one big mistake in their lives, and leaving you was mine. I know I broke your heart, baby, but let me put it back together again. These past few months made me realize that I'm nothing without you."

"Well, you know what, Leroy?" Jessica said. "I guess you ain't ever gonna be nothing, because you'll *never* have me in your life. Believe it or not, I was never mad at you, Leroy. I was hurt. I was *very* hurt. You left me when I needed you the most. But you know what? It worked out for my good. It took a minute, but God showed me that it really did work out for the best. I am *so* over you now. Not only am I over you, but I thank God every day for allowing me to be put in that situation so that I'd know who really cared about and loved me."

"Don't be like that, Jess. I do love you and you know it."

"Save it, Leroy," Jessica said.

"Why don't we just go?" Sherry said as she finished strapping Denise in her car seat.

"In a minute," Jessica said. "I just want to thank Leroy."

"Thank me?" he asked.

"Yes," Jessica explained. "I'm not angry at you for leaving me, but I *am* upset at the way you left me. However, in spite of all of that, I thank you because had you not left me, I would have married you and that would have been a *huge* mistake."

"So that's it?" he asked with a short laugh. "You want me to believe that you don't want me in your life? After all we shared and all the planning we made to be together, you want me to believe that you don't still love me and that you never want to ever see me again? Baby, all I want is a chance to see a happy smile on your face again. Let me make that happen for you. I can do that if you'd just give me one more chance."

"Leroy," Jessica began as she reached in her purse and pulled out an envelope, "there is only one more time in my life that I'm giving you permission to be in my presence," she said. "If my happiness is what you want to see, here's your invitation to see it firsthand," she said as she placed the envelope in his hand and joined the others in the car.

Leroy opened the envelope slowly and read the invitation to attend the wedding of Dr. Gregory Paul Dixon and Miss Jessica Grace Charles. He watched in speechless awe as the Town Car pulled away with his onetime future bride waving out the window. He dropped the invitation in a nearby garbage can and walked away.

"You handled that real good, Jessie," Lena said as they drove toward home.

"Too many words, if you ask me," Mattie said.

"I just needed to say some things," Jessica explained. "I can't believe he actually thought I might take him back."

"A fool," Mattie mumbled. "That's what he is."

"Well, I think he got the message when you slapped that invitation on him," Lena said, laughing.

"Yeah," Sherry added, "and that diamond on your finger probably half blinded him when you waved out the window when we drove off."

With all of their work complete, Sherry finally pulled into the driveway of Lena's home. From the car, they watched Derrick and Greg play a competitive game of basketball in the yard. With his tongue hanging out in his best impression of Michael Jordan, Greg slammed the ball in the goal over Derrick's head.

"Now, that's a good sight to see," Lena remarked with a smile.

"Yeah, it's been a while since you've seen them play together, huh?" Sherry added.

"Well, yeah," Lena said, "but I was talking about the way my boy is beating up on that husband of yours in this game."

"What y'all got in the bags?" Greg knowingly asked. He and Derrick broke away from their sport and walked over to meet the women.

"Get away," Jessica teased as she greeted him with a kiss. "You can't see my dress."

"Yeah," Mattie said, frowning, "and get away from us with all that sweating and going on."

"I want to see it," Greg said while trying to peek into the zipper of the dress bag.

"Boy, that's bad luck," Lena said.

"No, it ain't," Greg said. "It's supposedly bad luck to see her with the dress *on*, not to see the dress itself."

"It's beautiful, Greg," Sherry said. "You're gonna die."

"Yes, it is," Mattie said, "but we had to just about beat her to make her buy it."

"Why?" Greg asked Jessica as they all walked into the house together. "You didn't like it?"

"No," Jessica said. "I love it. Sherry's right, it's beautiful. *Very* beautiful."

"So what was the problem?"

"The price," Lena said. "She didn't want to spend that much of your money. She thought it was taking advantage of your kindness."

"Shoot!" Derrick laughed. "I sure don't have that problem with Sherry. She never thinks she's spending too much of my money."

"That's right," Sherry said without reservation. "If he says go for it, I go for it."

"Sweetheart, that's why I gave you the card," Greg said. "I wanted you to get what you liked."

"You haven't seen the bill yet, Greg," Jessica said.

"It doesn't matter, Grace. When the bill comes, I'll pay it. I want this wedding to be everything your heart desires. I want it to be your fantasy come true—I told you that."

"Ain't that sweet?" Mattie smiled.

"I think I'm going to be sick." Derrick laughed as he played with his daughter.

"Thank you," Jessica said, kissing Greg's cheek.

"Well, she will definitely look like a princess coming down that aisle in this dress," Sherry added. "By the way, Greg," she continued, "are you sure you don't need help with the caterer or anything else?"

"All taken care of, sweetie," he told Sherry. "I've gotten just about everything on my end taken care of. I'm waiting on one phone call from one of my singers and it'll all be set."

"Who's doing the singing?" Jessica asked.

Greg shrugged. "Just some guys. You don't know them. I have this guy named Don who'll be singing 'The Lord's Prayer.'

Then there's another guy named Kenny who'll be singing a special dedication, and he'll have a backup group and a guy named Kelly and some homeboys of his who'll be singing when you come down the aisle."

"Who are these guys and where did you meet them?" Derrick asked.

"Yeah," Sherry added. "Why didn't you get Sylvia or Lonnie from the church? They can really sing."

"Because everybody who ever gets married at the church gets Sylvia or Lonnie or LaToya. I don't want this wedding to be like any other wedding that's been held at Fellowship Worship Center," Greg said. "Of the guys I've booked, I've only met one of them and that's Don. I met him about a year ago when I was in Los Angeles for a conference. He was singing at the church that I visited that Sunday before I came back.

"I've heard all of them sing though, and they're all good. Kelly is the one I haven't heard back from yet. I did talk to his brother and a couple of other folks who said that they were sure he'd come if I got the money there in time. The money has already been sent, so I'm expecting to hear from him soon."

"You're having to *pay* these people?" Jessica asked.

"Sure. It's not like they're my friends or anything. They don't know me from the man on the moon. They all attend other churches and I'm asking them to give up a day for me. Besides, they have to travel to get here. None of them live in D.C."

"You're paying out a lot of money for something that I'm really supposed to be paying for." Jessica sounded concerned.

"Grace," Greg said as he slipped his arms around her waist, "please don't worry about the dollars. I'm not going over my budget with this."

"He ain't making minimum wage either," his mother added. "That boy went to school a long time to make the money he earns."

"I know I'm just a resident doctor right now," Greg said, "but I have a savings account that I haven't touched since I started working at Robinson Memorial. I've always said that

I'd only mess with it for something very important and this is the most important day of my life. Please let me do this."

"Okay," Jessica conceded. "I'll try to stay out of it and let you do it your way. I just don't want you to look back on it and wonder why you spent so much money on a three- or four-hour affair."

"The wedding and reception are just formalities, baby. The marriage is the important issue here and that's an affair of a life-time."

"Is anybody else here feeling sick besides me?" Derrick teased.

"Speaking of feeling sick," Jessica said. "I saw Leroy today."

"Now why you go and tell him that?" Mattie asked.

"Where?" Greg asked.

"Outside the bridal shop as we were leaving."

"Are you okay? He didn't get out of line, did he?"

"Oh, he got out of line all right," Lena told him. "Begging like a dog for her to take him back."

"He got some nerve," Mattie added, "after leaving her like that in the hospital. I woulda knocked my purse upside his head if they'd have let me."

"Wasn't worth it, Ms. Mattie," Sherry said.

"So, tell me what you felt," Greg said.

"What?" Jessica asked. His question caught her off guard, but she could tell from the look on his face that the question he'd posed was a serious one.

"When you saw him, what did you feel?" he repeated. "Did you feel betrayed, anger, sadness, happiness, confusion? What did you feel?"

"I think we all need to go find something to do in another room," Derrick said.

"I agree," Lena said as they all headed to the back of the house.

"Why are you asking me this?" Jessica said once they were gone.

"I just need to know, sweetheart."

"Okay, then," she said after a brief silence. "I'll tell you the same thing I told him. I wasn't angry, but I was upset. There was never any closure put to my relationship with Leroy. I didn't have a chance to say anything to him. I didn't even have a voice in the breakup. He did that on his own without caring what I thought."

Greg turned away and looked out the window as she continued to speak.

"I was upset because—yes, I felt betrayed by him. He was supposed to *love* me, Greg. We were less than a year away from marriage at the time of my accident. I had already started making plans. So, yes, I was upset and I told him so. But, no, I wasn't sad or confused or unsure about anything. Leroy didn't even know that I was alive until he saw me today. He actually thought I had died, Greg. There is no way that I could begin to believe that I missed out on anything with him," she added as she walked over and stood next to him.

"I love *you,* Greg. I didn't revisit the past when I saw Leroy. I didn't wonder what it would or could have been like. As a matter of fact, I thanked him for what he did. In the midst of everything, I owed Leroy my gratitude. The one thing I will forever be grateful to Leroy for is for his leaving me. I am *so glad* that he left me."

"Me too," Greg said. He smiled and took Jessica into his arms. "I know you love me, Grace, and I know that you're over Leroy. I didn't mean to question what you felt for me, I just needed to hear it. I'm sorry."

"It's okay," Jessica said. "As long as you know."

"Okay," Mattie said as they rejoined the embracing couple, "y'all need to save all that kissing for the wedding."

"Mama." Jessica blushed.

"So, are you ready for graduation tomorrow?" Greg asked as he swept Jessica's hair away from her face with his finger.

"Yes, I am."

"Got your speech all written out and everything?"

"Yep."

"I think that was so nice of them to give you a special place to speak on the program," Mattie said, beaming. "Graduating with honors and being able to say a speech. That's my baby."

"I was surprised," Jessica admitted. "They usually only give the top two graduates a place to speak—but they said that I was an inspiration to the school and that's why they put me on."

"That's wonderful," Lena said.

"And we'll be there cheering you on," Sherry said.

"The barking will be me and Greg," Derrick said.

"That's right," Greg said.

CHAPTER 16

Greg hadn't visited the campus of the University of Maryland since he'd given a college friend a ride there three years ago to attend another graduation ceremony. The school still looked the same and his surroundings felt familiar as he and the others walked inside the prepared building.

"It sho is crowded in here," Lena remarked. They found their seats with no problem.

"I feel sorry for anybody that doesn't get here soon," Greg said.

"I know," Derrick said. "Seems like they would've had this at a larger place."

"We'd have been in trouble if Jessica hadn't gotten reserved seating for us," Sherry said.

"I thank you so much for coming, Pastor," Mattie said.

"Oh, I'm glad to be here," Pastor Baldwin said. "I wish Clara could have made it, but she had to go and see about our daughter. She's due to have that baby any day now."

"We should've brought a video camera," Lena said.

"I got it covered, Mama," Greg said. "The same folks who will be videographers for our wedding are taping this. They're here somewhere."

"Boy, you think of everything, don't you?" Mattie said, laughing, as his cell phone rang.

"I hope that's not the hospital calling you," Derrick said.

"Jessie will be so disappointed if you have to miss this," Sherry added.

"Hello," Greg said as he stopped up one ear and spoke into his cell. "Hold on for a minute," he said. "I can't hear you, let me walk to a quieter area."

"Is that the hospital?" Lena asked.

"I'm not even sure, Mama. I can't hear a thing. I got noise on my end and it sounds like noise on his end too. I'll be right back," he said as he walked toward one of the exit doors.

"That is one busy young man," Pastor Baldwin said. "Seems like everybody needs him to be somewhere or do something all the time."

"Well, I hope they don't need him today," Sherry said, "because this is just about the last day he has off before the wedding rehearsal."

"Good afternoon, parents, students, faculty, family, and friends," the announcer said as he took the podium. "Welcome to our graduation ceremony. We are preparing to welcome our graduates for this semester. The graduates who will be entering first will be our honor scholars. They will be wearing gold cords around their necks. They will be followed alphabetically by our remaining graduates. Please stand for the entrance of our graduates," he concluded as the music began playing.

"Just in time," Greg said as he returned to his seat.

"Not the hospital?" Derrick asked.

"No, that was Kelly, my other singer for the wedding. Well, it wasn't him but it was one of his managers. He'll be there."

"Cool," Derrick said.

"There's Jessica." Sherry pointed.

"That's my baby. Eighth in line in her class," Mattie bragged.

"She made the top ten," Pastor Baldwin observed with a smile. "That's highly impressive."

Once the entire class had entered, they returned to their seats and listened as speaker after speaker came to the podium and gave words of encouragement and congratulations to the class graduates. A male student entertained them by singing Tevin Campbell's "One Song."

"That was a nice song," Mattie said.

"They should have gotten Sister Jessica to sing," Pastor Baldwin remarked.

"They don't have enough ushers to control this crowd if the Spirit got loose up in here," Lena said as they laughed.

"At this time," one of the deans was saying, "we are going to have a special address shared with us by one of our students who was in a car accident several months ago. She came about as close to death as a person could come without stepping over the dividing line. Her recovery and subsequent comeback are remarkable, and her ability to continue her excellent G.P.A. upon her return to classes has been an inspiration to us all. Please welcome with me honor graduate Miss Jessica Grace Charles."

The class and audience stood amidst cheers and applause as Jessica made her way to the podium. She fought tears at the reception extended to her by her peers and the strangers that she didn't even know.

"Thank you," she said as everyone finally returned to their seats. "Good afternoon," she began nervously. "First, as always, I would like to thank my heavenly Father for sparing my life so that I could be here in this place today.

"I am so honored," she continued after the applause subsided once more, "that I have been asked to speak on this wonderful occasion. I had prepared a speech," she said, holding up her note cards as proof, "but I just want to say a few words that I have in my heart.

"I am grateful for my learning experience here at the University of Maryland. I think that we have some of the best teachers in the nation and I thank each of you for the lessons that you instilled in me over the past four years. The UM School of Music has been my home away from home for quite a while. I have learned so much and you have given me goals to set for myself as to what I would like to accomplish in my field from this point. I give thanks where it is deserved, and I'm thankful for each and every one of you," she said as she faced the faculty who sat to her left.

"To my mom, Ms. Mattie Charles—I love you dearly. Through the years you may not have always been there when I wanted you to be, but you have definitely been there when I needed you. Thank you for your love and support."

Mattie wiped her eyes with the handkerchief that she held in her hand.

"Ms. Lena Dixon, thank you for putting up with my mama. I know it hasn't been easy, but you do it so well and I appreciate you."

"No, she didn't." Mattie laughed.

"She know my struggles," Lena said. "That's a sweet child."

"Derrick and Sherry Madison," Jessica continued, "thank you for all that you do and thank you for my very first godchild, Denise. I love all of you and I'm glad that I got a chance to get to know you. Pastor and Mrs. Baldwin, along with all the members of my new church home, Fellowship Worship Center, I love you all. Thank you for welcoming me with open arms.

"Although they aren't here to hear it, I want to extend a heartfelt thanks to Dr. Simon Grant and the entire staff of surgeons, doctors, nurses, and therapists at Robinson Memorial Hospital for the wonderful care that they gave me during my two-and-a-half-month stay in their facility.

"In closing," she continued, "I believe that God spared my life for a reason. I don't believe and cannot be convinced that my being here is by chance or by some stroke of good luck."

"Amen," Mattie said.

"I believe that I have discovered a part of that reason, and the other part I know God will show me as time goes on. I have someone I'd like for you all to meet. Come here, Greg," she said to his surprise as she extended her hand in his direction.

Cautious applause turned into deafening female screams and

cheers as Greg made his way from the stands to the podium and took her outstretched hand.

"Isn't he beautiful?" Jessica beamed with pride as laughter, more applause, and agreeing comments followed.

"This is Dr. Gregory Dixon and he is the doctor who performed my brain surgery at Robinson Memorial in Washington, D.C. He, with God's help, not only saved my life, but gave me a reason to live. He was once my doctor, he is now my hero and my friend, and he will forever be the love of my life." Jessica's voice broke as her fellow graduates and the audience applauded.

"May God bless each of you and may you be blessed to be half as blessed as I am today," she continued. "Thank you," she ended as her audience gave her a standing ovation while Greg kissed and embraced her warmly before walking her back to her seat.

"That's *my* baby!" Mattie yelled as she stood, clapping.

"That was beautiful," Sherry said, hugging Greg as he returned to his seat.

"Yes, it was," he agreed.

"And now," the president of the university said, we will begin handing out our diplomas and degrees. We will begin, as always, with our honor graduates."

"Well, at least we ain't got to wait all evening for them to get to Jessie," Lena pointed out.

Jessica was number eight and her fan club was already on their feet even before her name was called. Greg remembered how good he had felt after completing eight years of college in preparation for his life's profession. He knew his mother was proud when he walked across the stage, but he found it hard to fathom that her pride was any greater than his was right now, watching the woman who'd once been expected to die accept her reward.

Her name was finally called. "Jessica Grace Charles."

Scattered throughout the audience were members of Fellowship Worship Center. The cheers and applause were loud and lengthy as Jessica walked across the stage proudly. When she shook the last faculty member's hand, she turned to Greg and the others and threw out a big kiss. They continued to cheer until she stepped off of the stage.

"That was a wonderful ceremony," Pastor Baldwin said as he hugged Jessica following the dismissal.

"Thank you." Jessica smiled.

"Sister Baldwin sends her love," he continued. "She had to go and see about one of our daughters."

"I understand. Tell her that I said thanks for her well-wishes."

"Congratulations, baby," Greg said as he kissed her warmly. "I'm so proud of you."

"Thank you."

"So, where are we off to now?" Mattie asked after she'd hugged her daughter.

"Somewhere where food is being served," Derrick said.

"Dinner is at my house," Lena announced. "I got plenty. You're welcome to come too, Pastor Baldwin."

"Thank you, Mother Dixon, but I have some things to take care of before Sunday. So, if not before, I hope to see you in service Sunday morning."

After being hugged, kissed, and congratulated by several other church acquaintances and classmates, Jessica was finally ready to leave. Greg had sat along the side wall and waited patiently for her to finish mingling with the others. Sherry and Derrick had left earlier, saying that they had stuff to do before joining the others at Lena's for dinner. His mother and Jessica's mother had left shortly after Pastor Baldwin so they could have the meal warmed and prepared by the time Jessica got there.

"I'm sorry to keep you waiting, sweetie," she said as she joined him.

"You only get to graduate from college once," Greg said. "Well, I guess that's not exactly true. I mean, I graduated twice, but you know what I mean."

"I'm so glad that you were here to share this day with me,"

Jessica said as she sat next to him. "I kept thinking that you might be called away."

"Well, it wasn't *impossible*, but I had already told Dr. Grant that unless it was something that absolutely no one else could handle, I needed the day off."

"Thank you." She kissed him softly.

"Thank you," he said.

"For what?"

"You said some pretty wonderful things up on that stage. I felt embarrassed, proud, and loved all at the same time."

"I do love you, Dr. Gregory Dixon. With you, I feel so blessed."

Greg looked at her and smiled. "I love you too," he said, "and the blessing is all mine."

"I guess we should be getting to Ms. Lena's," Jessica suggested. "We don't want to leave her and Mama together alone for too long."

"This is true." Greg laughed as they stood and walked hand in hand through the thinning crowd to make their way to his car.

"You *go*, girl!" one of her classmates yelled while Greg opened the door to his freshly washed Jaguar to let Grace get in.

Jessica took off her graduation gown and laid it across the backseat as they headed to D.C.

"It's a shame that dress had to be covered up the whole time," Greg remarked. "It really looks nice on you."

"Thanks," Grace said. "You have good taste. Some guys don't know how to shop for women, but you have a natural talent."

"I'm glad you like it." He smiled.

"Sherry and I booked a florist, did I tell you?" Jessica said.

"Sherry told me this morning. Are you ready for this wedding? Are you ready to become Mrs. Jessica Dixon?"

"Yes." Jessica smiled. "I get nervous sometimes when I think about it, but I'm ready."

"Well," Greg said, "I think getting nervous is natural. I just started getting that way about it this week. I guess I was so busy getting the wedding organized that I didn't have time to feel nervous before."

"I think it's great the way you're handling everything, Greg. I mean, you got the church reserved, booked our photographer, videographer, vocalists, musicians, and catering company."

"I enjoyed every minute of it," he said.

"Not to mention," Jessica continued, "you paid for, not only my dress, but the mothers' dresses and Sherry's dress as well."

"I hear your dress is quite a knockout. I can hardly wait to see you in it."

"Just three more weeks," Jessica said. She leaned back on the seat and looked at Greg silently as he maneuvered the car through the light traffic.

"What?" Greg said as he glanced at her from the driver's seat.

"Nothing," Jessica said. "It's just that sometimes I think you're not real," she continued. "You know that saying, that things that seem to be too good to be true probably are? Sometimes you seem too good to be true."

Her words brought another glance and a raised-eyebrow smile from Greg. "Baby," he said with a slow shake of his head, "if you think I'm good now, I don't know if you're gonna be able to handle me after October sixth."

Jessica blushed and turned away. She and Greg shared a warm laugh before silence took over once more.

"Have you driven since the accident?" he suddenly asked.

"No," Jessica said.

"Is it because you're scared to?" he asked. "I know that happens a lot with accident victims."

"I'm not scared," she told him. "I just haven't gotten another car yet and I hate driving Mama's old car."

"You wanna drive mine?"

Jessica sat up straight. "I'd love to," she said as he slowly pulled the car to the side of the highway. They quickly switched seats and strapped themselves in.

"Adjust the mirrors and seats however you need to," Greg said. "She picks up speed kind of fast, so you might want to watch the pedal pressure."

"Oh, this is so cool," Jessica said excitedly as she drove all the way to Lena's house.

"You let her drive the Jag?" Derrick said upon their arrival. "You don't even let *me* drive the Jag."

"Whole different kind of love, my man," Greg said as they walked to the house.

"Well, it's about time," Lena said as they entered. "Did y'all have to stay and lock up the place?"

"I'm sorry, Ms. Lena," Jessica said. "It's my fault. I stood around talking for a while."

"Well, I guess you won't be seeing much of them folks no more since your schooling's over," Lena said. "So I guess I'll let you slide for staying behind and running your mouth with them."

"Y'all go on and wash up and come on in so we can eat," Mattie said.

"Derrick, you want to grace the food?" Lena said as they all held hands around the table.

Following his blessing, they quickly began chattering and passing the serving dishes around the table. The women had pulled together and fixed some of Greg's and Jessica's favorite foods.

"The graduation ceremony was really nice, Jessica," Sherry commented. "And your speech was really sweet."

"Did you hear all those girls hollering and going on when my son walked up them steps?" Lena chimed in.

"Wasn't that something?" Mattie said.

"Yeah," Derrick put in. "I started to walk up there with him, but then none of the women would have noticed him."

"Yeah, right." Greg laughed.

"Well, now that the graduation is finally over," Sherry said, "we can wholly concentrate on the wedding."

"Everything is done, now—ain't it?" Mattie asked.

"I think everything is covered," Jessica said.

"I have to get back in touch with all my vocalists to be sure that they'll all be here," Greg said. "And since they all cashed their checks, I don't expect to hear any excuses."

"Well, I sho am excited," Lena said. "The two of you belong together and I'm glad it's happening soon."

"Me too, Mama," Greg said. "I won't be seeing much of anybody for the next two and a half weeks, though," he continued. "Other than my two hours on Sundays, I don't have any scheduled days off. I'm sure I'll get at least one day off a week for the next three weeks, but I won't be taking two days at a time like I have in the past. Not until after the wedding."

"Do whatever you need to do," Sherry said. "Just make sure you're at that altar on October sixth."

"What happens if they call you in on the day of the wedding?" Derrick asked.

The entire table got quiet as they pondered what would happen in a situation like that. Jessica looked at Greg and seemed to hold her breath waiting for an answer.

"Pastor Baldwin prayed *you* through," he finally said. "Let's hope he could do the same for the patient that came in on my wedding day."

"Realistically you'd have to go, right?" Jessica seemed worried.

"Absolutely not," Greg said. "There are several very capable surgeons on staff. They'd just have to use one of them. From October sixth through the twenty-fourth I am totally unavailable."

"Can you do that?" Lena asked. "Can you just tell them white folk up at that hospital that you ain't coming in?"

"Yes, Mama, I can."

"Even doctors get vacations, Ms. Lena," Derrick said. "I

mean, they have to realize that you'll have stuff to do after your wedding."

"That's what I'm saying," Greg said and he and Derrick gave each other a high five.

"Greg." Jessica blushed.

"Y'all not being mannish over there, are you?" Lena warned.

"Who . . . us?" Greg said innocently.

"No, ma'am," Derrick added. "You know you have a lot of stuff to take care of after weddings, Ms. Lena. You have to wash clothes and—and, sweep the floor, and uh, take out the trash, and—"

"Boy, close your mouth and eat your food," Mattie interrupted. "We ain't crazy. You might *think* we crazy, but we ain't."

"I'm telling y'all," Derrick whispered aloud, "that's my mama."

Sherry laughed, changing the subject. "How many invitations did you all send out?"

"I only sent out a few," Jessica said. "Greg sent out a lot of them."

"I think all total we sent out around four hundred," Greg said.

"The church only seats around 750," Sherry said. "Let's hope all four hundred invited guests don't come and bring somebody with them."

"Well, rehearsal is at 5:00 P.M. on the fifth. It's only a few of us, so it shouldn't be hard to run through a rehearsal quickly. All of our vocalists will be meeting with the musicians in a different location on that night because they may need a lot of time to rehearse. So, at the rehearsal, we'll just use recorded music."

"Are you nervous yet, Jessie?" Lena asked.

"Sometimes."

"Are you, Greg?" Lena asked her son.

"Every now and then, I am," he admitted, "but I'll be so busy at the hospital for the next couple of weeks that I won't have much time for nerves."

"Well, I know that everything is gonna go smooth. I just know it," Mattie assured them.

"Evelyn sure has been sad lately," Sherry said. "I hope she snaps out of it soon."

"She'll be fine," Lena said. "And if she don't—who cares?"

"I think she'll be fine after the wedding is over," Derrick said. "As long as it hasn't taken place yet, she still probably believes there's some hope."

"I really don't want her to attend the wedding," Greg said, "because if she does anything to disrupt, it ain't gonna be pretty. I don't need her to mess with Grace's day."

"Oh, I'm sure she'll be fine," Sherry said. "I don't even expect her to attend, but if she does, I wouldn't expect her to start any trouble."

"What would be the purpose?" Derrick added. "That wouldn't win her any brownie points with Greg."

"Do you think she'd try to mess up the wedding?" Jessica worried.

"Well, I'm holding out hope that she doesn't come," Greg said, "but if she does, I'll make sure that she doesn't interrupt what I plan to be a storybook wedding for you."

In the days that followed, Greg saw very little of his bride-to-be. Some nights following his shift, he'd sneak by the Charleses' home for a few minutes to steal a few precious moments with Jessica. When he could, he'd stay awhile and watch a movie with her—sometimes falling asleep in the middle of it. Just his efforts to spend time with her seemed to be enough to keep her happy.

Those final weeks of waiting seemed like a lifetime for Greg, but he knew that it would all come to an end soon.

"Well, Dixon," Dr. Grant said as he walked with him down the hospital corridor on Greg's final day of work before his big day, "you only have a couple of days left to change your mind. Any second thoughts?"

"Dr. Grant," Greg said, "my wedding rehearsal is tomorrow

night and I am more certain today than ever that this is what I want."

"Well, I am happy for you, son. If you're half the husband that you are the doctor, this should work out just fine."

"Thank you, Grant. You are coming to the wedding aren't you?"

"I'll be on call, but I will be there. I believe that Dr. Pridgen, Dr. Young, and Kelly will be there as well. Several of the nurses are coming. They said they're all wearing black."

"They can wear whatever they want," Greg said, "as long as they don't do or say anything to mess with my wedding."

"Oh, they won't," Dr. Grant said.

The rehearsal started at 5:00 P.M. sharp, as planned. The atmosphere was laid-back and both Jessica and Greg appeared to be quite calm and relaxed. The team of florists was busy decorating as the rehearsal proceeded.

Jessica had decided that it was best that they block off the aisle of the church where she'd be entering so that no one could walk down that aisle while being seated. She told the florists to cover that aisle with fresh white rose petals on the morning of the wedding. Though she didn't have the traditional flower girl, she still wanted to walk in on flowers. Greg loved the idea.

By the time rehearsal was over, the florists had finished the decorations. The bouquet that they had prepared for Jessica was beautiful. It was a thick bouquet of white roses with blue-petal flowers scattered throughout the design.

"Everything looks so beautiful," Jessica said as she looked around the church.

"I'm sure it'll all pale in comparison to you tomorrow," Greg said as he kissed her.

"Aw, man," Derrick said, "I'm gonna be sick."

"I just love the candle arrangements," Mattie said.

"All the candles will be lit prior to the ceremony," Greg said.

"We don't have people walking in and lighting them. They'll already be burning when the guests arrive."

"Well, the rehearsal went well," Pastor Baldwin said as he prepared to leave. "I just hope your singers do well."

"Yeah," Sherry said, "that's the only problem. We didn't get to hear them."

"It's okay," Greg said. "I'm sure they'll do fine. I told the musicians not to end rehearsal until they knew they had it right."

"You got a lot of confidence in these folks who you ain't even heard firsthand," Lena said. "I hope you don't get disappointed."

"You think we should go by their rehearsal just to listen for a minute?" Jessica asked.

"No, baby," Greg said. "If it'll make you feel better, I'll go by there when I leave here. You just go home and get some rest. Tomorrow is our big day and I don't want you worrying about a thing. I promise you that this wedding will be your dream come true. Everything will be perfect. Trust me."

CHAPTER 17

October 6

"Is everything going okay in there?" Jessica asked her mother for the third time.

"Baby, nothing is happening yet. The ushers are still seating the people."

"Sit still so I can get your hair right," Sherry said as she styled Jessica's once-again short locks. "I really like your hair at this length," she added. "It's so easy to work with."

"How's it coming in here?" Lena asked as she joined them in the room that they were using to get prepared.

"Ms. Lena, are there a lot of people out there?" Jessica asked.

"Yeah, Jessie. The church is nearly full already."

"How's Greg?"

"He's fine, baby," Lena answered. "He's nervous too, but he's looking real good in that white tuxedo."

"Really?"

"Yeah. My boy looks like royalty over there."

"Well, Jessie's gonna look like royalty too when I'm done," Sherry said.

252 Kendra Norman-Bellamy

"You two look good, by the way," Jessica said to Lena and Mattie.

"Who does the dress look better on?" Mattie asked.

"It looks equally as good on both of you," Jessie said.

"Umph," Lena said. "She just don't want to hurt your feelings."

"I hope Ricky's tie is straight," Sherry said. "He always manages to have it crooked and I have to straighten it out."

"Rick, will you straighten out that tie?" Greg said as he paced the floor in the room where they waited.

"Fifteen minutes to showtime," Pastor Baldwin said. "Anything you want me to do?"

"Yes, can you please dial the number to conference room number two and see if all my vocalists are here?"

Pastor Baldwin picked up the phone and began dialing.

"You do have the ring, right, Rick?"

"I thought you had it," Derrick said.

"I gave it to you this morning," Greg said.

"Chill, man, I'm only kidding." Derrick laughed as he held up his hand. "I was only kidding. Get your nervous self together."

"Yeah, well, at least I brought fresh drawers," Greg said.

"Ha-ha, very funny," Derrick said as Pastor Baldwin joined them.

"Okay, the singers are all here. The Kenny fellow was just getting there when I called. I heard them singing in the background. The harmony was really good."

"Great," Greg said as he took a deep breath to calm himself.

"Why don't we have prayer before we go out?" Pastor Baldwin said as he stretched out his hands to join with Greg and Derrick.

"Good idea," Greg said.

"Our Father, our Father, our most righteous Father," he began, "thank you for this blessed day that you've given to us. Bless this ceremony that we are about to begin. Touch this brother and his bride-to-be. Let this day and all its plans run smoothly. Take away fear and nervousness and bring peace and serenity to the body and to the heart, in your name I pray, amen."

"Amen," Greg and Derrick said.

"Thank you," Greg said

"It's 2:00 P.M., let's have prayer," Lena said as the women held hands.

"Lord," she began, "we just want to say thank you for everything that you've done for us. Thank you for this day and the beautiful sunshine that you allowed to hover in the sky to make this day as wonderful as this occasion. Touch all of us, but especially Jessie and Greg. Let everything go according to plan with no interruptions or disruptions. Please, Lord, don't let Evelyn make no trouble, 'cause you know me and Mattie won't mind choking the life out of her. Let your will be done in our lives forever, amen."

"Amen," the women said.

"Baby," Mattie said as she held Jessica's face in her hands, "you are the most beautiful bride I've ever seen. You gonna take his breath away."

"The music is beginning to play for your entrance," Sherry told Mattie and Lena. "You'd better go on and meet the ushers in the lobby so you can go in and light your candles."

"Oh, Sherry, I'm so nervous," Jessica said as she looked at her reflection in the mirror. "Do I look as nervous as I feel?"

"You'll be fine, Jessie. You look absolutely gorgeous."

"I guess we need to be heading out, huh?"

"Yes," Sherry said as she hugged her tightly. "Now you just remember not to start walking in until you hear the first solo start," she continued as they took their place at the closed foyer doors.

Jessica stood back and watched as her best friend walked through the doors and let them close behind her. She could hear the tune of Richard Smallwood's "Center of My Joy" being played as Sherry walked down the aisle. The church got quiet for a moment as the introduction to the bridal march was being played. The ushers pulled the doors open and the audience gasped at Jessica's beauty as she stood in place for a moment.

She wondered why policemen stood around the wall near the front of the church. Turning slightly to her left as the photographer continued to take pictures of her as she stood at the door, Jessica noticed Evelyn sitting expressionless near the back of the church. A uniformed policeman was sitting directly by her.

The music stopped and changed as Jessica prepared to make her grand entrance. She recognized the tune as she began walking down the aisle. She also soon recognized the voice. The audience also recognized the voice as the singers walked out on the stage. Gasps ran around the room.

There, stepping onto the pulpit singing as she entered, was Brian McKnight. She placed one hand on her chest in surprise as she continued her march. With a single wink of his eye, Brian smiled at her as he sang his onetime hit song "Every Beat of My Heart." Gospel artists Take 6 were backing him up. It was a surprise she never expected. They sounded heavenly as she joined her smiling but teary-eyed groom at the altar.

"You are so beautiful," he whispered as he took her hand.

Pastor Baldwin began the ceremony as Brian and the others quickly disappeared from the stage. Pastor Baldwin always seemed to become quite the intellect when he performed weddings. He seemed to make an effort to speak clearly and correctly in all that he said. Mattie stood as he asked who was giving away the bride to be married.

"I do!" she said in a proud, strong voice that the audience found humorous.

"Let us pray," Pastor Baldwin said.

Greg and Jessica joined hands and bowed their heads. The music began playing softly and another recognizable voice began singing. Jessica looked up and Donnie McClurkin was now on the pulpit and singing "The Lord's Prayer." Once again, the crowd reacted. She knew it was inappropriate to speak at this time—and she probably couldn't have, if she tried—so she squeezed Greg's hand. Though his head was bowed and his eyes were closed, he smiled and squeezed back.

Following Donnie's soul-stirring song, Pastor Baldwin said a prayer of blessing over the couple. By the time the prayer ended, Donnie had left the stage. Pastor Baldwin continued with the ceremony as the couple walked to the unity candle and lit it using the candles that their mothers had lit earlier.

"And now," Pastor Baldwin said as he handed Jessica a microphone, "in lieu of traditional wedding vows, we will have words of love and dedication from the bride to the groom."

Jessica had originally planned to say vows that she'd written on her own, but instead, and at the spur of the moment, she began singing. Not having rehearsed it with the musicians, she sang the unexpected musical tribute a cappella. "For Always," the song made famous by CeCe Winans, had never sounded so beautiful.

The song stirred both the crowd and Greg. A stream of steady tears flowed from his eyes. Derrick handed him a handkerchief, whispering, "I think I'm gonna be sick," in his best friend's ear.

When Jessica finished, Pastor Baldwin handed the microphone to Greg. "And now words of love and dedication from the groom to the bride," he announced.

"Well," Greg said as he tried to regroup and regain his composure, "I thought that *I* was the one with all the surprises," he said as their onlookers laughed.

He turned to face Jessica and took her hand in his. "There is a song that's been on my heart ever since the day I met and fell in love with you. The words, although I'm not quoting them verbatim, say this day has been a long time coming but it's definitely been worth the wait. It goes on to say that you are really something special—and you are.

"Grace, I believe in my heart of hearts that you really are every man's dream come true, and not a day goes by that I don't thank the Lord that I found you. God didn't bless me with the talent to sing; therefore, as you listen, just know that these words are from my heart."

Greg pulled the microphone away from his mouth and the crowd reacted once more as Babyface stepped out onto the stage followed by Boyz II Men. It was Grace's turn to use the handkerchief as they sang Babyface's "Every Time I Close My Eyes."

"Your credit card companies are really going to love you when these bills come in," Pastor Baldwin said following the song, as the crowd roared with laughter.

He then took the rings from Derrick and Sherry and said a prayer over them. Afterward, the bride and groom placed the rings on each other's fingers.

"By the powers of God and of the State of Washington, D.C., that are invested in me," Pastor Baldwin said, "I pronounce you husband and wife. Dr. Dixon, you may now salute your bride."

Cameras flashed from every corner of the audience as Greg pulled back her veil and gently but deeply kissed his new wife. Neither of them could hold back the joyful tears as they embraced.

"I present to you," Pastor Baldwin said as the couple continued to embrace one another, "Dr. and Mrs. Gregory Paul Dixon."

The audience stood in thunderous applause as Greg and Jessica turned to face them as husband and wife. They watched and laughed as their mothers jumped up and down in celebration. The recessional music started. Jessica looked around to see if yet another surprise singer was going to appear on the stage. Greg pulled her arm as they began their exit. Sherry and Derrick gathered the train of Jessica's gown and followed the bridal couple down the aisle and out the back door.

Drs. Grant, Pridgen, Young, and Lowe gave the couple the thumbs-up symbol as they passed them. Kelly wiped tears as she stood with several other nurses, who as promised were wearing black as they all cheered the happy couple.

Following photographs and interviews for the wedding video, the couple and the crowd finally assembled for the reception. The decorations in the youth-center-turned-reception hall were exquisite.

"Oh, sweetheart," Jessica said as she finally got a private moment with her new husband once they were seated at the bridal table, "everything was so beautiful. You were right. It was my fantasy come true. Oh, my God!" she exclaimed, "I thought I'd die when I saw Brian step from behind those plants when I was walking down the aisle."

"I wanted to make this day as special for you as possible," Greg said as he kissed his bride once more. "It wasn't easy, but every one of them that I asked came through."

"You tricked all of us," Sherry said as she and Derrick joined them. "You gave us all these crazy made-up names for who your singers were going to be and you came up in here with Motown and stuff."

"I may have tricked you," Greg admitted, "but I didn't make up any names. Think about it. I said Don and that's Donnie. Then I said Kenny and that's Babyface's real name, and I said Kelly, which is Brian's middle name. I just referred to Take 6 as Brian's homeboys, which they are, and I think I just referred to Boyz II Men as background singers, which they were."

"That's pretty good, dog," Derrick said, obviously impressed.

"I knew something was strange when I saw all those policemen," Jessica said. "At first I thought something was wrong until I saw Brian."

"Yeah, that was a part of the contract deal," Greg explained. "All the vocalists had to be comfortable with getting in and out without a problem. Then I got an extra guy for Evelyn."

"I was *very* surprised that she showed up," Sherry said.

"Oh, children," Lena said as she kissed her son and new daughter-in-law, "everything was so beautiful."

"Yes, it was," Mattie agreed as she followed with kisses of her own. "You look like an angel, baby," she continued.

"I thought I was gonna need oxygen when I saw you walking up the aisle," Greg said. "It's so amazing that no matter how beautiful you are when I see you last, you manage to outdo it the next time I see you."

"Thank you." Jessica blushed.

The host and hostesses served the dinner party and the guests lined up to be served in the buffet-style line.

"So where are the celebrities now?" Sherry asked as she looked at the live band that now kept them entertained.

"Probably already on their planes headed home," Greg said. "They did what I paid them to do. I knew they'd be getting out as soon as they did their part."

"Well, I'm just glad that it's finally over." Mattie sighed. "Now I guess life goes back to normal."

"We have a honeymoon to go on first," Greg said. "We'll be gone for about two weeks."

"Well, if you want," Lena said, "me and Mattie can babysit all them gifts for you till you return."

"That would be perfect, Mama."

"That Pastor Baldwin did a nice job of performing the ceremony," Mattie said.

"He sure did," Jessica agreed.

"I especially liked the part in that prayer where he prayed for your future children," Lena added. "I sho can't wait to get my grandbabies."

"Can we just enjoy each other for a little while, Mama?" Greg asked.

"Enjoy each other?" Lena said with a grimace. "What y'all need to enjoy each other for? Y'all can enjoy each other while y'all making my grandbabies," she said to Jessica's embarrassment.

"One year, Mama," Greg said. "Give us one year as a couple and then we'll start on the babies, okay?"

"I agree," Jessica said.

"One *year?*" Mattie interrupted in disgust. "In a year, y'all could've given us one grandbaby and have another one on the way."

"Jeez!" Derrick laughed.

"And *you* shut up," Mattie told him as Sherry laughed. "They got to have us some grandbabies. We need sweet little granddaughters. Dee here need somebody to play with."

"Dee can play with her baby rattle," Greg said.

"Boy, don't make me come over there," Lena warned with a point of her finger. "Never mind them granddaughters, though," she continued. "We need some grand-*sons* so they can grow up strong men like their daddy is and like their grandfather was."

"My baby is strong," Mattie defended. "They can always be girls and grow up like her."

"Yeah, but then we take the chance of them growing up like *you,*" Lena said as Greg, Jessica, Sherry, and Derrick laughed.

"Lena Dixon," Mattie said as she held up a drumstick chicken piece and shook it at her, "you walking on thin ice. Just 'cause we family now don't mean I won't come over there and beat the living daylights outta you."

"Well, you better bring some help, sister," Lena said, " 'cause you sho can't do it by yourself."

"Greg and Jessica Dixon," Sherry said, laughing, "*this* is your life." She pointed at their mothers.

Lena turned to Sherry as Jessica and Greg continued to laugh. "And what you trying to say, Ms. Thang? I beat your little hiney when you was thirteen years old and you ain't too grown now."

"Now, Ms. Lena," Derrick said through his laughter, "you know I ain't gonna just sit here and let you take a switch to my wife."

"And what *you* gonna do?" Mattie jumped in, now shaking the chicken at Derrick.

"Will you all calm down?" Greg said. "You're getting an audience," he said as they noticed people laughing at the tables closest to theirs.

Mattie turned and flashed the chicken at the tables around her. "And what *y'all* laughing at? Ain't y'all ever seen a family discussion before?" she said as the guests laughed at her expression.

"Ma." Derrick patted Mattie's shoulder. "Is that you, Mama? Are you in there? Can you hear me, Mama?"

The group shared a hearty laugh as Derrick looked at Mattie closely from head to toe and pretended to think Julia Madison was somehow inside her.

"This is gonna be soooo much fun," Greg said as he kissed the back of Jessica's hand.

"So, how many babies do you want?" Jessica asked as their mothers continued to debate.

"When the time is right, I want as many as you're willing to give."

"Sounds like a plan," she said.

"Right now," Greg continued, "you're the only baby I want. I want to spend time making you happy and getting you used to sharing a home and a life with me. I want to be able to walk into services late on Sunday mornings. Not because I had to rush from the hospital or because I overslept, but I want to walk in late 'cause I had stuff to do."

"That's what I'm talking 'bout, dude." Derrick laughed as Jessica blushed.

"You are so *silly!*" Sherry playfully punched her husband's shoulder.

"I love you, Mrs. Jessica Grace Charles-Dixon," Greg said as they shared a warm kiss.

Jessica smiled. "I love you too."

"And furthermore," Lena was saying, "if they do turn out to be girls, don't you name a single one of them, 'cause Jessica and Grace do *not* go together."

"You workin' on my last nerve, Lena Dixon," Mattie warned.

"And the legacy lives on." Sherry laughed.

"Welcome to the family, Grace," Greg said as he held his glass up in a toast, "and may heaven help us all," he concluded.

"Hear! Hear!" Derrick said as the four of them touched glasses and shared a warm laugh.